Praise

The Key to
Happily Ever After

"*The Key to Happily Ever After* gave me so many emotions: I loved and cheered for all three sisters, and wanted to shake each of them in turn; I swooned for all of the romance; and I got choked up about their struggles and their victories. But mostly, I loved the de la Rosa sisters so much, and I can't wait for the whole world to love them."

—Jasmine Guillory, *New York Times* bestselling
author of *The Proposal*

"A charming, fun read. I love these sisters! Clear your calendar—once you start, you won't be able to put down this wonderful story."

—Susan Mallery, # 1 *New York Times* bestselling
author of *California Girls*

"A beautiful story about the bonds of family and the challenges of love—I was cheering for all the de la Rosa sisters!"

—Jennifer Probst, *New York Times* bestselling
author of *All or Nothing at All*

"This is the most aptly titled romance. A true gem filled with heart, laughs, and a cast of delightful characters. I read (and adored) *The Key to Happily Ever After* in one sitting!"

—Nina Bocci, *USA Today* bestselling author of
On the Corner of Love and Hate

"The de la Rosa sisters are much like the flower in their name: delicate and poised but also fiercely strong. As the trio takes over the family wedding planning business, they will need all those traits and more to transform their careers for a new generation. As they forge their paths both together and separately, these three sisters discover that love—like a wedding—is all about timing. Full of wisdom, wit, and, of course, wedding gowns, Tif Marcelo's latest charmer proves that sometimes *The Key to Happily Ever After* comes along when you least expect it. This endearing, deeply poignant trip down the aisle(s) is full of romance, unexpected twists, and the perfect helping of family drama."

—Kristy Woodson Harvey, author of
The Southern Side of Paradise

"Devoted sisters, swoony new loves, and wedding drama—what more could you ask for in a perfect summer read? *The Key to Happily Ever After* delivers it all with Tif Marcelo's enchanting prose. By the end, you'll want to be a de la Rosa sister, too!"

—Amy E. Reichert, author of
The Coincidence of Coconut Cake

The Key to Happily Ever After

TIF MARCELO

Gallery Books

New York   London   Toronto   Sydney   New Delhi

Gallery Books
An Imprint of Simon & Schuster, Inc.
1230 Avenue of the Americas
New York, NY 10020

First Gallery Books trade paperback edition May 2019

GALLERY BOOKS and colophon are registered trademarks of Simon & Schuster, Inc.

For information about special discounts for bulk purchases, please contact Simon & Schuster Special Sales at 1-866-506-1949 or business@simonandschuster.com.

The Simon & Schuster Speakers Bureau can bring authors to your live event. For more information or to book an event, contact the Simon & Schuster Speakers Bureau at 1-866-248-3049 or visit our website at www.simonspeakers.com.

Interior design by Davina Mock-Maniscalco

Manufactured in the United States of America

10   9   8   7   6   5   4   3   2   1

Library of Congress Cataloging-in-Publication Data

Names: Marcelo, Tif, author.
Title: The key to happily ever after / by Tif Marcelo.
Description: First Gallery Books trade paperback edition. | New York : Gallery Books, 2019.
Identifiers: LCCN 2018023291| ISBN 9781501197581 (trade pbk.) | ISBN 9781501197598 (ebook)
Subjects: | GSAFD: Love stories.
Classification: LCC PS3613.A73244 K49 2019 | DDC 813/.6—dc23
LC record available at https://lccn.loc.gov/2018023291

ISBN 978-1-5011-9758-1
ISBN 978-1-5011-9759-8 (ebook)

For the women I call sisters

part one

What's in a name? That which we call a rose by any other name would smell as sweet.

—William Shakespeare

one

Mood: "At Last" by Etta James

The bronze skeleton key jingled among the other shop keys in Marisol de la Rosa's palm, and the hopeful clinking noise brought a smile to her face. The key was multi-toned, some parts glossy, other parts dull, with one tooth notched in three places, its bottom blooming into a metal rose with six petals.

No longer a working key, it was an antique, representative of the deep roots the de la Rosas had in Old Town Alexandria, scuffed from being dragged and thrown about, stuffed in pockets and bags, jammed and twisted forcefully into keyholes. Given to Mari's parents two decades ago as part of the deed of sale of this Burg Street business front, they'd considered the intricate rose design auspicious. And so, right then and there, in what had been a stuffy Colonial town house of dark red brick with hideous puke-green trim, drafty windows, and a nonexistent furnace, her mother had decided that the business would be named Rings & Roses, after that key and their last name.

Now in Mari's possession, the key signified the turning of the tide, the passing of the baton. This morning, on this glorious first Saturday in March, Mari had walked into Old Town's preeminent wedding boutique—the absolute best in the DC/Maryland/Virginia tristate area, if she said so herself—as one of its new owners.

Now if only the entire team took the transfer of power just as seriously.

"Didn't I say nine? I explicitly texted *nine a.m. meet-up*," she said to her middle sister, Janelyn. Mari hooked the carabiner of keys on a belt loop of her tapered jeans, bent down, slung a satchel on her shoulder, and loaded her arms with baskets of tulle-wrapped bubble favors and cigars. With a grunt, she stomped through the showroom and front lobby of Rings & Roses toward the front door. Weaving around eclectic flower-print upholstered chairs and a rack of wedding dresses—a select few to lure in the would-be bride—the tulle and lace fluttered as she brushed past. Jane followed behind her, lugging a box filled with seating cards, the guest list, and Mari's event binder that contained every piece of information related to the "Jarvis"—or the Jardine-Davis—wedding. Her footsteps thumped against the restored original heart pine floors, a contrast to the clacking of Mari's sling-back kitten heels.

"Technically? We still have five minutes," Jane answered reliably, as the family's mediator. She shut the door behind them, the bolt locking automatically. "Pearl should be here soon."

Mari huffed as she stepped out onto the cobblestone sidewalk of Burg Street. She shivered in her thin white blouse. With her hair up in a bun and her neck exposed, the cold cut into her like a knife. March was known for its tricky weather. It changed with the position of the sun and the whip of the wind. Emerging from under the shop's cherry red awning, they sidestepped pedestrians, Mari smiling brightly despite the struggle. These days, there were as many tourists as there were locals on Burg Street, where independently owned shops like Rings & Roses flourished. But one thing remained despite the changes over the years: a smile went a million miles, and in their business, the smile was paramount. It set them apart from stuffy, and lesser, wedding boutiques.

But once the sisters had jammed their supplies into their trusty hand-me-down Volvo station wagon and climbed into its leather seats, Mari continued her rant. "*Should be* is the key phrase. This is the first wedding since the changeover. I want it to be seamless."

"It will be. You and I are here," Jane said. She took out her phone and texted their youngest sister anyway, and Mari's phone buzzed with the text in their group chat. Where are you, P? Ate Mari and I are driving out in 3 min. Otherwise, meet you at the Distillery.

Jane, thirty, was only two years younger than Mari, and both were type A. Pearl, their baby sister? She was six years younger than Mari and type B all the way.

So long as Pearl had been completing her respective job at Rings & Roses, her parents had never given a stink about her tardiness. Now that each of the sisters were one-third owners of both their business and their shared residence a half mile down on Duchess Street, Mari would have to set some ground rules, starting with the absolute requirement of on-time attendance. Especially on Saturdays—Wedding Days.

No rest for the ambitious.

Yes, she was setting the rules, because she was still the oldest, naturally the leader of the crew, with or without her voted title of CEO. Making the rules was her birthright as the eldest sister, the *ate*. Besides, her instincts told her that while her sisters seemed equally committed to the shop now, she was sure to be the only one left standing. Jane, now the shop's CFO, was a single mom to a seven-year-old and had recently emerged from what she called the "baby-toddler haze." What if she decided wedding planning wasn't actually her dream? And Pearl . . . well, Pearl worked like she dated. Despite her request to become a full-time wedding planner—she was the shop's social media director and in charge of day-of event coordination—she had other interests, which sometimes showed in her lack of commitment.

Mari only had one love besides her family: Rings & Roses.

She pointed across the street to the Colonial with red-orange brick and one-way privacy windows on the second floor, where a simple trifold chalkboard sign perched at its front door on the sidewalk read *8 a.m. Flow.* "I bet she's there, at Ohm, posing instead of working."

"Stoooop." Jane drew out the word and ran her hand through her windblown, black, chin-length bob. "Don't get yourself riled up. Let's get to the Distillery. She'll be there—I'm positive. A little late, sure, but just in time."

"That makes no sense. But fine." Mari fired up the engine. It sputtered and whined but, after a couple of pumps of the gas, revved to life.

"Let's discuss Pearl's birthday gift since she's not here. I still think the matchmaker gift certificate is the best way to go," Jane said as they pulled onto the cobblestone road for their ten-minute drive to the Distillery. She scrolled through her phone. "Here it is. It includes a phone consult, a speed-dating event, and a couple of matched dates."

Mari scoffed. "If there's anyone who doesn't need help getting dates, it's Pearl. We should get her an old-fashioned alarm clock since she's always late instead—"

"Ate Mari. Focus. Pearl's birthday is next Saturday."

"Just get whatever you think is best." Mari sighed. Pearl and Jane were like two peas in a pod despite their four-year age difference. Their opposite personalities gelled, while Mari's and Pearl's often clashed and emitted a spark that sometimes turned to fire. Jane had a better hold on what Pearl should get on her twenty-sixth birthday.

Her baby sister was turning twenty-six. *Damn.* Mari felt old. In her beloved historical romance books, at thirty-two, Mari would've been considered a spinster, too far over the hill to have her own life, marry, and have children.

Thank God for the twenty-first century—Mari could be an entrepreneur and didn't have to rely on a man. Although, sometimes with Pearl, Mari felt like she *was* wrangling a child.

T-minus two hours until the ceremony start time, and the Distillery was a flurry of delicate fabrics surrounded by wood, cork, and metal. With rectangular tables covered in taupe-colored linens set up in four parallel lines to accommodate forty guests each—over a hundred and fifty were expected today—the space was the perfect reflection of Mari's clients, Maddie Jardine and Frank Davis. The Distillery's catering team had arranged the buffet table at the rear of the space. Patty, of Shenandoah Petals, divvied up Virginia wildflowers—field chamomile, nodding thistle, and blazing stars—in pastel-painted mason jars tied with white tulle. Twinkle lights draped across the ceiling, softening the space's imposing wooden beams. "Boho and Boom" was Mari's original pitch for these clients, who were the classic opposites-attract, city-meets-country couple.

Mari all but skipped to the entrance, leaving Jane to set up the reception table, when one of her trusted vendors arrived. "I'm so excited to see what you have for me!" she said to Ben from Regalia Farms, who pulled a cart of stacked log slices. She picked up a slice. Rustic, natural, and romantic, it was heavy and solid in Mari's hands. A contrast to the fluffy and whimsical tulle and flowers, the logs were the foundation of the centerpieces. "These are absolutely, one-hundred percent perfect. Thank you for driving this all the way out here."

"Not a problem. Anything for Rings and Roses. Where should I put them?"

Mari directed him to the back, where the rest of the day's decorations were stacked. She stopped by her designated command center, a podium, where her binder was opened to her Full-Service Client Day-Of Event Checklist, and checked off the box next to centerpieces.

And when she looked up from her spot, at what would soon be the realization of her clients' dream wedding, satisfaction filled her.

Mari had been ready for this. She'd studied, jumped into, and completed a master's in business when, a couple of years ago, her mother had brought up becoming an expat and retiring. Regina de la Rosa was whip-smart, respected in the industry, and still sharp, but the workload had become overwhelming. Couples, over the years, had become more and more discriminating. Her mother had begun to don impatience like a second skin.

The next step in her parents' chapter had been inevitable—passing down the de la Rosa legacy so they could finally enjoy the fruits of their labor. To travel and cruise and golf and whatever else their father, Fred, had up his sleeve, and spend most of the year in the Philippines. The time had come. The couple's friends had slowly morphed into international snowbirds. Pearl was almost five years out of college and, though none of Regina's girls were married—this had been her prayer wish at Mass every Sunday—they were all independent and successful.

The turnover had been an easy process. A few signatures, dozens of initials for the Rings & Roses building, as well as their shared family residence. One meeting with their lawyer.

And with almost seventeen years under her belt at her parent's company, Mari took the helm like a superhero who'd worn her costume part-time and was finally free to shed her boring overgarments.

Mari's phone buzzed on her hip, knocking her out of her thoughts. Unclipping it from her belt loop, she saw it was Pearl responding to their sister group text: I thought you meant to meet at home! I'm driving to you now.

From across the room, Mari met her sister's eyes. Jane didn't have to say a word, but their communication defied science and Mari understood that look: *I told you she'd be here.*

It took less than ten minutes for Pearl to burst through the venue's front door—Mari timed it—which meant she'd probably sped through Alexandria. She was dressed in their standard Rings & Roses outfit, in neutral colors to blend into the background. Her ombré-highlighted hair was unclipped, down, and wavy.

The whole room stuttered to a stop at her entrance. "Hey, everyone," she said, wearing a guilty expression.

Mari's first thought: *Good. You* should *feel guilty.*

The next second, she shook her head. Mari didn't mean it. Pearl had been her charge since she was old enough to babysit. Mari had taught her how to flip off the swings, shown her how to kick a guy in the balls just in case, and actually had threatened one of her junior high boyfriends who dared to raise his voice at her.

It was only in this arena, the business, where their personalities clashed.

So, Mari didn't yell. She didn't nag. She swallowed her admonishments.

"I swear, I was only, like, two minutes late," Pearl said as she approached Mari, knotting her hair into a bun then grabbing a pencil from the podium to secure it in place. "I was just in the wrong place. Mommy always had us meet at the house first, and I had that on the brain."

Mari, distracted, pointed at Pearl's bun. "I needed that pencil."

"But you've got a pen right there."

Mari breathed in, let it out.

Pearl scrunched her eyebrows as if it was the silliest thing, as if Mari's ways were foreign. Everyone in the shop knew how Mari worked, though: she utilized lists with standard operating procedures, a pen for permanent notes, a pencil for updates. A highlighter for incomplete items. Post-it flags for reminders.

Pearl removed the pencil, and her hair cascaded down her back. She handed it to Mari like a peace offering. "I'm sorry I'm late."

"It's okay. We're all still getting used to this." Mari smiled, forcing the moment forward. "Besides, there's no time to fuss about it now. If you could stay here with Jane and the rest of the crew to set up, I'm meeting the photographer at the bride's home in about twenty minutes."

"You've got it. But hey, I need to tell you something. When I got home, I found something on our sidewalk."

"Don't tell me." Mari pressed her fingers against her temple with the start of a headache. The de la Rosa town house, 2404 Duchess Street, was divided into four separate apartments, with Jane across the hall from Mari on the first floor, her parents' now-part-time apartment above Mari, and Pearl's apartment across from it, occupying the shared side with 2402 Duchess, the single-family town house next door. From the outside, 2402 looked similar to theirs: a traditional redbrick Colonial with three floors, each marked by a set of two thick-framed windows. Gas lamps on both sides of a red door. Each had a brass plaque nailed next to the buzzer with the house number and street name, marking it as a historic building. The only differences were that 2402's windows were framed with black shutters, and while the de la Rosas owned their building outright, 2402 was a luxury short-stay rental.

Recently sold, 2402 had become a playhouse for vacationers. Close enough to DC that its guests could be at monuments and museums within a half hour but far enough away from the stuffy suits of our nation's capital, the town house had been occupied by a different set of strangers almost every day for the last two months.

The short-stay rental attracted tourists to the area, true, but it also brought in partiers and noise. The rental had become a nuisance. How many times had they called the police since it had changed hands? Every couple of weeks? They'd already lodged several complaints with the property manager to no avail.

"It's our neighbors, right?" Mari asked.

"Yeah, so, the thing on our sidewalk? It was a car."

Mari gasped. "A car?"

"A smart car, literally on our front step. And color me impressed, but the thing fit. Anyway, I knocked on their front door. I could tell someone was inside, but they refused to answer."

"This is getting ridiculous. We can't let this go on." Mari slammed her book shut and gathered her things into her tote. "You know what? I'll take care of it. Let's kick butt with this wedding. Then, meeting, tomorrow ten a.m."

"But tomorrow's Sunday." Pearl whined, then grumbled, acquiescing. "Is this a family or a business meeting?"

"Both." Mari was too old for this crap, and now that she was in charge—okay, one-third in charge—she would not be pushed around. It was time to get everyone on the same page, sisters *and* neighbors alike.

two

Mood: "Respect" by Aretha Franklin

I absolutely refuse to spend my days off like this." Pearl de la Rosa scowled, pushing down on the plunger of Mari's French press with the same concentration she put into one of her yoga poses. Wisps of steam billowed from the canister's spout, the scent of java calming her despite the annoyance that had invaded her body. "We can't live and breathe work. It's not healthy. Neither is it sustainable, nor realistic. And worse, we're here for a meeting but all we're doing is watching her rant."

"You know that this has been a problem for a while. I'm tired of the noise. Since Ate Mari's the one willing to be confrontational, I'm all for it. Anyway, it's good for us to touch base after yesterday. We can't lose sync during the business transition." Jane said, eyeing Pearl with a politician's gaze, as she always did. Unlike Mari, *this* older sister had the knack of cutting through her emotions right down to the issue at hand. Hence, the reason Pearl confided in her first.

"I doubt she'll get a positive response with the way she's yelling at the poor guy. He can't get a word in," Pearl grumbled under her breath, not yet ready to concede, despite her sister's logic.

She felt sorry for 2402's owner, currently on Skype with Mari, who was seated at the dining room table in her open-concept apartment. For the last ten minutes, Mari's was the only voice Pearl had heard. Not surprising, because she was an outright nag. Pearl knew this fact well; usually she took the brunt of it.

She poured coffee into three cups while Jane fetched two creamers from the stainless steel refrigerator: coconut milk for Pearl, a French vanilla creamer for Jane. Mari liked hers as black as her heart.

Jane poured creamer into their cups, picked hers up, and leaned her elbows on the white Carrara marble kitchen island. "I think you'll be surprised. Our sister can be quite persuasive. I, frankly, am fed up with the bass thumping against my headboard."

Meanwhile, the volume of Mari's ranting dialed up from two to six, the pitch rising to soprano level. The man on the screen was fuzzy from Pearl's view, but she bet he was wishing for someone to save him.

"By 'persuasive' you must mean 'bossy,'" Pearl said, rolling her eyes, impatience burning at her chest. Mari always took over the conversation. She took over anything and everything.

Their parents had encouraged that kind of role playing. They'd perpetuated birth-order theories that Mari should take the lead, and Pearl, as the youngest, must follow. But being on this end of the equation was like getting the short end of the stick, the last slice of pie people left behind to make themselves feel better. Growing up, she'd gotten all the hand-me-downs. She'd tagged along to her sisters' activities, from dance recitals to Tae Kwon Do practices and band concerts. Whether she was twenty-five, fifteen, or five, Pearl's requests had been treated like a child's pull of a mother's arm: something to placate, a nuisance.

Through it all, Pearl had kept her mouth shut. She'd known her place in this family. As the youngest, she was doted upon, and she also had the most wiggle room. With less parental pressure, she got away with things her sisters hadn't. She wasn't under as much academic pressure. She partied. And despite the crises that befell every family—with an especially memorable one between her and Mari, aka the *Saul* incident—she had been spoiled, anyway.

But since their parents' retirement, something new had come over Pearl: a feeling of empowerment.

Her parents awarding the sisters equal ownership meant that they had intended for Pearl to step up, to stand up for herself as a businesswoman, finally, in a tangible way that no one could protest. If they'd wanted Mari to be the boss, they'd have given her a bigger share.

So: Game. On.

Pearl had decided to ask for a high-profile client at this meeting. Her pitch had been honed; she'd practiced answering the hard questions. She'd demand the much-needed promotion that she'd been hinting at for months, from social media manager and day-of event coordinator to full-time wedding planner. Or else.

Instead, they were listening to Mari berate 2402's owner. Sure, once, Pearl had stepped on vomit at their own front door. Another time, one of 2402's guests had streaked through Duchess Street. Residents turned over twice a week, sometimes three times. Not quite the Old Town vibe. But Mari herself had done her share of partying, some putting 2402's to shame, and yet here she was, acting righteous and unforgiving.

With annoyance now bursting from her, Pearl was going to stop this madness so they could get their meeting started.

Pearl circled the island and approached her sister from the right side. Now closer, the outline of the man on the screen focused, and uh-oh, he had a huge placating grin on his face.

No wonder her sister was pissed.

Mari was rattling off demands. "I'm asking you to put a no-party clause on your rental agreement. The HOA has specific quiet hours in our residential area. We live in a historic district, Mr. Quaid. Beyond that, we're a home of professionals that need our sleep. We need to feel comfortable in our own home."

Pearl inched forward to get into the camera's view, and once she detected her shadow in the box on the top right corner of the screen, she raised a hand and waved. Mari flashed her a look, the kind that said that she'd do all the talking. But, oh, it was a dare. Pearl pulled up a chair next to Mari and purposely willed a relaxed voice. "Hi, I'm Pearl. I'm Mari's sister and also a resident of 2404 Duchess Street."

"Hello, Pearl. I'm Reid." Humor played across his face. The man was handsome, clean-shaven, and wearing an open-collar oxford shirt. He had wrinkles around his eyes, his expression sincere. Behind him were the gray walls of what looked like a home office. "I apologize for the inconvenience my guests have caused you."

"It's not all your guests. We just don't want the behavior to escalate."

The man smiled. "Point noted. As I told your sister, um . . ." His gaze cut to Mari.

Mari's face clamped down into a frown, no doubt perturbed that Pearl had interrupted her speech and now had gone Benedict Arnold by having a decent conversation with the man. "*Ms. de la Rosa.*"

It took all of Pearl's patience for her not to roll her eyes.

"As I told Ms. de la Rosa, I was unaware of all the commotion. I'll look at our rental process ASAP. I don't want to upset the Old Town crowd. Or any one of you ladies."

"Thanks, Reid. That's good of you," Pearl said brightly, turning to her sister. "Right, Ate Mari?"

Mari ignored Pearl, shifting away slightly. "Mr. Quaid. I hope this is the last time we have to see one another."

"The feeling is mutual." He pressed his lips down into a tight smile. "But, Pearl"—he turned to her on the screen—"I wish *you* a wonderful morning."

Mari harrumphed at the man's jab. After she shut down the chat, she glared at Pearl, a lecture surely at the tip of her tongue.

Great. Wonderful was going to be stretching it.

"You know she hates to be talked over or corrected." Pearl's best friend, Kayla Young, said before she sipped her vodka raspberry mojito. A mischievous grin played across her mauve-stained lips. "Remember the time we were in the sixth grade and you helped her with her algebra homework and she lost her mind?"

"Yeah, I do." Pearl matched Kayla's smirk and licked her lips, relishing the citrus and salt of her Salty Dog. She leaned back and relaxed into the plush seating of the Coronation, a recently remodeled Euro-Asian fusion restaurant she was scoping out for Jane. Jane's top wedding client wanted a local DC "blazer-and-jeans with a hint of bling," as described by the client herself, venue for their reception, and so far, this place was spot-on. The restaurant had filled considerably in the last ten minutes, though it could have accommodated another hundred people. The vibe was upscale but accessible, the space furnished with black tufted leather seats, floor-to-ceiling windows that looked out over CityCenterDC, crystal chandeliers, painted cement floors, and hand-scratched tables. But she digressed. "I was sorry about it, but not sorry. I love my sister but—"

Kayla held up a hand; thin rose gold bangles jingled at her wrist, a rich contrast to her dark brown skin. "Please, I'm not judging. No need for caveats. You remember I have a twin, right? Who I love dearly but has crashed with me 'temporarily' and is already cramping my style? You'd think that he would have let up by now since we've lived apart, but nope. Trenton is all in my business about having a boyfriend. He sat Calvin down to, and I quote, 'get to know him better.' I am too old for this." She scrunched her nose. "By the way, I hope you don't mind I invited T to crash girls' night. My call schedule has been bananas, and in my lack of sleep I totally forgot to text you to make sure. This pediatric residency is kicking my ass."

"No, I don't mind at all!" Pearl's answer came out louder than she'd intended. She lowered her voice despite her racing heart. "I mean, it'll be good to catch up."

Pearl shifted in her chair. Crap, was she sweating? At the mention of Trenton, she was catapulted back in time, her squabble with Mari all but forgotten.

The Youngs and the de la Rosas were thick as thieves; she'd known Trenton and Kayla since kindergarten. Pearl's mother and Mrs. Young had bonded at the Filipino-American club in Alexandria, and when they'd found they lived within walking distance of each other with kids the same age, the bond was soldered. Together, the mothers had dragged the American-born Filipino de la Rosa girls and biracial Black-Filipino Young twins to Fil-Am cultural events with the intention of educating them on their Filipino roots.

There had been a period of time in middle school when Pearl had thought Trenton was "gross," but ninth grade did something, turned him into her Prince Charming and childhood crush. Tall, dark, and handsome. A gentleman. Beautiful to watch on the lacrosse field. The right guy to study with because he'd been as serious as a heart attack when it came to school.

Pearl hadn't seen much of Trenton since he left for the Army seven years ago. Scratch that—she'd seen pictures, of course. They were friends on several social media platforms. She'd kept up with where he'd moved and deployed. Kayla had relayed all the necessary gossip. But tonight, right now, any second would be their first face-to-face since high school.

"Speak of the devil." Kayla broke through Pearl's train of thought with an impatient sigh at the end of her sentence.

And when Pearl spotted Trenton in the crowd, her heart did something she had yet to accomplish at yoga: *sirsasana*. It flipped upside down, on its head.

Dressed in a light blue button-down and slim-fit jeans and leading with an infectious smile, Trenton screamed *born and bred in DC*, like he'd never left. "Sis." He leaned down and kissed Kayla on the cheek. Then, he turned to Pearl. "And my sister from another mister."

By God, he was going to kiss her, too. She stiffened at first, but relaxed as she took in his scent of laundry detergent and body wash, of what was undeniably him: unpretentious, silly Trenton.

You're a grown-up. He called you his sister from another mister. If ever there was a shove to the friend zone, that was it.

"It's so good to see you! What's up? How are you?" Pearl recovered and took a sip of her drink to ease her parched throat.

She waved their server over. She was going to need another drink. In a taller glass. With more alcohol.

"Nothing much." He shrugged, nudging his sister. Kayla sighed dramatically and shifted to make room in the booth. He sat across from Pearl. "Old-fashioned, please," he said when their server was at their table.

Of course an old-fashioned. Because he was exactly that: classic, chill, steady. Unlike Pearl's brain that was ping-ponging with questions about his life. Like, did he currently have a girl-friend?

"I'll take another mojito," Kayla chimed in.

"Surprise me with something festive and sweet," Pearl cooed when her turn came. Part of picking a venue was ensuring that the establishment's bartenders could deliver a variety of crowd-pleasing cocktails. Not forgetting about Trenton, she nar-rowed her eyes in jest at him when the waitress left. "Um, seven years isn't nothing."

"You're right. But it's all boring stuff." He waved the ques-tion away, as if two deployments, three moves, a full marathon, getting out of the Army, and finding a government job *just like that* was nothing.

Not like she was keeping track.

Not really.

Pearl's cheeks burned.

"I wanna hear about you, Pearly-Pearl. I hear you're moving up in the world," he said.

Pearl dipped into the last bit of her drink, keeping her grin at bay at the nickname he'd given her in grade school. But two could play at that game. "Nothing new, Triple-Threat Trent. Still just planning the small weddings. Still the day-of coordinator. Still the social media director."

"You did not just call me that."

"What? You're no longer about love, lacrosse, and *the ladies*?" Pearl lowered her voice to imitate his freshman year declaration that always made Kayla cackle. Which she did now.

"All right, all right. I see you both still like to pick on me."

Pearl shrugged.

"But seriously, I hear you're part owner of Rings and Roses now."

"Thirty-three and a third percent." She lifted her chin proudly.

Kayla palmed the space in front of them. "Yes, and our Pearl wants a *top*."

Trenton's eyebrow shot up nearly to his hairline. "Top?"

"Also known as a top client," Pearl explained. "An elite and all-encompassing client. My current ones only need me for day-of celebration services. I want a client I can follow from start to finish. I want to be right there for every decision. A client with a budget to match the attitude—sky-high." She raised her hand and Kayla slapped it from across the table.

"You tell it, P," Kayla cheered.

"I'm ready for it."

"Yes, you are."

Trenton assessed this back and forth. "So what's the problem?"

The round of drinks arrived at the table, interrupting the chatter.

"That was quick!" Pearl mused, impressed.

"We had a couple of free hands at the bar." The server set a drink in front of Pearl. "A Jack Rose. It's made of applejack, lime juice, and grenadine."

"Thank you," Pearl said. And just in time, because she was going to need the reinforcement to verbalize what she'd kept from her sisters today. After Mari's conversation with Reid Quaid, and with little time for the rest of the meeting, the business portion was rushed. Pearl had chickened out.

She took a grateful sip, letting the liquid courage flow over her taste buds. The drink was yum—the final passed test for the Coronation as an official reception contender. "My sisters don't think I'm up to it. And I . . . I think that if they don't give me the chance, I might ask them to buy me out. So I can start my own business."

"Oh. My. God." Kayla choked on her drink. "Are you serious? You're willing to leave Rings and Roses?"

Pearl straightened her back, though she felt shaky at her sudden burst of honesty. "I don't know. I think so? I want more, you guys. To be autonomous is the dream, and if I can't have it with my sisters . . . Anyway, I think I deserve it, and I have to be ready to hold my ground whenever I bring it up. The worst-case scenario would be for me to leave. You all know Mari and how stubborn she can be."

"When are you going to tell them?"

She swallowed her fear. "Soon."

While Kayla stared at her with a dumbfounded expression, Trenton responded with a wicked grin, bigger than she'd ever seen. His warm brown eyes reflected back understanding. He raised his drink. "To more, and not being afraid to ask for it."

Kayla followed suit. Pearl touched her glass to the others' glasses, this time with bravado. "To more."

At night's end, Pearl helped Trenton coax a drunk Kayla out of the Uber and into the Youngs' town house. Pearl tucked her friend under her white goose down comforter, tempted to jump in with her like they had when they were kids. For a moment she wanted to be back in the comfort of that childhood bubble, of knowing that other people would take care of your needs.

But she was a grown-up now. It was time for her to step out of that bubble fully, even if it was going to be challenging and messy.

Pearl snuck out of Kayla's room and picked up her purse from the couch. Now in a space exponentially brighter than the Coronation, the truth of what she'd revealed rang clear in her brain.

Holy crap, she'd admitted out loud she was willing to leave the family business. She'd given voice to a thought that had been festering inside her since she graduated from college five years ago.

Was she the kind of person who'd abandon the family legacy for her own success?

Was she that selfish?

Was it right?

Panic rose inside her. A squeak of a voice left her body. "I'm gonna go."

"You sure? I'm making coffee." Trenton's voice drifted from the kitchen. The bones of the Youngs' house hadn't changed much in two-plus decades. Mr. and Mrs. Young had preferred a closed floor plan and parquet flooring throughout, but after they'd retired closer to Virginia Beach, Kayla had changed out the superficial necessities like carpet, furniture, and lighting when she took on housemates. She'd stripped away the chintz wallpaper and repainted in light gray.

"I can't drink coffee this late," Pearl replied, slipping on her low boots at the front door.

"I can make decaf." His body followed his voice with a rush. His shirt was untucked now, wrinkled at the bottom, giving off a boyish charm that made her insides skip. Pearl understood she saw Trenton with childhood-crush colored glasses—he was always going to be that guy.

"Nah." She smiled. "I've got to be up early. But thank you."

"Wait." He scooped a beanie from a basket next to the front door and jammed it on his head. "I'll walk you home."

"It's three blocks to my house."

"Still, it's late." A slithery snake of a scarf materialized in his hands, and he slung it around her neck, tying it into a haphazard knot.

Pearl turned away so she could bite her lip and compose herself at this sweet, natural gesture, then followed him out the door of the town house.

The street was dark except for the soft glow of the gaslights next to front doors. She crossed her arms against the cold. "When it's dark like this, every house looks exactly the same. A door in between two windows. Three floors. Top floor dormer windows. If you don't pay attention, you'll miss my house altogether."

"It's not a bad thing. It makes for a neat-looking street."

"Yeah, I suppose, but there's nothing wrong with standing out, is there? Being seen?" The thought came out in a tumble, and she winced at her own candor. This was her first solo conversation with him in the last seven years, and it wasn't the time to bare her feelings.

His voice echoed through the quiet street. "No, you are absolutely right. Everyone—I mean, every house—should be seen for what they are. I get it, you know. It's a fine line, being part of a neighborhood that's supposed to look a certain way, yet be a home with its own value. Because it's not just about the structure, it's about what's been improved, invested in."

Her face heated at his answer, at his ability to understand the meaning behind her words. "Exactly. Some people never re-model."

"Some make massive changes," he added.

"Right," she said. "And unless there's a chance to show it off, no one would be the wiser."

They'd arrived at 2404 Duchess Street. Pearl turned to Trenton for a swift goodbye. She needed to be alone, to process the information she'd revealed today. "Thanks for walking me home."

"Anytime." He kissed her on the cheek.

All Pearl could do was nod. Geez, it was like she was thirteen all over again. *Get over it!*

She turned and stuck her key in the lock.

"And Pearl," Trenton said, now a couple of steps away. "There is absolutely nothing wrong with *you* wanting to stand out. I see you."

Pearl watched him walk off without another word. Once her heart calmed and the goofy smile on her face receded, she walked into her town house to dream of something more tangible than that compliment Trenton gave her and truer than the crush she still harbored.

She was going to dream about a future to work toward.

three

Mood: "It Had to Be You" by Frank Sinatra

The whole shop was in upheaval, at the stage of decluttering where everything had been dragged out of its nooks and crannies. Boxes were piled up in random places, papers dug out from years of storage, and with barely enough room to navigate through the shop, Mari hung signs that expressed her apologies for the mess.

In between greeting customers and tidying the shop, she eyed Pearl in the accessories area, talking up a client. With an iPad in her hand, Pearl scrolled through the screen with a finger and alternately pointed out veils hanging on a wall display behind her. The client was engaged, animated, eyes glued onto her sister's face.

Her baby sister was so good at that, at making customers feel comfortable, at getting them to stick around the shop. She was a saleswoman, and her smile was disarming. She held people's gazes with confidence, acknowledged their thoughts, and knew how to turn it all around into one pretty pitch. These were her strengths.

But Pearl had been late again this morning by two minutes. Not a big deal on a time clock, since Mari opened the shop daily, but it grated on her like the squeak of a metal hanger on a clothes rack. Today was Friday. Next to the usual Wedding Day, Saturday, Fridays were the most hectic with the shop's management, as well as with prepping for events. Add their first ever inventory to the list . . .

At the sisters' first meeting five days ago, Jane had reported that in her initial evaluation of the finances, she'd discovered cracks in the foundation: incomplete expense reports, discrepancies in the books. Her solution: a total shop inventory.

With no perfect time to close the shop, Mari agreed to undertake the task immediately.

Mari now climbed the creaky wooden steps to the third floor, the only one currently kept immaculate, into what she'd described time and again as the "area of hope": the wedding dress, fitting room, and alterations area. Three tall mirrors reflected light from south-facing windows; no need to turn on the lights until late afternoon. A wall of exposed brick, painted an antique white, played off the bright multicolored area rugs covering hand-scraped wooden floors. Three rows of dresses hung from high racks in the middle of the room, with aisles wide enough for two people to squeeze through the fabric that billowed from the racks. It had been Mari's idea to add rugs to this floor, to muffle the sounds of footsteps. And to aid in the intimacy of dress shopping, the de la Rosas spaced out their clients so only one roamed the stacks at a time.

On this floor, brides cried, they squealed, they bore their disappointments. It was where brides decided, officially—*YES!*—that they would indeed march down that aisle and take the biggest risk of their lives. And in less than an hour, Mari's top client was arriving for her first fitting. Her dress, special-ordered from Israel, had finally arrived.

Mari took note of the condition of the room with her Third Floor Checklist in mind. Temperature comfortable? All the light bulbs working? Windows streak-free? Rugs vacuumed? Did it smell more like lavender and pine rather than fabric?

For now, it was a yes to all.

A cough and the scrape of a hanger against metal alerted Mari to where Jane and their intern, Carli Swanson, were in the rows. She found them in the furthermost row. Jane was reading SKU numbers and descriptions, while Carli looked through a white binder, acknowledging each entry with a "yep."

Not wanting to bother them, Mari headed to the backmost office, beyond the client dressing room and behind a curtain, to where their lead seamstress, Amelia Garland, worked in her lair. The sound of Louis Armstrong's distinct singing voice filled the air, wrapping around Mari like a ribbon.

The song tugged her into the space. Mari knew all of the greats by now, with Amelia part of the Rings & Roses family since it all began. Amelia had played Etta James and Duke Ellington and Nat King Cole on repeat Mari's whole life. She never got tired of it.

The blond woman was alone at the moment, behind her sewing machine, hands buried in the ivory fabric of a dress for one of Jane's clients. A pincushion was wrapped around her wrist like a bracelet of shiny studs. The needle of the industrial machine stitched against the bodice of the dress, marked with blue washable ink and clover-topped pins.

Amelia didn't look up from her work. "How are things going out there?"

"Great." Mari answered back brightly. She pulled her stool

from the back of the room, behind a wall of ribbons and bolts of fabric. Although they didn't make wedding dresses at the shop, they found it necessary to have extras of every type of fabric and ribbon known to humankind. Amelia was a magician at bridging the gap between the original design and what brides envisioned. The dresses on the rack were simply the beginning of the process, the blank canvas of what would eventually become a fully customized wearable work of art.

Mari had been a full-time wedding coordinator the last decade, but this space, amidst the smell of sewing-machine oil and the purr of the motors, was her place for a breather, a reset.

It was where she was least expected to perform. Mari was always cerebral. Not like Jane, with her penchant for numbers and science. Unlike Pearl, with her constant chatter that put people at ease.

Mari's head was always full of stuff: of ways to do better, to be better. She checked her motivations and efforts against action. She was always asking herself: What else could I have done?

In Amelia's space, Mari could shrug her shoulders down, slouch into her stool, and simply relax.

"Great? Is that it?" The sewing paused as if the machine, too, was waiting for Mari's answer. "You've sat in that same spot a thousand times the last twenty years, and there's always a reason why, Marisol." Her cheeks wrinkled as she smiled, leathery from her visits to Bethany Beach, where she spent every available long weekend during the year. She owned a four-bedroom beachside home steps from the surf.

A quick thought came to Mari: Amelia was a short-stay rental landlord herself.

Speaking of . . .

"Darn right, there's a reason." Mari beamed. "I'm thrilled.

We've all slept better because there have been zero parties next door."

"Ah. Your ultimatum worked." Her eyes twinkled. "But I was talking more about Rings and Roses. How did your first week fare?"

"All right. Mommy only called me twice this morning. We're slowly adjusting to managing the shop among ourselves—not having an extra person is a blow, and we're still scrambling to fill shifts. I'd like to hire an assistant or salesperson soon. Inventory should wrap up today. I'd say things are moving along well." She paused, mesmerized by the needle threading through the fabric. "But it all feels too smooth."

Amelia had gotten to the end of the stitch, and she snipped the thread from the fabric. She rose from her chair, snapping the fabric straight, and with a magician's flair revealed a scallop-trimmed bodice adorned with beads.

As usual, it took Mari's breath away. A dress on the rack was beautiful in its own right, but once it chose an owner, it came to life.

"What do you think? Is it lovely, or is it lovely?" Amelia held the dress up to herself and blinked flirtatiously, making Mari laugh. "Good," she said, as she walked the dress to a rack, but not before she looked askance at Mari. "I wanted to hear that laugh. For a second there, I thought I heard doubt in your voice."

"It's not doubt." Mari picked at a piece of lint on her pin-striped slacks, gaze rooted downward and inward at how Amelia could wade through the muck that Mari came in with and find the pearl. "I'm just being realistic. I did run this business next to my mother. There were good and bad times."

"And there will always be both those times, so enjoy the moment." She fluffed the dress in between the others on the rack.

"You're in a much better spot than when your mother and I came into this business. You have the knowledge and the experience. Not to mention the help of two other sisters who are every bit as talented as you. They are your biggest assets."

A grumble made its way out of Mari's throat. Amelia had meant her advice to be helpful, but at the mention of the intricate and complicated relationship she had with her sisters, especially Pearl, the truth came down like a red velvet curtain at a theater.

They might be her biggest assets, but they were also her biggest challenges. She'd felt the undercurrent at their last meeting, more so than in the many years they'd worked together. Under one boss—their parents—there had been someone to rally against.

Now, it was as if they'd been let loose after being held back by gates. Pearl with her lack of seriousness, Jane's detachment from the business, still understandably putting her son first. Was there truly such as a thing as an equal share? From the couples she'd worked with, she'd learned equality wasn't possible each and every day. It was a give and take, a constant negotiation.

"What's your biggest worry?" Amelia perched on her chair. Using a small brush, she swept the lint and thread off her workspace and into her hand.

Mari inhaled, the words at the tip of her tongue. The anticipation of relief was mere seconds away. She'd finally reveal that the pressure to succeed weighed on her shoulders. The need to take Rings & Roses to the next level bore heavy on her mind twenty-four seven, and wrangling her opinionated sisters in the process seemed insurmountable.

But the cell phone in her hand buzzed, slicing the moment in half. It was a text from Pearl: Hazel Flynn arrived. Settling her in your office.

"Your top?" Amelia teased.

"Yep." Mari hefted herself onto her feet and nodded toward the singular dress hanging on a tall rod. A glory of lace and beads, angelic and provocative all at once. "Ready for another round?"

"But of course. Let me put on my lip gloss. Let's give her the time of her life, shall we? But Mari?"

"Yes?" Mari had a hand on the curtain. She looked back at Amelia, who leveled her with the kind gaze she'd come to rely on.

"It's okay to worry. But don't let it consume you. We're all here to help, and you can rely on us."

She smiled, her mind already on the next step. "I know."

Hazel Flynn's smile was the kind a wedding planner wanted to see first thing in the morning: wide and disarming, open and sincere, and not the transactional smile Mari sometimes encountered from clients who saw her as just another employee rather than an expert in her field.

Hazel's smile was like a friend's.

So, aside from Hazel's unlimited budget and exquisite taste, if she'd asked for the world, Mari would've found a way to package it in a turquoise box and wrap it with a satin ivory ribbon.

"The future Mrs. Brad Gill." Mari entered her office with open arms, and Hazel, an easy half foot taller than Mari's five-foot-two frame—five-four in her black patent leather two-inch heels—fell into it like Mari's nephew had done time and time again, with part relief, part excitement. Like she'd needed a hug. Jean Patou's Joy, a scent so light it was as if she'd skipped under a mist of it, brought a smile to Mari's face because the perfume was perfectly Hazel. Delicate and sweet. She stepped back. "Are you ready for today—" She faltered, noticing Hazel was alone. "Where's your matron of honor?"

Unlike other brides of Hazel's social stature—old money, well connected, and lovely to boot—Hazel had her Louboutins firmly planted on the ground. She'd planned for an intimate wedding of seventy-five attendees, and only one in her entourage: her matron of honor. A recent transplant from Atlanta, she'd given Mari four months to bring together all the chaotic moving parts of the most important day of her life.

The event was sure to be glamorous, classic. But the plans had been fraught with issues, as could be expected, especially because of the short timeline, with only three months left till the big day.

"She's on crutches." At Mari's raised eyebrows, Hazel's lips quirked downward. "She fell while dancing the Cha-Cha Slide in four-inch heels at a charity banquet and broke her ankle. I can't even make this up. I hope you don't mind my stepbrother coming. He's in town for business the next couple of weeks, and I didn't want to do this alone. Is that okay?"

"A hundred percent okay. I'll let the ladies know to expect him." Mari's fingers flew on her iPhone, sending a group text to her sisters and Carli. A pang of worry shot through her. Mari had chalked up the lack of participation from Hazel's friends to her need for privacy and that they were only, technically, a month into the planning. But Hazel's mother was also MIA. Hazel seemed alone. "Let's head to the dressing room. Or would you like to have coffee before we head up? Wait. Can you have—" she glanced down at Hazel's belly.

Hazel nodded. "Coffee is still allowed. But I had my cup today. Water will be fine. Or soda? Oh no, I shouldn't have soda either, I think. Sorry, I'm nervous."

Mari peered at her, knowing exactly what she needed. She sent another group text. "Since we're waiting for your stepbrother, let's relax a bit before we begin." She led her back to the tweed armchair and sat across from her.

"Mari, I have to be upfront. The reason why I'm nervous is because I have to tell you something."

"Anything."

"It's about my family . . . they don't know I'm pregnant. And I don't want anyone to find out, not until after the wedding."

Mari stilled. When Hazel had walked into her office a month ago with her wish to marry in a hundred and sixty days, Mari had initially refused her. Budget be damned, the timeline was nearly impossible for where they wanted to marry, at the Carnegie Institution for Science in DC. But the woman was distraught, practically begging, finally admitting she was six weeks pregnant with the baby of a man she'd only met two months prior but whom she'd fallen madly in love with. In the end, Mari had said yes, but she hadn't realized part of her job was to lie. "Hazel . . . wow."

"My stepbrother has given me a hard enough time with the timing of the wedding and me moving here to Virginia. I don't want one more thing to add to the stress." She lay a hand on her belly. "I don't want bad vibes for this little one."

A knock on the door produced Carli, carrying a tray of iced peach tea and delicate Filipino-style meringue cookies in pastel colors from Barrio Fiesta, a local Filipino store and restaurant.

Hazel accepted her glass gratefully; she sipped it like it was chocolate milk after a race, color rising to her cheeks. "Oh, that's so perfect. Thank you."

"Of course." When Carli walked out, Mari said, "Okay. I will do my best to keep it under wraps. We'll have to update Amelia, our seamstress, and my sisters as well. I'd mentioned your pregnancy as part of the alterations and general wedding plans. But I don't foresee it being a problem."

"Thank you." Another gulp of her tea, and Hazel's glass was half empty. "Not gonna lie, it's been stressful with Brad traveling a bunch. I moved in with him so we could plan this wedding together, but he's not been around to do it with me. I mean, obviously, we discuss the wedding, since we keep making changes." Her voice dipped into a whisper, and her gaze dropped. "We're still getting to know one another."

The "Glynn" nuptials were turning into the classic "Monday morning fiancé" situation. Brad Gill, always unavailable because of work, micromanaged Hazel from afar, and usually, after the decision had been made.

Mari pulled a speech from her internal catalog of wise sayings. She softened her tone to put Hazel at ease. "I promise none of the decisions you'll make are wrong. The most important part is you and Brad. We can change things as necessary."

Luckily, changes were especially easy with Hazel's unlimited budget. Besides having family money, Hazel was an entrepreneur and an interior designer. Brad was from old money himself and a highly sought-after residential architect. He'd managed projects in the tristate area, though he was expanding into Seattle, which was where he was until the third week of March.

"You're right." Relief settled over Hazel's expression. "I just wish he was here."

"More fun for us." Mari winked.

A knock at the door pulled their attention. It swung open, and Carli walked in. "Mr. Quaid is here."

Quaid. Mari racked her brain as she rose—the name was familiar—and faced the suited man. He was tall, over six feet, in a slim gray coat and slacks, with an open-collar shirt. His hair was cropped close on the sides, though wild and curly up top. His green eyes canvassed her face. The next second, recognition flashed in them.

Mari's brain fired awake. Stunned, she could only stick a hand out.

"Reid Quaid, Hazel's stepbrother." He returned the handshake.

Mari choked out a haphazard hello.

Reid. The owner of 2402 Duchess Street. The guy she'd told off was the stepbrother of her most important client.

four

Mood: "Don't Stop Believin'" by Journey

When it rained, it poured, and right now, Pearl was in the middle of a category 2 hurricane. With the shop a mess, customers were especially rambunctious—they'd assumed open boxes on the showroom floor was carte blanche permission to rifle through them. This morning she'd acted as referee and bouncer, keeping track of the foot traffic in the shop, preventing runaway children from pulling on the lace of the dresses, and answering questions as they were rocketed at her, all with a smile on her face.

Her pocket buzzed with texts from the Ortega-Robinson, or "Orbinson," couple. Their wedding was tomorrow, St. Patrick's Day, and the bride and her groom were having a potentially wedding-breaking argument. Will Ortega had staunchly insisted on wearing one of his own suits instead of the barong tagalog, a sheer, embroidered Filipino formal shirt, which he and his future bride had agreed upon, citing that "it wasn't comfortable." A first-world problem, true, but a problem nonetheless, because Chrissy Robinson had planned on wearing a vintage 1940s traditional Filipino Maria Clara gown, complete with butterfly sleeves, but with added sequins to the bodice and refitted into a mermaid profile. The bride herself was not Filipina but had Irish roots, and it was her idea to incorporate each of their families' customs into the celebration. For him to wear a suit to his own black-tie event was unacceptable.

But Pearl pushed that current crisis to the side. More pressing news had come down the wire. When Carli descended from the second floor, Pearl rushed at her. "Can you cover for me down here? I need to talk to Ate Mari."

"No prob." Carli held the serving tray tightly in her hand as a customer brushed past. "But Mari's in a fitting right now with her top."

"Oh, that's right. Thanks."

"Also, your fortieth wedding anniversary event in May? Mrs. Gonzalez called again—another argument, another crisis with her husband."

Pearl internally sighed—since starting to coordinate the details of their event, she'd received at least two phone calls a week from someone in the Gonzalez family. But she smiled. "I'll take care of it."

Pearl bit her lip as she climbed the stairs and the bustle of the shop fell behind. She *could* wait to approach Mari with the news. She *should* wait. Then again, her eldest sister was the first to advocate for drive and communication.

And if Pearl didn't do it now, she might lose her nerve.

Pearl was both blessed and cursed to have two mothers in her life; the second was the woman on the third floor who'd never let her get away with a thing. Mari didn't pick her battles. Pearl always had the overwhelming urge to push her buttons, to challenge her theories and her strict processes. But today, she would render herself immune to Mari's words so she could get her message across.

Today was the day.

With every step, Pearl imagined a protective brick sliding into place. By the time she reached the third floor, she was encased by a full imaginary barrier. Hazel Flynn's fitting was in progress, so despite Pearl's heart pounding in her ears, she lightened her steps, almost tiptoeing. The scent of fabric filled her nostrils and bolstered her.

Hazel stood on a wide platform, two stair steps above the floor. Her back was to the entrance; she was facing the mirror. In a stunning mermaid wedding dress covered in Victorian lace with a dramatic flair at the bottom, she turned slowly to the left, and then to the right as Amelia, barefoot and wearing black in stark contrast, fiddled, inspected, and pinned fabric to its future shape. Finally, she stepped back.

Hazel beamed. Her hair was up in a haphazard clip, exposing the Sabrina neckline and deep scoop of her dress back. Pearl recognized this dress. It was a Galia Lahav design, ivory and long-sleeved and utterly romantic and sexy all at the same time. The lace peeked into the bodice, showing off Hazel's hourglass figure. No sign of her baby bump yet, but it wouldn't have mattered—the dress was forgiving in the midsection because of its corset back. Besides that, Hazel glowed.

"And let's not forget." Mari appeared from the right side of the mirror with a sample veil in her hand. With Amelia's assistance, Hazel bent at the waist as Mari clipped the veil to her hair. With a sweep of her hand, the fabric cascaded down Hazel's back, completing the dream.

Hazel choked back a sob. "It's perfect."

"Of course it is. You are magnificent." A man's voice echoed from the couch. His profile was visible though fuzzy from the door. Pearl approached her sister, who stood silently with her hands clasped at her front, now on the left side of the mirror.

It amazed Pearl that Mari appeared so collected among her clients and knew when to give them space. With her sisters, Mari often charged in like a bull and demanded what she thought was right.

After a closer inspection of Mari's expression, Pearl detected that something was off. Her sister's face reflected something apart from the usual joy for her bride and calm competence. Pearl sidled up next to her and gazed upon her point of interest: the groom.

Or was it the father of the bride? The man was a few years older than Hazel and looked nothing like her, but his expression was of pure affection.

Pearl's brain slowed as she recognized the cheekbones, the unruly hair. And then . . . "Oh, isn't that—" she whispered.

"The very."

"Awkward."

"Yep. He's her stepbrother." Mari's cheek caved in as she bit it.

"Dear God. Did he . . . bring it up?"

"No, which makes this a little complicated. Do I?"

As if the man had heard them, his gaze swung their direction. Drama was written all over it.

Pearl spoke up before she lost her focus. She could feel her resolve slipping. "I'm sorry to interrupt, but I found our next client."

"Oh?" Mari's phone flashed with a message, and her attention went to it. She scrolled up with a thumb.

"If I snag this bride for the shop, I want her as *my* client." She forced Mari's attention by addressing her formally. "*Ate Mari.*"

Her big sister inhaled and exhaled, then turned her body slightly to give Pearl her full attention. "Sorry. Repeat, please."

"I found a top." At the sound of the *T* word, Mari stood straighter. Pearl continued, emboldened. "And I want her as my client. As a full-service planner. I'm ready. The last of my day-of clients is done in November. The rumor mill is betting on the wedding happening next fall. I can make myself free. Carli is ready to take on more than the regular shop duties. She can handle our social media accounts."

The words plopped out in succession, leaving Pearl out of breath. Mari's face was deadpan—indicating that she was thinking, hard. She had a poker face down to a science. "Who is it?"

"Daphne Brown."

"*The* Daphne Brown?"

"The one and only." Daphne was DC's *it* girl. The diamond in a roomful of pearls. She was a senator's daughter, a Harvard Law grad turned lifestyle guru, and had a mega media empire built on her love for the DC area. "Her rumored three-month whirlwind romance with Carter Ling, the British investment banker? It's for real, and he proposed earlier this week."

"How do you know all this?"

"Her now fiancé is a yogi." Pearl smiled triumphantly. "Haven't I told you that hot flow is magic?"

Mari frowned, not understanding. Pearl sighed, pulling the threads of her meandering thoughts into one. "Kayla goes to seven p.m. hot flow on Friday nights at Ohm, you know? She's invited me more than once, but it's not my speed to go that late. Might as well give me a shot of espresso; it would keep me up all night"—Mari shook her head, never one for free-flow convo, especially about yoga, so Pearl sped up—"Anyway, Carter has family in Old Town and pops in to get his yoga on. He's been chatting it up with Kayla, they became yogi friends, and voila." She jazz-handed for effect. "It's truly insider scoop."

"So you want to convince her to come to us?" Her eyebrows furrowed.

"Yeah. You don't think I can snag her?"

"It's not that. We're not in the business of solicitation. That's not our style. That's not what we do here."

"I know what we *do here*. And it's not solicitation. It's marketing. Anyway, if and when she asks us to plan her wedding, with my slight *encouragement*, I'd like for her to be my client." She stuttered, remembering to throw in a nicety to ease the skids. "I . . . mean, if that's okay with you."

"Ready to get undressed?" Mari said too loudly, her words now directed toward Hazel, who was looking at them expectantly.

At the sight of the full beauty of the woman in front of her, Pearl dropped the subject with Mari. Part of their service was to make clients feel like stars, but there was no question Hazel truly was one. Hands out, Pearl emerged from the shadows behind Mari, took Hazel's hands into hers, and squeezed. "You are going to wow your groom."

Pearl bent down and gathered the dress's train while Amelia took Hazel's right hand. As Hazel stepped down the platform stairs on her three-inch heels, Reid Quaid rose from the couch and took his sister's left hand. His expression was like a father's: choked up with a slight bit of fright on his face. "Might as well practice now, I guess."

Minutes later, after Reid had departed down to the main floor, his duty complete, Pearl tapped her foot as she waited for Mari and Amelia to help Hazel out of the dress. When Mari finally popped through the curtain, Pearl rushed her for her verdict. "So?"

"So, what?" Mari's tone was distant, as if Pearl hadn't asked her the most important question in her career.

"Top bride. Me. Next."

"I don't know." Mari sighed. "Look, I don't want you soliciting brides."

"First of all, you know that other planners are already up her butt. Secondly, I won't, but it doesn't mean I can't gently lead her to us. Kayla can make the introductions—"

"And." Her gaze was pointed. "Your focus should be on your current clients. Like the Orbinson wedding tomorrow. Are you all set?"

Pearl shut out the burning texts in her pocket. "Of course I am."

Mari crossed her arms. "So you're using the Day-Of Event Checklist we all agreed to use?"

"As if I don't know how to pull off a day-of event, but yeah . . . okay? I used the checklist." Pearl fibbed, because Mari and her checklists were ridiculous. Her checklists were the kind of bureaucracy that hindered progress. It took longer to fill out her checklists than it took to actually do the tasks. And truth be told, the sisters did not *agree* to use them—Mari simply mandated it.

Someone cleared their throat. Amelia was giving the two of them the eyes, eyebrows raised. *Quit fighting*, those eyebrows said.

Mari made to turn, but Pearl reached for her forearm.

"Ate Mari."

Mari waved her away with irritation in her voice. "Yes, okay. *If* she comes to us, then she's yours. But only if. And then we'd have to talk about the details."

"Okay, whatever. Cool," she said to her sister's back. Inside, Pearl pumped her fist. *Yes.*

Pearl discovered in childhood that the key to thriving under the shadow of her two older sisters was to celebrate their strengths. She'd used Jane's notes to help her through school; she'd asked Mari for backup when she begged her parents for a later curfew.

It was never about *who* was better among them in the family, but who was better *at what*.

Pearl applied the same theory to marketing. One had to have contacts, connectors, resources, and sometimes, spies, and Pearl didn't have a shortage of any of them. It helped that Rings & Roses had been around forever. Their reputation preceded itself. Vendors wanted to work with them and their high-profile clients. The de la Rosas were known as discerning; they partnered with businesses that wouldn't disappear overnight.

Pearl's list of partners was short but reliable. Ohm Studios was on this list. Like spa gift certificates or a wine-tasting tour, bridal and couple yoga sessions sold like hotcakes. While Pearl didn't subscribe to the "shedding for the wedding" ethos, a peaceful mind she could get behind.

Coincidentally, Ruby Dunford, one of Ohm's co-owners, was Pearl's dearest friend. And she'd confirmed that a certain couple had indeed signed up for tonight's hot flow class. Since tomorrow was the Orbinson wedding and she had already planned a night of last-minute prep, Pearl had nothing to lose. *Bring it, insomnia.*

She checked her watch: ten minutes till seven and she was running late. The Orbinson rehearsal at St. Mary's Catholic Church went off without a hitch, with the groom promising to think about switching back to the barong, but what took longer was Pearl's research on Daphne and Carter. As usual, she went down a rabbit hole with Daphne's engaging blog. If the woman wasn't going to be her client, Pearl would have to beg her to be her friend. Her posts were funny and self-deprecating but fabulous.

Pearl speed-walked down Duchess Street in her yoga outfit, hair up in a high ponytail, mat bouncing against her back with each step. Kayla, who'd agreed to let Pearl tag along so she could make introductions, was surely pissed; she was as anal about time as Mari was.

She startled as she came around the corner of Burg Street. Trenton was standing at her and Kayla's meeting spot, under the glow of a streetlight. In shorts and a long-sleeve tee. With a rolled yoga mat under his arm.

Her legs slowed. The bones in her body softened. The question of why he was looking at her expectantly was superseded by her raging hormones. Trenton had become a man, all right. Goodbye late-teen lanky body, hello muscle.

"Hey, Pearly-Pearl."

"Hey." She was out of breath. "What's up?"

"I've been sent in my sister's place."

"Oh." She frowned. "Why?"

"Someone didn't show up for call, and Kayla was next on the roster. She felt bad about bailing last minute."

Disappointment rocketed through Pearl. She was counting on Kayla's connection and familiarity with Carter. But resolve replaced it the next second. She had this—her promotion depended on it. She led the way to Ohm. It wasn't far—a short five blocks. "No, it's fine. Um, have you practiced yoga before?"

"Nope." He rested his hand on the back of his head. "But it shouldn't be too hard, right? I thought, hey, I need to go for a run anyway. Might as well stretch beforehand."

A cackle escaped her lips. "A nonbeliever. Well, yoga challenges and relaxes your mind and body, all at the same time. And believe me when I say that hot flow will surprise you."

"I hear there's some sweating to be had."

"An itty-bit." She squeezed her thumb and pointer finger together for emphasis, then gave him the side-eye, gauging his real interest. "Did Kayla tell you the real reason why I'm going to this class, since it's not my usual?"

"Yep. Luring a client. I'm down with it. I don't start work for another couple of weeks. Apparently, I owe Kayla my life for crashing with her and backing you up will help cover it. Besides, I want to see you work your magic and get this couple to sign on the dotted line while in that cat-dog position." He nudged her with an elbow.

"That's cat cow and down dog." She rolled her eyes at his teasing.

His laugh trailed off as they arrived at Ohm. Tiny bells jingled when Pearl opened the door to a lobby lined with benches. Instrumental music filled the room, and the water feature in the corner added to the ambience that kept everyone in hushed tones.

She approached the front desk. Ruby was propped straight on her stool, fingers on her laptop's keyboard. As usual, her friend was stunning. Red hair piled on the top of her head, body strong and lean, muscles formed without flexing. Behind her, her husband, Levi, was folding T-shirts.

Ruby's gaze darted from Pearl, to Trenton, and back, blue eyes swimming in pleasure. "Well, hello, Pearl. So glad you could join us for couples' yoga."

Pearl frowned. "Couples?"

"Yep." She lowered her voice. "Oh my God, didn't I mention it? We switched schedules around this week. We received numerous requests and this was the only time Levi was available, so, you know, we could demonstrate together."

It was only then that Pearl noticed the other class participants sitting on the benches, in pairs. Pearl shook her head ever so slightly, stiffening.

"I'm so sorry."

"I'm down for that," Trenton said in Pearl's silence, nonchalantly. "I'm Trenton, by the way. Kayla Young's brother."

"Ruby Dunford. Kayla told us you're back in town after being stationed elsewhere with the Army. Thank you for your service. I'm a co-owner here, but I know Sanjana—the other co-owner—would agree that you should try a class out for free. We have a military and veterans discount, if you decide to grab a membership. Oh, let me introduce you to my husband . . ."

The two continued to yammer while a knot of anxiety bloomed in Pearl's belly. How was she going to do this? Couples' yoga meant touching. At hot flow sessions, women peeled their clothing down to boy shorts and sports bras, and guys stripped down to their shorts. Pearl had never felt shy before since she was usually too focused—but with Trenton? And all while having to lure Daphne to Rings & Roses?

The bells of the front door jingled, snatching Pearl's attention. Daphne and Carter sauntered through as if they owned the place, their voices not in keeping with the studio's peaceful vibe.

All at once, Mari's doubtful face flashed in Pearl's memory, transforming her anxiety into sheer determination. Shyness be damned. She wrapped her arm around Trenton's waist, his abs contracting, to her delight, and with a singsong tone said, "Ready to get our mats set up? I am *so* needing a break from Rings and Roses right now. It's definitely wedding season."

Ruby's lips wiggled to keep a smile at bay. Pearl never talked about work while in class. Yoga was her tool to calm her nerves, to silence her brain, since it had a tendency to run amok. While Mari coped with cooking and Jane found solace reading, Pearl looked to yoga, especially the most important bit at the end, the *savasana*, or corpse pose, as her center.

But right now yoga was for networking.

Trenton was quick on the uptake, picking up Pearl's yoga mat for her as they both kicked off their shoes. And before they walked into the already heated room, she glanced at Daphne and smiled sweetly, as if she hadn't just planted a seed that she would soon water and sun.

five

Mood: "Poker Face" by Lady Gaga

It was 8:30 p.m., and Mari's feet were killing her. Now in flat canvas shoes, she walked home from Burg Street with the straps of her heels wrapped around her finger, her leather bag slung over her shoulder, and two paper bags stuffed with three baguettes and various meats and cheeses from La Crémerie, the cheese shop two doors down from Rings & Roses. Her tummy rumbled at the smell of the savory prosciutto. She couldn't wait to dig into the flaky bread.

But this was her commute home, and she was going to take her sweet time.

People in the DC area complained about the commute like it was an Olympic sport. It was common for folks to be on the road or the Metro an hour, if not more, for their trek into and out of the city. Mari's walk, a short three blocks east and one block north, was ten minutes. Fifteen if she took her time.

Being so close to work had its disadvantages, though, much like living in the same building with the people one worked with. The main: privacy was almost nonexistent. Their town house on

Duchess Street might as well have been a college dorm. Mari and her sisters kept their doors unlocked until it was time for bed. During waking hours, it was open season for socializing and crisis management. They also had keys to each other's places, just in case. Mari was never surprised to encounter one of her sisters in her kitchen—she was the default family chef and had a stocked pantry and refrigerator—or someone rummaging through her closet.

Her walk home was the only time of day, besides bedtime, when she was alone, and she took advantage of the peace and the beauty of Burg Street at night. Shops outlined their awnings and topiary trees with white lights. A street musician played his guitar, serenading the tourists, setting the stage for what could be a Hallmark movie. Historic Alexandria had a small-town feel, with just enough charm plus the inclusive environment of a diverse metropolitan city nearby.

She'd needed this. Today had been a whiplash of emotions. Work exhausted her daily, sure. Surprises arose in this business with such frequency that a lack of drama would be unusual.

But Hazel had thrown her a curve ball with her request, and even though Mari had agreed to keep her secret, she now had reservations. And on the slim chance that Pearl did, in fact, convince Daphne Brown to sign with Rings & Roses, Mari wasn't sure if her sister was ready for that kind of client—a client that would monopolize her every day, who would hold her to the fire of a schedule. Mari couldn't allow for failure to occur under her watch.

Which meant another fight between the two of them was on the horizon, another discussion where she was made out to be the uncompromising individual.

Sometimes it was so exhausting to have to continue to defend oneself, to fight for one's position. It was simply tiring for the past to keep nudging into the present to impose its shadow and affect how everyone saw her and treated her.

And yet none of that topped the shock of seeing Reid Quaid in her office.

This was bad.

Would she have to disclose their fight to Hazel? Had he done so already? Would their disagreement affect her working relationship with Hazel?

I'll have to apologize. Mari worked on her bottom lip with her teeth, strategizing. Apologizing was not a thing she did often . . .

And Reid Quaid? He was gorgeous.

Hence the stop a La Crémerie. A late-night snack would soothe her thoughts, would refocus her, and help her act like the professional that she was.

Now in front of 2404 Duchess Street, Mari set down her bags and shoes, and dug her keys from her pocket. A quick glance to her left, and she noticed the first-floor lights of Reid's building were on. She pursed her lips. Another renter.

But as she stuck her key into the lock, 2402's door swung open. A shadow stepped out, followed by the deep timbre of a man's voice. "Ms. de la Rosa. I was hoping it was you."

Mari stilled. *No.* Her heart fluttered in her chest; her stomach hollowed out. Was her hair a wreck? She didn't have a lick of lipstick left after she'd noshed on their leftover meringue cookies.

She straightened herself, inhaled a deep breath to squelch the heat that had surged through her. "Mr. Quaid. What . . . what are you doing here?"

"I live here."

She frowned. "I . . . don't understand."

He crossed his arms, leaned against the brick. "Well, this is my house. I usually stay in Crystal City when I'm in town, but since this is vacant, it only made sense to occupy it."

This was good, right? No more loud renters, not for a while. But how long was he staying? Would she see him every time she stepped out of her house?

She shook her head at her own nonsense. Her clients lived everywhere in the tristate area, many within a ten-mile radius of Alexandria. Then again, she'd never had a contentious relationship with any of them. "Well, that's nice. Have a good night." She attempted to pick up her things from the ground, but failed, with the weight of his stare and the need to escape pressing against her. She dropped a shoe. A bag tipped precariously out of her arms.

"Do you . . . here, let me help." Reid stepped toward her. "I was reading by the window and saw what I thought was a camel, and realized it was you, with your two bags." He eyed her packages and scooped one under his arm. "Three, actually."

"No, I'm fine." But Mari wasn't. Her heart was beating as if she had a heart condition, and suddenly she couldn't breathe. Her face flushed with embarrassment, that he could be so nice after she'd lashed out at him. But it was more than that. Reid was out of his slacks and crisp white shirt, now wearing jeans and a black long-sleeve V-neck, and he was hands down adorable in casual clothes. She glanced down at her forgotten shoe. "I've got it."

It was too late. He bent down as she stooped. Their eyes met; she darted hers away, catching herself. What was wrong with her? Fumbling, she stood, popped the front door open, then stepped into the foyer, leading him to her apartment, the first door on the right.

He looked around. "Interesting. How many apartments are in here?"

"Four, one for each of my sisters and one for my parents, though they're only now living here in the US part-time. The top floor is an unfinished attic." Speaking of her sisters, Mari took a moment to train her ears. Thank God, it was silent. Very few men entered the apartments in 2404. None of the sisters wanted to subject their dates, love interests, or "special friends" to the scrutiny of the two other women. Her sisters would have a field day with this one. She could see it now, the teasing, the *I told you so* from Pearl that Mari shouldn't have contacted Reid to begin with. "It was converted about a decade ago. My parents kept a lot of the old charm, so the baseboards and moldings are original. The fireplaces are intact, though not all of them working. But the heating, ductwork, plumbing were all updated."

He nodded, appraising the molding. "I'm in real estate and am investing in three homes in Grant Park in historic Atlanta with some renovations in the plans. Trying to mix in old and new. I'd love to get a tour of your building . . . for research," he said, casually.

"No." The word shot out of her mouth before she could stop it.

His eyebrows lifted.

"I mean, yeah. But a tour, ah, it's late. And I'm exhausted and starving. Another time?"

"Marisol." The smooth way he said her name refocused her wayward thoughts. "Can I call you Marisol?"

"Sure."

"I know we started off on the wrong foot, but I want to thank you for the work you've done with the wedding. Hazel only has had nice things to say."

She nodded, her body relaxing. He'd wanted to thank her— that was all. "It's what I do."

He grinned. "I have a feeling that it's more than a job."

Mari's cheeks pinched into a smile despite herself. In this business, not many people cared to say thanks for her sincere effort. Some were more willing to throw money at services, at problems, than they were to express true gratitude. "It is. And, you're welcome."

"And our conversation the other day on video chat? I hope it's water under the bridge. It's obvious I have some plans to make for this property, and until then, it will be for private use."

"I appreciate that." She glanced at the door and then at Reid, unsettled at the silence. This would've been the perfect time for her to apologize for her own behavior, but the suddenness of this conversation and his candor had properly thrown her off her game. "So when you're in town . . . you'll be here?"

A grin sliced across his face. "I promise—no raging parties. I'm quite boring after a long day."

"Oh, okay. Well, good night, Mr. Quaid." She leaned in and gestured for the bag he was carrying.

He piled it into her arms. "Reid. Please."

Mari placed a hand on the antique glass doorknob, twisted it slowly. "Until next time, Reid. With Hazel, I mean. If she needed you there . . . again." *Stop it, now.* The air was too thick, too heavy. She spun toward the door.

"Don't forget your—" he said behind her.

The knob jiggled under her fingertips, and the door swung open wide to her nephew, Pio. His eyes widened, matched by an even more mischievous grin. "Tita Mari?"

Mari sighed, but it wasn't because of her nephew's reaction to the stranger at her front door. It was because of her two sisters behind him, both barely holding back distinct looks of curiosity and amusement at Reid, who was holding up her shoe.

She really had to change her locks.

———

Her sisters were out for blood. As soon as the door shut behind her, and after Reid exited the building, Pearl and Jane swooped toward Mari, unburdening her of her physical load but attacking her with questions.

She dropped her shoes. "You guys. It's nothing. Quit it!" Except instead of annoyance, she laughed, swept up by her sisters' excitement.

Her sisters worked on each other's love lives like Cupid's assistants, but they tackled Mari's as if there were a grand prize at the end of it. As if getting hitched at thirty-two was a feat, a lost cause. As if it was a requirement.

There wasn't such a thing as a timeline where Mari was concerned, nor was there a fire raging inside her to find a partner. She was perfectly happy with her easy, casual dates. Exposed to every single one of the different types of grooms, she'd seen the gamut from sweet to douche; it took a lot for a man to impress her. Not to mention a certain Saul—she cringed as the name of her ex materialized in her brain—had forever smudged the possibility of a shiny new relationship.

She was also never truly alone. She was like a mother to her sisters, and Pio had given her the baby, toddler, and cuteness fix she needed, with the advantage of sending him right back to his mother when it was time for discipline.

No, it was this interaction, this closeness with her sisters, that gave her joy. Even if the teasing was at her own expense this time.

Pearl set plates on the island while Jane pulled the food from the bags—Mari always bought extra in anticipation of sharing with her family—and arranged the meats and cheeses on a wooden breadboard. Pearl sliced oranges from their fruit basket. Pio hopped up on a stool, and they all took their places around the island. Their quick-style meals were unfussy but checked the box just fine. While their parents had been sticklers at the dinner table—cloth napkins, a pitcher of water, and a somber prayer before meals that sometimes spun off to a Joel Osteen lecture—the sisters' tradition was simple and their prayer had morphed into a one-line "Thank you for the food, God" before they dug in.

Pio, as usual, took over the conversation, and the sisters indulged him. And, right on time, after a few minutes, he declared he was full. Jane excused him so he could watch television.

He'd just rounded the corner and Mari had barely layered a mouthwatering slice of goat Gouda on a cracker, when she felt the heavy stare of two pairs of eyes. She knew where this was leading. "He saw me walk by, is all. It was nothing."

"I just have never seen a man make it all the way to your apartment door," Pearl teased.

Her sister was right. Mari, if she'd even conceded to letting a date pick her up or drop her off at 2404 Duchess Street, usually ended things at the building door.

"Don't forget Lolo," Pio mentioned his grandfather from the couch. His back was to them.

"Pio. Not your conversation." Jane's voice was stern, though Mari couldn't help but giggle.

"He's right." Mari stuffed the cracker in her mouth.

"Seriously," Jane said. "You guys were out there for minutes."

Mari swallowed and picked up her glass of water, swirling it around. "Just small talk."

"He is *way* cuter in person, right?" Pearl asked.

"I'm not even going to justify that question with an answer. You know I don't look or think twice about people I work with."

"Except"—Pearl lifted her glass, then tipped the edge toward her lips—"you aren't really working with him."

"Oh, yes, I am. He's my top's brother."

"I'm just saying."

"And I'm ignoring it."

"Well, since we're talking about things ignored"—Jane lay both palms on the table—"I'm glad we're all together before another Wedding Day tomorrow, because I have something to discuss. This is business related, not personal."

Pearl groaned. "I don't like the sound of that."

Jane's gaze cut to Mari. "You won't like it either, Ate Mari."

"Shit." Mari pressed a napkin to her lips. "This has everything to do with inventory, right?"

"Numbers rule. Unfortunately, it looks like our parents didn't think so." Jane nodded somberly and took her phone out of her back pocket. After a series of swipes and taps, she placed the screen in the middle of the island. "I know this is going to be pretty hard to see. There are a ton of numbers on this page. What you need to focus on is this." She zoomed in to the screen using her thumb and pointer finger. "See that? That figure is the value of product we're missing from the store."

"What?" Mari picked up the phone and stared at the low five-figure number highlighted in red. Pearl came around the countertop and peered over Mari's shoulder. "What do you mean 'missing'?"

"Meaning it was either sold, given away, or stolen, but not accounted for. It could also mean we never got the item in the first place, though we had it listed in our inventory. Now, look at these items." She took the phone back and after two long swipes, presented it to Mari and Pearl. "This is a list of accessories and dresses—yeah, dresses, too—that we have double stock on. And for the pièce de résistance." She swiped down. "This is a list of the events that we did for free last calendar year."

Next to her, Pearl whistled the tune of a bomb incoming. Mari's tummy bottomed out. "Eight? Mommy did eight events for free last year?"

Jane nodded. "Most of it was for day-of coordination. Basically, all your events Pearl. She also gave discounts."

"This is a mess." Mari's brain felt suddenly fuzzy, like it had been crammed with cotton balls. Her heart sped up. Her fingers tingled with the first signs of anxiety. "This isn't good. This is setting us up for a crisis if we have one big emergency."

Pearl stepped back. "But we can still fix this, right? We can take on more clients. I can use our growing social media platform to reach out. The bridal expo we signed up for is a good way to pull in some clients." She waggled her eyebrows and grinned. "And when Daphne Brown signs with me, that's another top on our list."

Mari shook her head. "Hold on. Let's not get ahead of ourselves."

"What is that supposed to mean?"

"Nothing, but let's stay focused on next steps. Jane, what can we do right now?" Mari turned to the logical sister and ignored the growing frown on Pearl's face. This wasn't the time for another pitch. During an emergency wasn't the time to take a big risk.

"We stop spending. Seriously. Like, as in, zero new branding efforts, Pearl. I know we have it all set to plan for a new website and graphics, but we have to hold off."

"That's crap." Pearl crossed her arms. "Publicity and marketing has to remain the number one priority. We can't service clients we don't have. But wait—the bridal expo. Please tell me we're not backing out of it."

"The expo will be fine. The booth is paid for, though we'll have to be careful with our swag expenditures." Jane took a breath. "Next, salaries. We can't take on another employee or paid intern, and we have to pay ourselves less. If I had it my way, just living expenses for now."

"We can do that." Mari glanced at Pearl, who nodded.

"Finally, we have to charge in full for future family events."

Mari winced.

"I know." Jane frowned. "That is going to be our most unpopular decision. The family won't be happy."

The title of family went beyond blood relatives, to extended relatives and close friends. In line with the de la Rosas' cultural ideals, family—literal and figurative—was given five-star service for a two-star price. But that was before the red numbers on Jane's screen. Before Mari became CEO. "Okay, I'll take care of it."

Mari's appetite all but disappeared. The positive: they had a chance to turn the business around if they focused. One thing was clear. Not a single risk was to be taken that could derail the de la Rosas' bottom line. Time to live frugally and spread the bad news to the family that the gravy train was over.

part two

A rose must remain with the sun and the rain
or its lovely promise won't come true.

—Ray Evans

six

Mood: "Raise Your Glass" by Pink

The NBA had the Finals; the MLB had the World Series. The NFL, the Super Bowl. Rings & Roses had Wedding Day, the culmination of months of coordination, of weaving the intricate and the mundane, of fielding panicked phone calls and emails. Wedding Day was *the* romantic conclusion.

In Pearl's eyes, Wedding Day was also always deliciously dramatic.

This morning, the Robinson-Ortega wedding was in its final quarter. From the sanctuary of St. Mary's Catholic Church, a hired quartet played a Celtic version of Pachelbel's Canon in D. The groom's party stepped out in perfect time to the music—all were wearing the barong tagalog, including the groom; Pearl internally patted herself on the back for this win—toward the priest at the front of the church. The pews were packed. Everything seemed perfect.

The church's foyer told a different story. Currently, Pearl was trying to mitigate an MOB and MOG, or mother of the bride and mother of the groom, catfight. Despite the women wearing delicate attire, their scowls were a sure sign neither one was afraid of throwing down.

Standing between Mrs. Robinson and Mrs. Ortega, Pearl sorted out the details of their disagreement:

One of them had put the other in charge of purchasing the veil and the cord, two critical items for a Filipino Catholic wedding ceremony. At the dress rehearsal yesterday afternoon, where they acted out the ceremony using an imaginary cord and veil, Pearl hadn't thought to ask who was bringing the actual items this morning.

Pearl discovered that neither family had purchased them.

This type of mishap was yet another reason why Pearl wanted to be part of the planning stages. Details fell in the cracks when there were too many chefs in the kitchen. She'd only had a month with Chrissy, when she'd pieced together the timeline and her already hired vendors. After charcuterie with her sisters last night, she'd ensured the groomsmen hadn't parked themselves in some bar somewhere too long. This morning, she'd double-checked that the cake was securely at the Fil-Am Community Center and that the head table had been relocated to the middle of the room.

Oh crap. Pearl's heart sank. She hadn't told catering that huge detail. She pulled her phone from her back pocket, streamlining her thoughts. She glanced at Carli, her assistant for the day, who was waiting for her instructions. The noise in the foyer rose; Pearl's heart beat in her ear.

"Carli, do you mind backing the bridal party up a few feet for some space, please?" Pearl gestured to the frightened Chrissy and nodded at her MOH, or maid of honor, in silent communication. The MOH hastily gathered Chrissy's extended train. Carli ushered them and the six bridesmaids and four flower girls deeper into the church's hallway. Meanwhile, the two mothers continued to bicker.

"Mrs. Robinson, Mrs. Ortega, please, there's a solution to this." She kept her voice low. No doubt, the rest of the church inside had heard the commotion, even above the music. Pearl dialed the shop in silent prayer someone was there to answer. Jane, too, had a wedding today, starting in an hour. Mari was her assistant. They could be in transit. "We can fix this."

Mari answered the other line. "Hey, what's wrong?"

Pearl's relief switched to humiliation. *She expected me to mess up.* But she swallowed her pride and took a breath. "I need a cord and veil from stock, please. And I need it at St. Mary's ASAP."

Mari sighed. "This is on our Day-Of Event Checklist, Pearl. You said you were all set. I hate it when you do that, when you say things just so I lay off—"

"I . . ." Pearl started. Next to her, Mrs. Ortega huffed at Mrs. Robinson, stomping once in her short heel. Her makeup cracked as a deep scowl created a wrinkle between her eyebrows.

"How much is that going to cost? *Naku*, this is your fault, Sara," Mrs. Ortega said.

"Oh, who cares?" Mrs. Robinson's hand flew in the air, exasperated. "I'm paying for everything anyway."

Someone in the foyer gasped. Carli, who'd stepped up to the circle, bit her lip to stop a giggle.

Yes, it was entertaining, and if Pearl had been a bystander, she'd have pulled up a chair and grabbed some popcorn to watch it all unfold. But she had been hired to fix this. She had been hired not to have forgotten items in the first place.

She had also been hired to make sure the head table was set up in the right place.

The procession music repeated. The low rumble of voices

from the pews reminded Pearl that time was ticking by and her pride had to take a back seat. She hated to do it, but it was time to beg.

"Ate Mari. Please." She interrupted her sister's rant while she feigned a smile to the bridal party who was watching her intently. "The least ornate of the stock. And hold for one moment." With a soothing voice, she settled her face into a warm smile and turned to Mrs. Ortega. "It won't be but a small charge. And it can be here in less than ten minutes since the shop is just up the road."

With that, the two ladies calmed, but Mari snapped in her ear. "You can't send Carli down here? I have to head to Jane in five minutes."

"The procession has begun," Pearl said, then gritted her teeth. Her blood pressure escalated at her sister's inability to just go with it. Mari *knew* emergencies happened, that wedding planners forgot things, too. It was like her sister was hell-bent on proving that Pearl wasn't ready for a big client.

"Fine," Mari said.

"Great. Hold on." She gestured for Carli to reposition the bridal party. She led the parents of the bride and groom to the church doors and cued their entrance. When everyone was in place, she found a quiet corner. "Ate? I need another favor."

"Yes?"

"Please call Ivanna at Fanciful Catering. We need the head table set up in the middle of the room."

"Pearl!"

"No lecture, please. Help me?"

"Of course I'll help you. These are amateur mistakes, is all."

"I know, I know. But I've got to go. Thank you." Pearl hung up, 100 percent upset but confident that all would be fine. If there was anyone who could remedy mix-ups, it was Mari.

Pearl marched down the right aisle of the church. She signaled Father John with a thumbs-up. The groom, standing to the left of the priest, visibly relaxed at her cue.

Thank you, God. That was close. And remembering she was at a church, she whispered, "Please, let the rest of it run smoothly." She'd told Mari she was ready for a top. She couldn't make any more mistakes.

St. Mary's Church had a modern, minimalist feel with a simple altar and a large hanging cross, bringing attention to its curved archways and stained glass panel windows. Sun shone through the glass, and warm beams of maroon, gold, and blue gave the place a feeling of hope. A generous swath of white fabric draped the center aisle and a trail of greenery marked each pew.

The quartet quieted after the wedding party entered. Pearl cued the organist. With a flourish, the musician raised her arms. "Wedding March" piped through the space and the congregation stood. And when Chrissy proceeded down the aisle to meet her groom, the swell in Pearl's chest grew. Tears sprang to her eyes, right on time.

The tissue was already in her hand, taken from her discreet dress pocket. She stepped deeper into the dark corner of the church and dabbed her eyes.

This moment. This moment was worth the stress, each and every time. The trouble, the fights, the mad rush in the end. Even the unforeseen disasters. This scene in front of her was her reason. This happily ever after, if even for just this day, for this couple.

The phone in her hand buzzed. Trenton. You ok?

The Ortegas and Youngs were cousins by marriage, though it didn't dawn on her until then that Trenton might have been invited to the ceremony. They hadn't spoken since their couples' yoga class, except for a quick text she'd sent thanking him for jumping in. She scanned the packed pews and spotted Kayla and Trenton. Kayla was taking a photo with her phone—illegal and she knew it. Chrissy had requested no cell phone photographs during the ceremony. Pearl's fingers flew on her phone screen.

To Kayla: Put that phone away, you!

To Trenton: Now that C is down the aisle, I'm good. :)

Trenton: You've got this.

Pearl: Did you ever have any doubt?

Kayla: Party pooper.

Trenton: Not after you kicked my ass at crow pose I don't. I mean, butt. Sorry, God.

A grin snuck onto Pearl's face. He'd been a good sport attempting the intermediate poses despite being an amateur, but as the heat had risen in the room with the grunting, stretching bodies, he'd lost steam while she kept on, lifting herself into the crow position: both hands on the ground, body crouched, legs off the floor, bottom raised, knees resting lightly on her triceps. She'd even gotten an approving nod from Daphne behind her.

She bit her bottom lip: I need a favor. For this Friday the 23rd? You can say no if you're not free.

Trenton: Pearly-pearl, yes, I will be your plus one at your next yoga class. Adding it to my calendar now. Consider it a birthday present.

She blushed. Twenty-six today and she'd almost forgotten. Thank you.

The phone buzzed again, though this time, it was Carli. OMG. Caterer called. DJ arrived drunk.

Crap. Pearl skirted the perimeter of the church while scrolling through her phone for the DJ's number, heart pounding in anticipation of the butt whooping she would have to lay on him.

Forget birthdays. Weddings—they gave her life.

⁓

Pearl's number-centric sister, Jane, once did a study of the shop's clients and concluded that Rings & Roses successfully ushered ninety percent of their clients to the altar. Unfortunately, one out of ten weddings would never come to be. One example was a couple from Manassas, Virginia, who broke up a week before their wedding. It hadn't surprised Pearl; they'd fought over all the details, down to the color of the napkins. Pearl also remembered a bride who'd left her groom at the altar for their officiant. The groom had been waiting patiently at the end of the aisle, alone, anticipating the yawn of the double doors for the pastor and his bride, only to be heartbroken when it never opened.

Today would not be a sad day. Despite being lectured by Mari, and the fight between the mothers, aside from a grooms-man passing out during the ceremony because his knees locked, despite the ring bearer untying the claddagh ring from the ring pillow and dropping it onto the marble floor of the church, beyond finding another DJ within an hour's time frame, the close call of the table arrangements, and the most embarrassing maid-of-honor speech from a woman as high as a balloon that had slipped from a little girl's hand, the Orbinson wedding would go down as a win.

Now that it was all said and done, Pearl was going to enjoy this glass of Riesling in her hand.

She sat at the pop-up bar at the corner of the reception area. The guests had cleared and the cleaning staff was out in full force. Carts with dishes and silverware clinked passed her. The occasional instruction from a supervisor rose from the clanks and thumps of tables being moved, dismantled, and stacked. She'd sent Carli on the final run back to the shop while she oversaw the rest of the cleanup.

"There you are." An accusatory high voice called from behind, followed by a signal guaranteed to snag the attention of any de la Rosa, and any Filipino, in Pearl's opinion: *Pssst.*

Mari.

What was she doing here? Pearl scanned her brain for more of the day's imperfections. No wedding was ever flawless, but Mari was a brilliant executioner. Her weddings *appeared* flawless, even to Pearl. Things always clicked into place for her. During crises, Mari had such a smooth facade; she was the epitome of calm. She was the best in the business, and right now, this thought infuriated Pearl. For while Mari wasn't her boss, per se, pleasing her was the key to stepping up at Rings & Roses. She was the gatekeeper. As it was, Pearl knew she was due an earful because she hadn't used her checklist, and for lying—Mari's pet peeve.

Pearl set her glass back on the bar top, anticipating an admonishment that she shouldn't have been drinking on the job, and took a long, deep breath. She turned in her seat and promptly relaxed, a laugh bubbling from her lips.

Mari wasn't alone, nor was she empty-handed. With her was Jane, who'd raised the distinct blue bottle of her favorite Moscato in the air.

"Happy Birthday!" they said in unison, dancing in her direction despite the absence of music, and Pearl cackled at the silly sight. Mari reached over as the bartender passed her a corkscrew. Jane handed her an empty glass, brought two stools over, and created a circle. Mari poured a generous helping of Moscato into their glasses. From her pocket, she fished out a small bottle of

San Pellegrino—she must have lost the bet and was dubbed the designated driver—and twisted the cap.

"You guys don't know how much I needed this," Pearl choked out as her sisters parked themselves on the stools, though she couldn't quite look at Mari. "What are you both doing here?"

"Jane's cleanup went much faster than expected so we thought we'd surprise you. And after your last phone call we thought you needed the wine . . ." Mari said, kindly, but the words stung anyway. "We couldn't let the night go without making this part of the highlight reel. Hey." She nudged Pearl.

Pearl raised her eyes to her sister's. Their knees touched.

"You did it. You have a happy couple. That's what matters. The rest are lessons we learn from, okay?"

Pearl didn't understand how Mari could compartmentalize situations. How she could go from being cutthroat to comforting and expect for Pearl to just go with it. Mari treated situations as black and white. On and off. Now that Pearl's event was over, suddenly they were back to being good?

"Pearl?" Mari had raised her green bottle up in a toast.

Pearl raised her glass.

"To the *bunso* of the family on her birthday." Jane touched her glass to theirs. She was the toastmaster of the three, despite seeming the quietest. An objective person might have assumed that it meant she was shy, unsure of herself. Pearl and Mari knew better. Jane had the most to say.

"We are so proud of you." She gazed at Pearl lovingly. "You might be the youngest, but you are the toughest, and the only one who could have handled today with such grace. Including an inquisition from one of our own." She peered at Mari.

Mari shrugged. "Sorry?"

"May this year bring what your heart desires."

"Hear, hear!" Mari cheered.

Pearl sipped her Moscato, cheeks burning at the toast, at what her heart desired . . .

A full-service client.

A true seat at the business's table.

Autonomy.

But if the worst-case scenario happened, and she had to leave Rings & Roses, she would have to leave her sisters, too. She might not have agreed with her sisters' decisions, but they had this partnership, this bond that couldn't be re-created with another group of people.

"And"—Jane pulled out a credit-card-sized silver box—"your present."

The box was tied with black ribbon and adorned by a tag with her name written in calligraphy. Over the years, the sisters had started going in together for a gift for the other—leading to creative results. Jane was still riding the heck out of her cruiser bicycle, complete with basket and bell; she hated driving when she could ride. And Mari—well, suffice it to say, their fiber levels were at peak from the fruit strips she made using the food dehydrator they'd given her last year.

Pearl didn't bother being gentle. She tore the ribbon off and tossed the cover open, revealing a silver card, embossed with *LU* in block letters. She read the text. "Happy Birthday! You are now a Silver Member for Love Unlimited." Pearl looked up at her sisters, both with frozen, slightly bemused smiles on their faces. "Love Unlimited. As in the matchmaker?" she asked.

"The one and only." Jane sipped her wine.

"I . . . I don't know what to say." Was she supposed to laugh or be insulted? Did they think she needed help? That she needed a man? That she was a failure at dating?

Okay, sure, she'd had some bad luck lately. Nothing seemed to be working. She tackled dating like it was a part-time job. She worked those apps for a half hour a day—at least—searching for *the one*. Because yes, one day, she'd like to have a happily ever after, too. Pearl wanted a partner, someone who'd understand where she was in her life, at the cusp of something great, and who'd support her endeavors. And yes, she also wanted the entire kit and caboodle: the ball gown silhouette dress, the tiara, the red-carpet entrance, and the money dance.

"Was this your idea?" she asked Mari.

"What? Why am I always the bad guy? It was Jane's idea!" Mari burst out, glaring at Jane. All at once, the two bickered.

The sisters' arguments were like the feathers of a torn-open down pillow during a pillow fight: words drifting without rhyme or reason.

Pearl laughed. Between the exhaustion from her day, the stress of wondering what she wanted for her life, and now with this weird gift her sisters got totally wrong and right at the same time, she couldn't help cracking up. "Stop, you guys."

Mari and Jane quieted.

"It's perfect," Pearl said. "Absolutely perfect because it was from love." She leaned into a group hug, settling the chaos. What else could she have said? Feeling anything other than grateful wouldn't have helped. She wasn't in the mood for another fight. There were no refunds on these gift certificates; they'd spent good money on it.

Right now was all about celebrating her win over Wedding Day and the start of her twenty-seventh year. A year that would bring her into the great world of true independence. And she was going to enjoy the hell out of this Moscato.

seven

Mood: "Feels So Close" by Calvin Harris

A re you ready to meet the first challenging client of the day?"
Mari said to Pearl as she pulled up the emergency brake in
the Volvo. She flipped on the dome lights, which cast a dim glow
above their heads. With white and red lights flashing, a stream of
cars passed behind them through the narrow parking garage lane.

"Yep." Pearl took a breath next to her. "Thank you for letting
me tag along today."

"Yeah, well, you're not just tagging along. I'm going to need
you to back me up, too. Glynn is our afternoon appointment, and
you've met Hazel. But our first couple, 'Bito,' isn't a top, though
they're giving me heartburn like one. Let me give you the
skinny." Mari turned her planner to Reanna Vito and Francisco
Bell's page. "A September wedding at the Gaylord, National
Harbor. One hundred guests. Pink and brown color scheme. On
point budget. On paper? Straightforward. In real life? Not."

"Is she indecisive?"

"No. She's um . . . particular." Mari held back from divulging
her real opinion—that Reanna was loud, demanding, and a

mouth without a filter. Pearl was still a colleague, and right now, she wasn't listening to her as a sister, but as a mentee.

Her sisters might have complained that Mari was overbearing and hotheaded sometimes, but she wasn't ignorant. Mari excelled at listening. She didn't get to her position by imposing her choices on clients; she provided the best options she'd deduced from what she heard and observed that her clients wanted.

She was aware Pearl was getting antsy. Her restlessness resonated in her SOS phone call at the Orbinson wedding three days ago. It was in the way she shifted uncomfortably when Mari corrected her. But a gap existed between a day-of coordinator and a full-service wedding planner, and Pearl had to witness it. The job wasn't just more work—it required more commitment. It meant sticking it out despite personality challenges.

Not only must Pearl understand this learning curve, but Mari had to be comfortable with her taking on the role. Today was about watching Pearl in action while dealing with her two most challenging clients.

They sidestepped their way around cars out of the parking garage and into the full sunlight of Georgetown. It was the first day of spring, and the weather did not disappoint. The sky was a cornflower blue with streaks of white. A hint of chill remained in the air—the area was possibly due for another snowmageddon toward the end of next week—but the buds on the occasional tree on the cobblestone sidewalks dared to burst through. The narrow streets resembled Old Town, with its historic town houses, but prominent, beyond the roofline, were the two steeples of Georgetown University's Healy Hall.

They came around to a corner shop with its window framed with flowers. "Here we are. District Petals." Mari paused at the window and spied a brunette perched on a stool at a high round table. She shot Pearl a look. "And she's already here. Note that this is the third florist I've visited with this client. The first florist backed out citing personality conflicts. Reanna thought the second florist was trying to cheat her out of her money."

Pearl's eyes widened. "Oh dear."

"Stay positive, and she'll soften up." With a breath, Mari opened the front door and entered, overly chipper—the only attitude that had carried her through meetings with this client. "Good morning, everyone!"

"Finally." Reanna looked at her oversized watch face. She was hard-edged everywhere. Stiff blown-out hair, drastic eye makeup, a gaze that could cut glass. "Aren't you supposed to beat me here? I'm starving and ready to get this over with."

Behind her, Louisa, District Petal's proprietor, rolled her eyes. Already a bad sign.

Mari moved things along and dragged two stools to each side of Reanna. "Then let's do this, shall we?" The quicker they picked flowers, the faster they'd depart. "Reanna, Louisa, this is my sister, Pearl."

"Aw, is this 'bring your baby sibling to work' day?"

"No, actually," Mari said. "She's a wedding planner, too."

"God, you look like you just stepped out of a sweet sixteen party. Do you have experience? Because I hired experience."

Pearl's eyes flashed, but to Mari's relief, she kept her voice calm. "I understand your concern because I have such a baby face, but I've worked full-time at Rings and Roses the last five years."

"Okay," Reanna said after a beat, eyes narrowed, tone suspicious. She turned to Mari. "She'll pass. As long as she knows how this works. I call the shots."

Pearl popped up on a stool and said sardonically. "Oh, I can already tell that you do."

Mari internally groaned. No. This was not the time for Pearl to rise up. But instead of Reanna calling her out, she cackled, hiking a thumb at Pearl. "I like this girl." Grabbing the portfolio binder right out of Louisa's hands, bypassing the owner altogether, she handed it to Pearl. "Tell me, sassy girl. I've had a pill trying to pick the right bouquet. Everything is so"—she waved her manicured fingers in the air—"frilly. What's your recommendation?"

Mari jumped in, compelled to protect her sister, as well as to mitigate the tension before it got really out of hand. She stood and leaned over to grab the portfolio from Pearl. "Reanna—"

"Actually?" Pearl's voice lifted, taking over. "I don't even have to look through this binder to know the kind of flowers that represent you." She tapped her chin, was quiet for several beats. "You're strong, bold, with a hardy exterior. But with a softness just below the surface. And majestic."

Mari hung back, intrigued. Her sister's aura had transformed. She was confident, unwavering, and, Mari would daresay, a little subversive. But her client was eating it up; Reanna had leaned forward in her seat.

"Peonies," Pearl declared. "Peonies with their resilient blooms. They're audacious. Bewitching, much like you. And with your pink and brown color scheme, it won't be a problem to pinpoint the exact color. But may I suggest a contrasting color to wow your guests? Like a Tiffany blue."

For the first time, Reanna Vito was utterly silent. And Mari was knocked back onto her stool, impressed.

~

Mari's smile hadn't left her face since getting into the Volvo and driving herself and Pearl twenty minutes downtown to the Carnegie Institution for Science.

"You were amazing back there." Hands on the steering wheel and maneuvering through traffic, Mari glanced at her sister. "I was worried at first—"

"I thought she was going to eat me up alive," Pearl said.

"And she ended up eating out of your hand. You took her from indecision to transaction. You said exactly the right things."

"I did, didn't I?" She settled back into the seat with a triumphant grin—smug, even. "All I did was reflect how she wanted other people to perceive her. And thank goodness for Daddy and his gardening habit. Remember? He planted peonies one year? He used the word *audacious* to describe the bloom. Anyway, I thought of those two things and guessed right. Honestly, I think I could have picked any flower and she would have gone for it. Reanna just wanted someone to see her. It's really what most want, you know?" Pearl pointed up ahead. "Holy crap. An open space."

Mari swerved into open street parking across from the building. Today was their lucky day. "Your intuition was spot-on. But could you work with a client like her? Full-service?"

"I could. Reanna put up a good front, but I think I see what you see in her, too. That once she softens up fully, she'll let go. I would do a good job." Her voice was determined.

Mari nodded, proud. No doubt, what Pearl had done at the florist's—she'd gotten the client to decide, order, and pay within the hour—was indeed a feat. And her raw instincts exceeded those of Jane, who was methodical, sometimes clinical as she learned her clients' tastes. But one lucky break did not readiness—or reliability—indicate.

"Okay, then. Show me your magic a second time. We're early, so we can discuss our suggestion for the floor plan before Hazel arrives." They got out of the Volvo and darted across P Street. Banked by Victorian- and Empire-style historic homes with manicured and gated lawns, the Carnegie Institution's gray exterior with its prominent columns and its steep cement stairs could not be missed.

With a hand on the front door of the building, Mari paused. "Here's the thing. You and Jane know I took this job not just because of the budget but because I liked Hazel, and that she's pregnant."

"I remember. For a grinch you have such a soft spot for babies." Pearl grinned.

"Ha. But seriously. Apparently, Hazel hasn't told anyone in the family. And since Reid will be here today—"

"Reid? As in our *neighbor*?" She accentuated the word and trailed her sentence with a giggle.

Mari rolled her eyes. "Pearl."

"Fine, okay. I won't say a word about how you and he make such a cute couple. Or about the pregnancy." Her voice became a whisper. "I think he makes you nervous. Am I right?"

Mari groaned. Since Friday night, her sisters had teased her subtly. Neither had accepted that Reid had simply been a Good Samaritan by bringing in her groceries. They'd crowed that he had an ulterior motive. She'd tolerated the ribbing, assuming Reid's attendance at Hazel's dress fitting would be his last appearance until the wedding. Then Hazel texted last night and sprinkled in casually that Reid would be at today's venue tour.

"See, you're thinking about him," Pearl said.

"That man is the last thing on my mind."

Pearl crossed her arms and scrutinized Mari.

"Okay, fine. I thought about him. A little." How could she not? He was *fine*. Yes, she was drawn and attracted to him—and that was a feat in itself. In retrospect, in their brief moment together, Mari knew he found her intriguing, too.

But she'd done a tiny bit of research on this perpetual bachelor out of curiosity. Alas, he was a party boy. He was successful in his own right, true, but one Google search brought up pictures of him on social media with several different women.

Mari had been with a man like him before—impressive, charming, assertive—and she was better off staying away from that sort.

They were startled by the door opening. Reid was on the other side of the threshold wearing what Mari now knew was his business attire; this time navy slacks, coat, with a white dress shirt underneath.

Mari jumped back, hands on her chest. Pearl cooed, "Hello, Reid. It's you."

"It *is* me. Good afternoon, Pearl." His eyes cut to Mari. They danced with mischief. "Ms. de la Rosa. We thought we heard voices out here."

Mari lacked a witty comeback, her mind combing through her conversation with Pearl. Had she said anything incriminating? How much had he heard?

He stepped aside for Mari and Pearl to enter, and Mari shuffled ahead, desperate for distance from him and her wayward conversation with Pearl, with Hazel and the institution's event coordinator in her sights.

This was the ultimate reason Mari could never be in a serious relationship: she only had enough headspace to take care of the things that mattered. She'd sowed her oats, made her mistakes, and now was the time for real living. For building herself and this business, and being the best CEO, big sister, and aunt she could be.

The tour wasn't going as planned. Hazel was tearful and distracted. Despite the grand marble architecture and the perfect potential ceremony layout in the rotunda and for their sit-down dinner in the ballroom, she showed little enthusiasm. Her fingers flew over her phone as she texted every few minutes.

"Excuse me, Bill?" Mari interrupted the institution's coordinator, approaching him. "Can I get a few minutes with my client? Do you mind?"

He looked beyond her, to her client, and understanding flashed in his expression. "I'll be in the other room, setting up for an event this evening. Feel free to walk around."

"Thank you." Mari waited until he disappeared behind the door. "Hazel?"

"Almost done," she answered, still texting.

Mari trained her eyes on Hazel and took in her demeanor, her uncertainty, and remembered her tearful meetings with the woman. A nagging feeling tickled the back of her conscience.

She was accustomed to finicky brides, sometimes to angry brides. But she found the worried, tearful bride the trickiest to interpret. One didn't know if the tears were from joy, sadness, or anxiety. Right now, Hazel was clearly far from content.

It could've been the pregnancy or the hormones affecting Hazel's mood, but not for the first time in the last month, Mari wondered if it was a good idea for Hazel and Brad to marry. She'd met Brad just once, at the initial consultation. She hadn't been able to put her finger on it, but something about their interaction didn't sit right. It triggered deep insecurities within Mari, and when Hazel was upset like this, her mama bear protectiveness threatened to burst through.

Which was breaking the first cardinal rule: don't judge the couple.

Hazel clicked her phone off. "Sorry."

"Is everything okay?"

She looked askance at her stepbrother.

"How about we take a walk." Mari eyed Pearl, who picked up on the cue. Pearl found something interesting about the rotunda's dome and directed Reid to look up at the ceiling, striking up a conversation.

Getting a few feet ahead of the two, Mari sidled closer to Hazel. "What's going on?"

"Brad's upset he's not here. That we didn't postpone this tour until he was back home."

"I understand he must be feeling left out, but we didn't have much of a choice. In fact, we have to make a decision today. This is a sought-after venue. We were really lucky to snag it."

"I don't want him to be mad at me."

Mari searched her brain for the right thing to say. Weddings were about two people coming together in a lifetime of compromise. When working with wants and needs, conflict was inevitable, but it shouldn't be this painful or sorrowful.

Mari loved and believed in her role in a couple's nuptials, but she'd already decided that when it came time for her to tie the knot—an idea about as far-fetched as a daily commute between DC and the Philippines—it was going to be done quickly and intimately, and the only thing planned would be the after. As much as the details were important, planning sometimes took the meaning out of the most important part of the bottom line: the marriage.

But she was the wedding planner, and she had been hired to carry this couple across the finish line, to their happily ever after. For better or for worse.

"You know what?" Mari cheered. "You and Brad need to

speak. Meaning is lost through texts, but maybe a short phone call or a video chat is in order. What do you think?"

Hazel's voice shook. "Okay. Can you guys give me some time alone? I'll call him now."

"Of course." Mari called to Reid and Pearl, "Let's check out the ballroom."

"I need to use the restroom," Pearl whispered as she passed. "Meet you guys in a sec."

Mari nodded, then turned, expecting Reid next.

The man hadn't moved and lingered around his sister. He was acting like the protective older brother, but he had to realize that this problem was not his to solve. Hazel had the sole power to rise above her insecurity, and the only way she was going to learn how to exercise it was to practice, without her brother's scrutiny.

Mari raised her eyebrows at Reid. Three, five, eight seconds passed. Then, finally, the man's gaze faltered. He arrived at her side with a huff.

In close proximity, she was struck by his spicy and mouthwatering cologne. Oh, good golly, he smelled nice. So nice that she wanted to bury her nose in his neck and breathe him in. Her imagination took over: of her unbuttoning his shirt in a crazed lust, peeling it off to a hard body. Of running her fingers down his chest . . .

"Marisol?"

"What?" She shook her head, refocused. Reid was a few feet ahead of her, inside the ballroom. *Holy crap, get your mind out of the gutter.* "Coming."

The institution's ballroom was simple but elegant with understated wainscoting and column moldings, though with grand crown moldings. From the middle of the room, Mari envisioned a slew of options for seating Hazel and Brad's guests. For now, she joined Reid, who perched himself on a knee-high window-sill. Legs out straight and crossed, he seemed to be staring at the tops of his shoes.

"Is everything okay?" She stood under the warmth of the sun teeming through the window.

"He's acting like an ass."

Mari nodded, her stomach hollowing out. Reid didn't have to explain who he was talking about, but she had to tread lightly here. Very lightly. "And by he, you mean . . ."

"Brad. I can't work out if I want to do something about it."

Mari's heart softened. This. This was the part of the business she loved. Getting to the bottom of things, putting the puzzle together. Finding the solution.

This was also her cue to tap into her slew of standard neutral questions about their family but they escaped her now. She and Reid were quite honestly past it, the time for small talk smashed when she'd let it fly about his short-term rental property a week and a half ago.

Mari winced all over again. Before she could go on, it was imperative she clear the air, once and for all. "Before we move on . . . our video chat—I see now that I could have approached it differently."

He shook his head. "My property manager wasn't doing his job, and things got out of hand. It was a lucrative venture, but I'm considering selling the place." He smiled sheepishly. "I'm here often for business, but I'm not much of a fan of the DC area and don't see myself coming here for pleasure."

"Except to see Hazel."

"True." His lips turned up. "Maybe I shouldn't sell, then. We're close, and I miss her. Her mother married my father—his second marriage—but he passed about five years ago."

"I'm sorry."

"I appreciate that." He inhaled. Exhaled. "He was the glue. Her mother—well, she's not exactly around, with her being in Miami and all."

Mari nodded. "Hazel *did* say that she wouldn't be as involved."

He shifted to the right. "Want a seat?"

"Sure." Mari settled herself onto the sill, inwardly thankful to give her feet a rest.

"Patricia loves the hubbub of events, holidays, the good stuff. But she always kept a distance from us kids. And when my dad passed away, she simply stopped being in touch."

"And your mother?"

"She passed a long time ago. Hazel is all the family I care about. I consider myself more a dad than a brother—and I feel somewhat responsible. To be honest though, this wedding stuff is not my thing."

"So the scowls and the hand-wringing . . . that's not your usual demeanor?"

"You caught those?" When she nodded, he laughed. "Yeah, I'm not one for . . . all this pomp and circumstance."

"You're anti-wedding." Mari clamped her hand over her mouth, shocked at her own words. Apparently with Reid, her manners had taken a back seat. She spoke through her palm. "I'm sorry. No idea why I just said that—"

He barked out a laugh. "Since you asked so bluntly, I guess I am, a little. I almost found myself at the end of the aisle once, but it didn't work out."

"I see." She lowered her hand. "I didn't mean to pry. It wasn't my intention. Reid, I'm sorry for casting judgment, and for your experience."

"Don't be sorry—I appreciate straightforwardness. I find it

refreshing, more palatable than the games most people play. But I admit, my past affects how I feel about Hazel marrying Brad so quickly. And seeing her like this, how she succumbs . . . you should've known her, before she met Brad. She would have never left her friends in Atlanta—"

"Or you." Mari completed the thought, then halted, and broke out into a laugh herself. "I seem to keep putting my foot in my mouth—"

"No, you're right." He sighed. "She left me. I guess that took me aback, and it's probably why I want to strangle the guy." He frowned for a beat. "I get she makes her own decisions, and I respect they run their relationship their way, but he wants to support her. Seems ideal, right? But here's the thing: he doesn't want her to work even if she loves it. He checks in repeatedly, and she can't seem to make a decision without him."

Mari threaded her fingers together, careful in her actions. Reid would've changed his tune if he knew the real reason why Hazel had uprooted herself from her home.

"Anyway, not my business, right? She says she's happy, and that's all that matters to me. Should, anyway." Reid raked his hair with a hand. An amused smile graced his handsome face, the moment changing. He pointed at her. "You. You're better than a bartender."

"Moi?" Mari chided, mirroring his posture, grateful he didn't hold her candor against her. She switched to a casual stance, letting her body go, releasing the serious vibe she hadn't expected to reach in any of their conversations. It was true, part of her job entailed some counseling, sometimes a little psychology, but Reid was the first to ever point it out.

"And I didn't even have to take a drink. Speaking of." His eyes sparkled.

"What?"

"Have you been to the Whistling Pig?"

"Of course I have. It's down the street from Rings and Roses. It's the dive bar of the neighborhood." Mari laughed. "Locals only."

"Maybe that's why my beer was warm. They know I'm an outsider."

"No. The beer was warm because they suck."

"Okay, well I'm looking for a good microbrewery, walking distance from the town house. Something to ease the pain as I help my sister plan her seating chart."

"That's an easy task."

"Good. You'll have to take me." His lips curled into a grin.

In the flow of the conversation, Mari nodded, but as the meaning of his words caught up to her, she stiffened. The request had been easy and smooth, but was this a come-on? She cleared her throat, face warm.

"Is that too much to ask, for you to show me the way?" Reid leaned on his elbows. "Is that out of your job description?"

"R-Reid—" she stuttered, not knowing how to answer. Rings & Roses was a full-service shop. If Hazel wanted microbrew, Mari would've marched along with them to meet the owners of any microbrewery in town. But this felt . . . different. And wonderful.

A lovely churning began deep inside her as he looked into her eyes. He didn't say another word, but the message was loud and clear. There was something between them. Though they wouldn't act on it—they couldn't—it didn't mean he wasn't going to try.

It would have to be up to her to resist.

"He said yes!" Hazel stomped in, cheeks pink and out of breath. "He'll go with what I want. Let's lock this place down."

Mari leapt to her feet like a teenager caught making out in the basement. "Great, let's seal the deal. Congratulations!"

Pearl entered a few steps behind, and her eyes lit up in excitement. "Congratulations? Did you break the news? Yay, baby!"

Hazel's mouth fell open.

"What news? What baby?" Reid asked, standing.

"No baby." Mari grabbed Pearl's elbow. Squeezed at the seriousness of her faux pas. She muddled out a random set of words she hoped would make sense. "She meant that . . . congratulations, because I'm having a baby, one day, in the distant future." She winced at her horrible attempt to buy time.

"I don't understand. You're pregnant?" Reid asked Mari.

"No, she's not, but I am. Yay!" Pearl said, face skewed into fright.

"Just . . . just stop. Thank you, ladies, but you both are horrible liars." Hazel stepped up to Reid, rested a hand on her belly, and smiled. "It's me. I'm pregnant."

eight

Mood: "Jump on It" by Sir Mix-a-Lot

Pearl understood she'd messed up. When she'd approached the group in the ballroom and heard Mari say "Congratulations," she'd naturally assumed Hazel had revealed her secret.

But right now—what Mari was doing? "Assisting" her with a Friday afternoon ceremony at the H. Carl Moultrie Courthouse, the easiest kind of event, where the extent of Pearl's duties was to wrangle the photographer and usher the small wedding party of six to their reserved restaurant location? It was unnecessary and humiliating. Just because she'd opened her big mouth didn't mean she wasn't capable of performing her duties.

Besides, her mistake did not ultimately end in disaster. Hazel had come clean to Reid, who had expressed his total support. She hadn't blamed either Mari or Pearl for the slipup.

Pearl had apologized no fewer than a dozen times in the last three days, and yet here Mari was, standing next to her behind the last row of the courthouse's ceremony room, watching her every move. As if seemingly disremembering Pearl's interaction with Reanna Vito at the flower shop, she left Rings & Roses to

Carli's care since Jane was on a venue tour with a client. Pearl was back to the first square of this convoluted board game where she couldn't seem to gain ground.

The officiant raised her hand, signaling Pearl that she was ready. Pearl cued the photographer with a nod. Mari fussed with the iPod.

Pearl cracked the door open. Her couple, Jacqueline Ansari and Ernest Henderson, "Henri," were on the other side of the threshold, in the hallway, holding hands. Both were in their sixties but breathed youth. Jacqui was stunning in a white long-sleeve vintage sheath dress with a fascinator clip and veil. Ernest wore dapper high-waisted white slacks and a brown vest and bow tie, with a camel-and-white pinstripe suit jacket. Jacqui clutched a bundle of six tulips in her hand, stems wrapped in thick ribbon.

"Showtime?" Pearl asked the couple.

They looked at each other. "We've been ready," Ernest answered.

Pearl cued Mari, who pressed the Play button on the iPod. Music filled the room through the portable speaker the couple had brought. She opened the door, and the couple stepped through, faces bright with anticipation.

The civil ceremony room was a standard government meeting room, lined with rows of chairs to seat about fifteen with enough space for a small aisle down the middle. At the front of the room was a wire arch sparsely covered with fake greenery and flowers, behind it a lecturer's podium, with the officiant waiting on the other side. On the wall was the District of Columbia's seal.

The couple had wanted this simple ceremony. They were each other's second marriage. Each of their three children were present; one carried their wedding bands. They had written their vows; Jacqui's were in verse. The ceremony was short, and in the end they shared a kiss Pearl knew bound them tighter than the signatures on the signed official document.

This was a ceremony of second chances. Separately, Jacqui and Ernest had had their own struggles and pain. They'd independently traversed the world and somehow found each other. Henceforth, they believed they would be invincible. Strength in numbers.

Pearl risked a glance at her sister, who dabbed her eyes with a tissue. Separately, each of the de la Rosa girls were proficient and tenacious individuals. With Pearl fully part of the team, what more could they do as a business? She could help them recover from their shaky finances. Together they would be unstoppable.

But Mari would have to trust Pearl. Mari would need to give her a second chance.

———

Time for Pearl to take her second chance. Later on that evening, she and Trenton had hung back, a block away, until Daphne and Carter ducked into Ohm, each with a stainless steel travel coffee mug in hand. Pearl waited until the couple were set up in the middle row. Luck had it there was space for two mats next to Daphne.

Pearl rolled out her yoga mat and unloaded her cinch sack. Above her mat, she lined up her blocks, strap, and water bottle. As people milled into the space, as predicted, the mats were pushed closer, bringing Daphne into easy hearing distance of Pearl and Trenton.

Now for the big guns.

Pearl snapped her hand towel, embroidered with the name

Rings & Roses, out of her sack. A skeleton key took the place of the stem of the letter *i*, with a gold ring for the dot, and a red rose for the *o* in *Roses*. It was a design she'd conjured up and had embroidered that she'd hoped Mari would approve; that is, before they'd halted their spending.

Pearl still wasn't in agreement about cutting paid marketing and publicity efforts. Currently, word of mouth had sustained the shop and brought in their current brides, but there were too many event planning companies emerging from the sea of DC transplants. Saving in the short run might cost them the marathon.

But becoming Daphne's wedding planner would be a step toward solving their current—and future—problems.

The room grew hotter, and Pearl's limbs loosened. It was time to work; she signaled Trenton with a nod. Ruby, today's instructor, entered the room and greeted her yogis, and the window to communicate with Daphne narrowed. As if reading her mind, Trenton nudged her, and almost too loudly, said, "I don't know how you have enough energy to do this at the end of the day. Don't you have a big wedding this weekend?"

"Oh, ah." She tried to be more natural with her part. "I do, but I needed this break. I love working with brides who know what they want, but with how much time I spent with *you know who* this week, yoga will do me some good. Gotta keep my head clear to plan the perfect wedding!"

Okay, so she was being dramatic, and she was totally fibbing. Her only wedding this week had been this afternoon's ceremony at the courthouse, and the sole event on the calendar this weekend was a bridal expo, where she'd hoped they could publicize Rings & Roses. She hadn't spent hours with any you-know-whos.

But the dialogue worked. Next to her, Daphne's ear tilted slightly toward her.

"Right. And you deliver, as you always do. I saw all those comments on Instagram about last week's wedding." Trenton's hand crossed the space between them, taking hers and squeezing it. "I'm proud of you, babe. I love watching you in action."

That last sentence wasn't part of the script, nor was the hand-holding and the pet name. If Pearl had been warm before, she was now melting. Her teen self was on the verge of freaking out.

"Excuse me. Do you happen to be one of the wedding planners from Rings and Roses?"

Daphne's airy voice interrupted Pearl's galloping thoughts. She let go of Trenton's hand, regaining her composure. She turned to the woman. "I am. I'm Pearl de la Rosa."

"Daphne Brown." She canvassed Pearl's face, no doubt curious if she recognized her. "I just got engaged."

Pearl wasn't going to show her cards. "It's nice to meet you, and congratulations! When's the big day?"

"September of next year. It's going to be at the Thatched Roof Winery in Loudoun County." She rolled her eyes. "I mean, that's where we want to have it." Sitting with her legs folded under her, she leaned back. "This is my fiancé, Carter Ling."

"Nice to meet you. This is my . . ." Pearl glanced at Trenton, stuck. They hadn't discussed their label for this fake relationship.

"Her one and only." Trenton beamed.

Maybe it was because they'd known each other forever, or that beyond her crush on Trenton was a friendship built on teasing and sarcasm, but she said, with pure honesty, "He's such a cheeseball."

"Aww." Daphne glanced at Carter for a beat. "You guys are cute."

"We are, aren't we?" Trenton said. "I keep telling her that."

Pearl was speechless. What universe where they in? What was happening?

Ruby spoke up from the front of the room, interrupting their chatter. "Good evening, family. Full house today, and there's more folks coming in from the lobby. Let's get cozier, shall we?"

People stood, mats moved. The room shifted to the right. Pearl's mat was now a foot away from Daphne's, so close that conversation was completely unavoidable, and therefore the move was to her advantage.

Anticipation grew inside of her. Though she hadn't gone to a wedding at the Thatched Roof Winery, she'd done a wine tasting there with friends. Loudoun County, northwest of DC by fifty miles, flourished with foliage during the fall, a landscape out of a painter's canvas. West coast wineries were king when it came to wine, but they did not compare to the backdrop of a transitioning East Coast autumn with its changing leaves. But yeah, she could see this wedding happening there, knew where she'd suggest to seat the guests, what view they'd look out on as Daphne and Carter said their vows. And with the research she'd done on Daphne, on the clothing she'd worn in her Instagram posts and from her blog's vibe, the theme materialized in her head.

"That's a beautiful spot," Pearl whispered, smiling. "I can see it. Rustic and sweet. Grapevine arches. Wine barrel markers. Classic ivory linen, with touches of burlap. Hints of red and pinks."

"Oh." Daphne gasped, ever so softly, next to her.

Music rose from the corner of the room and the lights dimmed, as if Ruby had been in cahoots with her pitch.

It was a sign. Pearl just *knew*. She knew she had Daphne.

And though it was time to channel all of her effort into the absolute present, into her breath, body, and into this mat, with Trenton on her left and Daphne on her right, Pearl wasn't sure how she was going to keep herself from hyperventilating.

By the end of class, Pearl had found her center. Sweat dripping from the baby hairs at her neckline, body awash with endorphins, and confident that she'd accomplished her goal, she set her rolled mat on the ground and plopped on a lobby bench next to Trenton. She jammed on her sneakers and spied Daphne and Carter chatting with Ruby.

Trenton wiped his face with a towel. His eyes lit up with the satisfied look of someone who'd done a major workout. Lips curled into a grin, he said, "I think I'm hooked on yoga."

"Really? Mr. CrossFit, converted?" Pearl teased.

Across from them, a yogi grabbed her coat and flashed Pearl a knowing smile.

Yoga always got such a bad rap.

Not able to resist passing on some knowledge, she spurted off her favorite fact about the practice. "Do you know that the mind-body connection goes beyond relaxation and muscle strength? It can even heal people after a trauma, like post-traumatic stress." Then, she bit her lip, regretting mentioning it altogether. She might have taken a couple of yoga classes with the man, but she didn't know enough about what happened to Trenton the last seven years. She didn't want to appear presumptuous, only to make a point that yoga had helped her with her own mental health.

"Say no more." He put a hand up. "I'm a believer. Now, is she?" His gaze flashed to Daphne.

Pearl was glad for the change of subject. "I daresay yes. But it might be time to back off, for now."

"You're the boss. I, for one, am starving. Want to grab something to eat?"

"Oh." She hedged on agreeing. It was one thing for him to fill in for Kayla, but another to grab dinner with him. "It's after eight, way too late. If I eat, I really won't sleep."

He stood, the muscles of his upper thigh flexing. Pearl looked away, her mind scurrying back into the studio, where he'd shown his physical strength. Today, he'd stripped shirtless, unveiling his defined abs. Unlike the men she'd encountered at their local gym, who ogled themselves in the mirror while they pumped iron, Trenton moved with a smooth, humble grace. It made him sexier.

His voice was playful, though still a whisper. "Oh, so I see. I'm a part-time pretend boyfriend now. Good enough to flaunt half naked but not enough to take out for a late-night snack?"

"You caught me." She grinned up at him. "I'm a player underneath all this Athleta gear and sweat."

"It's no wonder you were speechless when I called myself your one and only. Should've known I am anything but."

Pearl floundered at his teasing. If only he knew the truth! If Trenton had remotely suggested that they date for real, she would've dropped everything and said yes.

Maybe it was time to call Love Unlimited for her consultation after all.

With a hand on the yoga mat strapped across his chest, he gestured toward the front door. "C'mon Pearly-Pearl. My treat. We dropped ten pounds of water at this last session. I want to replace it with grub."

She regained her composure at his sincere smile. She

might've had a sad dating life, but they were friends, and that was special enough. "Okay, as long as we're someplace where we don't need to stand close to anyone. I'm odorific. And, I'm paying."

He opened the door. "So I'm a hired man now? I should raise my rates. And make sure you pay for drinks, too."

⁓

They stood at the corner of Burg and William Street, waiting for the light to turn. Pearl squinted against the bright lights of cars passing while her body acclimated to the thirty-degree change in temperature. "What do you feel like having?"

"Anything with meat and grease."

She laughed. "The Porterhouse it is."

A half block away, the Porterhouse was the go-to joint for burgers. Not exactly the fanciest place, or the quietest; it was a local haunt. In Pearl's opinion, their sweet potato fries were the best in town. Their local brew wasn't so bad either.

As they crossed the street, Pearl heard her name.

"Oh damn, it worked." Trenton put a hand on her back, to steer her away from a driver who cut it too close to the sidewalk. Her heart shot into her throat at the contact, but it proceeded to make her speechless when she turned to the woman waving from across the street.

"Pearl! Wait!" Daphne jogged across as the pedestrian light turned red, out of breath, with Carter behind her. "Where are you guys off to?"

"Post-yoga munchies," she said, though still in shock.

At the pause, Trenton jumped in. "How about you all?"

She glanced briefly at her fiancé. "We're about to grab something to eat, too."

"Care to join us? Interested in microbrew and meat?" Trenton asked.

"You're singing my song." Carter took Trenton's side and started an immediate conversation, leaving Daphne with Pearl.

As they followed behind the guys, Daphne broke the ice. "Pearl, to be perfectly honest, I was wondering if we could chat about some of your wedding ideas? I'm looking for a wedding planner."

The tension in Pearl's chest eased, and triumph overcame the endorphins by a mile. *I did it.* With confidence, she said, "You've come to the right person."

nine

Mood: "Signed, Sealed, Delivered I'm Yours"
by Stevie Wonder

Mari's priority as a wedding planner was to acquire what was right for her client, and a myriad of people were involved in the decision of what was right, from brides, to grooms, to family members who had a financial or emotional stake. With unlimited choices at the couple's feet, her role was to vet each option in accordance with her client's tastes.

Mari was paid to wrap it up; she was also paid to follow her instincts and know when her client had begun to stray. She led her clients to the next task, capitalized on their momentum and speed. And for the event to have a chance at being successful, the client had to feel comfortable with her.

The relationship between a wedding planner and a client had to be born out of trust.

Trust. The thing Pearl had irresponsibly played with three days ago. The thing that could've meant the difference between a client who stayed or left. The thing that Mari currently didn't have for Pearl after she'd blurted out Hazel's secret, and she'd felt compelled to assist her at the courthouse wedding earlier this afternoon.

Tonight, at Hazel's cake tasting, Mari planned to regroup. Assess her client's thoughts on what had happened the other day. Determine if Pearl had damaged the relationship by spilling the bride's biggest secret. A week had passed since the sisters' discussion about their finances—losing a top would not help ease the financial strain Rings & Roses was under.

Mari sat at a separate table at Just Cakes answering emails while Hazel and Reid were hosted by its proprietor, Carolina Just. On an open planner page in front of her were scribbled bits of information she'd gleaned from the running conversation next to her. Hazel had expressed interest in a three-tiered cake with textured vertical stripes and fresh flowers, colors to be determined when she and Brad finalized their theme.

"Reid!" Hazel snapped.

Mari jerked up from her planner and Reid looked up from his phone a half second later. As if reorienting himself to the two women in front of him, he said, "I'm sorry." He tucked the phone into his coat pocket.

"You haven't even had a taste." Hazel frowned, gesturing to three square bite-sized samples on a platter in front of him.

He sat up on the stool, ran his hand through his hair. "I'm ready now, li'l sis. Give it to me."

With upturned lips, Hazel handed her brother a napkin.

Mari exhaled a quiet breath. Things seemed to be good between them. Hazel's pregnancy announcement did not end in disaster. Reid had even appeared all the more doting toward his sister. So, despite the lovely jitters Mari felt around the man— she still couldn't get their last conversation out of her head— she must try harder to keep all their interactions aboveboard.

Nothing could come between Hazel and Brad and the altar.

Carolina jumped in with an enthusiastic cadence, waking Mari from her thoughts, as she pointed out each sample. "Ms. Flynn has narrowed it down to three choices: Traditional red velvet with cream cheese frosting. A ginger spice cake with salted caramel buttercream. And a Black Forest cake with almond buttercream." She had a saleswoman's flare, matched with what Mari knew was her ability to deliver delicious cakes, and most of all, provide the visual masterpiece her couples envisioned.

Only the best.

At that moment, a phone buzzed. Reid took his from his pocket and glanced at it. "Can you . . . can you excuse me?" Reid stood.

"Seriously?" Hazel sighed.

He grimaced. "Work. I'm afraid if I put it off, I won't be much fun the rest of the evening. I'll be right outside. I know whatever you pick will be perfect."

Hazel returned a grave expression.

Mari stood from her table. This was her cue. Nothing else would be accomplished today. Hazel needed someone in her circle to back her up. If she made this decision alone, there was sure to be a change of heart down the road. "Hazel, how about you sleep on it?"

"Yeah? Is that okay?" Hazel asked Carolina.

Carolina nodded. "Absolutely. There's still time."

"But I do want samples to take home. Think you can hook me up with a chocolate cake for my midnight snack?" Reid grinned.

"Of course, Mr. Quaid."

"Great." He kissed Hazel on the cheek, and with a final squeeze of her shoulder, headed outside, phone against his ear.

"I'm sorry about that," Hazel said. "He comes for me, not for the details. Like all men."

Mari corrected her. "No, not like all men, just some personalities."

"You're right. I'm taking it out on him when it's me who's difficult."

Carolina left to package up the remaining samples. Mari sat on the stool Reid had vacated. "No doubt, the timeline adds a little bit of pressure, but you aren't being difficult. You deserve what you want out of this wedding. If it means ginger spice, or a tower of doughnuts, then we'll make it happen." She tiptoed around her words now. Hazel was vulnerable, as all brides were months from the wedding. Their emotions were exposed wires. They absorbed every blip in attitude or slight shade of judgment from others. Worse, their vulnerability had the potential to turn into fear, and they could lash out. "But I think you should make these decisions for you. Make your choice and run with it. Brad told you he didn't have a preference on the cake—to me, that means ordering your favorite cake on the planet. And can I say something personal, something from my heart?"

"Yes."

"A bad decision is doing something against your spirit. A bad decision is going against your moral code. Maybe . . . maybe we can strike the word *bad* from any of the wedding plans—because nothing about this is bad. It's joyful and it's for you. You have impeccable taste, and you are obviously loved, not only by your fiancé, but by your brother." Her gaze shot to Reid, now pacing the sidewalk. "I am confident in your choices."

Hazel's expression softened; the crease in the middle of her eyebrows eased. She let go of a breath, her body deflating from relief. "I think I want the red velvet cake. And I don't want vertical stripes. I want a naked cake, with hardly any icing. I end up scraping icing right off the cakes I eat. It sticks to my teeth."

"Then your wish is our command," Mari said.

"What do we do with Brad? What if he ends up hating my choice?"

Carolina entered the room, now with a kraft box in her hand. "Then we make a groom's cake."

"That sounds ridiculous. Two cakes for seventy-five people?"

"This is the era of choice. We've done small weddings with several cakes offered. We bake cakes that cater to dietary restrictions. A gluten-free, diary-free cake, for example. A nut-free cake. The options are limitless. One cake, two cakes, cupcakes. Two cakes that represent the couple's individual Hogwarts houses, even. Whatever you want."

The front door jingled open. Half of Reid's body peeked through. "Listen, I'm going to be much longer than I thought, so I'll head on and walk back home."

Hazel responded with the customary little sister expression, with apathy and her eyes rolling upward. "Sure. Why not?"

Mari looked at her watch. This was a good stopping point. "I think we're done here, too. We don't see each other next week, correct?"

"Yep. Brad and I are headed up to New York City for *Hamilton*, but we'll be back for Easter. So, a week and a half from now."

"Excited to have him back?"

"Absolutely. It will be nice to have my fiancé and not my brother here for these appointments, not that Reid hasn't been wonderful. He flies out tomorrow."

"Ah." Despite the airy tone in her answer, Mari's insides fell. If she was really going to be honest with herself . . .

No, no, there was no room for honesty about this subject

whatsoever. She might've enjoyed Reid's company, but their meetings were not social calls.

Carolina gestured to the kraft box in front of them, waking Mari from her straying thoughts. "Leftover cakes."

"You are the best, Carolina," Mari said.

"I do what I can."

Hazel tapped her phone and it illuminated to a picture of her and Brad. "Yay. I might even have enough time to grab a pedicure today." Her gaze rose, shy. "Or, better yet, are you free? Pedicures are so much more fun with a friend."

A friend.

Mari bit her lip to keep the sudden rush of emotions from bringing tears to her eyes. Friendships were rare for her. She had acquaintances, but the rest of her life consisted of work and family. Her sisters were the only ones who appreciated her drive. More than once she'd been perceived as someone who didn't let loose, someone who didn't let her faults show.

And those people were right. Straddling the extremes of who she was before, and who she strived to be now came at the expense of pushing people away.

Which was exactly what she had to do now because this wasn't the time to mix business and pleasure.

"That sounds heavenly, but I'll have to pass," Mari grumbled lightly. "I've got a houseful waiting for me. And there's a bridal expo tomorrow to prep for."

"I understand. Do you mind bringing the cakes to my brother since you're next door?"

"Not at all."

"Speaking of . . . I'm sorry that the house gave you so much trouble. No wonder things were awkward between you and him in the beginning."

"Ah, it's in the past. Reid and I talked it out."

"It will for sure be in the past, since he mentioned selling it after the wedding. We'll need it for some of our company flying in, but the For Sale sign should be up by September."

"Oh." Although Reid had mentioned selling the property, the details surprised Mari. Self-admonishment followed. Why did she care? She stuttered the next answer. "That's great . . . I mean, I don't think it will stay on the market long. It's such a seller's market."

"I'm not in agreement. I like having my brother around. Anyway." Hazel stood. "Thank you, for today. For setting me straight. Sometimes I need to remember that I can do this." She leaned in for a tight hug.

"You have totally got this." Although Mari let go first, she clung to the word *friend*. Friends spoke what was in their hearts. Hazel had trusted Mari with her secret, and it only made sense for Mari to trust her, too, with her emotions. "Hazel, I'm sorry about what happened with my sister and spilling the news about the pregnancy—"

"You don't have to—"

"Yes, I do. It's not okay either professionally or personally. It was your news to tell. Pearl made a mistake, and I was in charge of that entire exchange. It won't happen again. You can trust me."

Hazel held her hands, squeezed them. "I know I can, and I do. You and I are fine, and I appreciate this. It proves I was right all along. Brad wasn't sure about having a wedding planner, but I insisted, and it led me to you."

Mari blinked away her anxiety. "And you get to have a naked cake."

Hazel half laughed. "Hell yeah."

They walked out of Just Cakes together, parting at the corner of Burg and Mary. Then, with the kraft box in her hands, Mari's relief flipped to nervousness.

She had a house call to make.

Reid's front door opened without Mari having to touch her knuckles to the wood, and a painfully gorgeous and barefoot Reid greeted her with a playful smile. "I couldn't stand it anymore. You were taking forever to knock."

To that, Mari had no words, no quick retort, though one thing rose within her: defiance. God, he was so confident. Attractive, yes. But borderline cocky.

And she loved it. All these years, she'd dated safe, dated men who were lovely and respectful, but who didn't light her up. At most, she'd spend the evening at their place, but eventually end up in her own bed, in her own double-brushed microfiber sheets, where she'd spread out like a starfish and fall asleep with the TV on.

With this man, because of his pure aura alone, she'd be willing to mess those sheets up. With Reid, a familiar coil curled within her, a delicious feeling of . . . being turned on.

As if reading her thoughts, Reid lazily leaned against the door frame and raised a brow.

She snapped out of it and stuck the box out between them. "Your cakes."

"Perfect timing. Thanks." His eyes wandered from the box to her. "Would you like to come in?"

The suggestion glued Mari's shoes to the front step. "Oh no . . . it's late."

He glanced at his watch. "It's eight. I can't eat this cake alone. Or is this against your rules, too?" At her hesitation, he continued, laughing under his breath. "Are you always like this?"

"Like what?"

"Always hard to convince. Because this isn't an out of this world question. It's cake, Marisol. We're neighbors. You're my sister's favorite person. I promise I'm not going to try to convince you to walk me to the Whistling Pig."

"Ha," she retorted, then her stomach growled—the traitor. Cake *was* tempting. She'd inspected the slices Caroline had packed up. Mari had a thing for dark chocolate.

And then it appeared again—a grin on his face that would be the end of her if she wasn't careful. A grin that knew her answer before she said it.

"Sure, okay," she relented, stepping inside, taking in the interior of the town house, flipping her thoughts to a blank page. There wasn't a lick of historic home left in it. From the front foyer, one could see clear through to the back windows, with most of the interior walls removed. Tray ceilings replaced crown moldings. Recessed lighting throughout gave a modern air. The floors were dark and sleek. The prominent wooden banister had been replaced with metal. "This is . . . wow."

Yep, this was so outside of what she envisioned for any home in this area.

"It's pretty sweet, right? The architect did a magnificent job. If only he wasn't such an asshole."

His words popped Mari out of her thoughts. "Oh?"

"It's Brad. Brad is the architect and designer. I brought my sister in to decorate; that's how Brad and Hazel met. And no, he's not really an asshole. As you put it, he took my sister from me, and I'm feeling a little sore about it. But now that I'm going to be an uncle, I'm going to have to accept Brad for better or for worse." He gestured as he turned to walk. "Kitchen's in the back."

Out of habit in her own home and respect for this home's impeccable, shiny floors, Mari stepped out of her shoes, and her stocking-clad feet were met with pure, utter comfort.

He nodded. "The heated floors are hands down my favorite feature of the place. It gets so damn cold here in DC. But the rest of the decor isn't me."

As they walked to the back, Mari absorbed all the details. The sparse furniture. The remodeled gray slate hearth encasing a gas fireplace. Bare white walls except for an occasional mirror.

They entered a miniature chef's kitchen, which had a five-burner gas stove with an overhead vent and a stainless steel refrigerator. Only one six-foot countertop. Top-of-the-line finishes, but in proportion to the rest of the house, it all seemed small. "Brad must not be a cook."

He set the box on the countertop and popped it open. He groaned at the sight of its contents. "Oh, Carolina hooked us up." Grabbing two forks from the drawer, he handed one to Mari with a flourish. "How could you tell that Brad wasn't a cook?"

"There's barely any prep space, the sink won't fit a tall stock pot, and the refrigerator is practically down the street." She pointed to the lone appliance separate from the rest of the kitchen. Laughing, she turned back to the heat of Reid's gaze. She cleared her throat and went on, brushing off her sudden shyness. "But all in all the renovation is pretty impressive. I've been in quite a few of these homes, since we know our neighbors well. Sometimes I pop into an open house."

"Ah, you do that, too." He nudged the cardboard box, a signal for her to take the first bite. She dug the fork into the chocolate cake. His fork took its turn immediately behind hers. "I do it for research; seeing who lives in a neighborhood gives me a connection to a place."

"I respect that. You don't want to take away from a neighborhood's character."

"Exactly. I would have kept this house as historic as possible. But Brad had other ideas."

"I like to go to open houses because I'm curious. I love looking at people's styles, at how people put together their homes. I think the worst-styled homes are the ones that come right out of a catalog. There's no personality in it. I don't mind clunky, mix and match, so long as it's real."

"Makes sense, especially with what you do."

Finally, she brought the fork to her lips, the scent of the cake already giving her a head rush. She moaned as she lapped her tongue under the fork, then nodded. "I love the challenge of giving a client their truest dream within their budget. But isn't that life? Taking what you have and running with it?" she said.

"What's the hardest part of your job?"

She looked at him intently, mulled over his thoughtful question. "The hardest part would be encouraging my clients to listen to their own wants and not others'. It's so easy to want to please everyone, but I've seen what happens when a person puts others first."

"And that is?"

"They lose themselves."

Reid ate his cake silently. Mari's body flushed from her honesty, from his gaze. It started from the tips of her toes and traveled to the top of her head, and instead of her usual instinct to meet his expression, to challenge him, she looked away.

He liked what he heard and saw—it showed on his slackened jaw, at the pulse jumping at his neck. This Reid had something about him, equal parts prestige and care, like two sides of a coin, perfectly balanced.

She licked her lips, tasting the last bit of chocolate.

"Thirsty?" Reid's voice was gravelly. "I've got . . . well . . ." He straightened and went to the refrigerator. He took out a Tupperware container, and peeked behind it. "Um, sparkling water, orange juice. Milk?"

Mari couldn't quite grasp the sight she was seeing—a refrigerator of homemade food in plastic covered containers. No take-out boxes. No week-old pizza. "Are those leftovers?"

"Yep. Or did you want wine or beer? I have a drink cooler for the good stuff." He gestured toward what Mari now noticed was the undercounter refrigerator.

She shook her head. "Oh no. I'm fine."

"I was going to open up a bottle of wine before you came over. I usually have a glass with dinner. Unlike Brad, I am a cook, but all the recipes I follow are for servings for two; hence, the extras."

"You cook?"

He nodded.

Dear heaven on earth. The man could cook. His house was clean. He had a good job. He was *oh so fine*. If he tried something right now, Mari would be hard-pressed to say no. She wouldn't have the willpower.

Which was completely inappropriate.

Panic shot through her. She had to get out of there as soon as possible. "That reminds me, I should get home. I'm the cook in my family, and I have a feeling my sisters are already waiting in my living room. They'll complain that they've starved half to death. Have you ever had little sisters just hang on you?" She was rambling now, so she put her fork in the sink. "Of course you have! Anyway, thank you, Reid, for the slice of cake."

"I'm heading back to Atlanta in the morning, but I'm back next weekend. Hazel invited me for Easter."

"Great! Have a good flight. I'll show myself out." Mari's footfalls echoed as she backed from the kitchen, where she gave him a final nod. Her breath remained caught in her throat until she entered the hallway and the front door was in sight.

"Marisol." After he called out her name, his footsteps followed. Mari turned.

A foot away, his gaze lazed upward to her face. "Thanks for bringing over dessert."

She jammed her feet into her shoes, struggled with one. "Sure, um . . . safe travels." And after almost tripping out onto the sidewalk, she shut the door behind her.

She inhaled the cool night air.

That was close.

ten

Mood: "Modern Love" by David Bowie

Pearl internally screamed.

Mari—not their intern, Carli, as previously planned—was assisting her at the Perfect Weddings Expo this morning in Bethesda, Maryland. And that sneaky oldest sister of hers hadn't informed her that she had reassigned Carli to manage the shop until this morning at 6:00 a.m., when she showed up at Pearl's apartment door freshly showered, clutching the rental van's car keys.

And now, Pearl was slumped in the passenger seat headed to what was supposed to be her project, listening to the radio her sister had commandeered, cranked up to high.

Pearl texted the only other woman who could feel her pain: How am I going to survive this day?

Jane texted immediately. This was a bye week for her, and she'd promised Pio a day of whatever he wanted: Hang in there. She'll chill out soon.

Pearl: Why couldn't it be you here?

Jane: Now that we're waiting to take pictures with the Easter

Bunny, I wish it was. Parents are trying to cut this line! I'm about to throw down.

Pearl laughed to herself and looked out the window as the van exited the beltway in Bethesda. The convention center's parking lot was packed. A line of chattering, enthusiastic attendees, some dressed in veils or matching outfits, snaked around the building. Pearl's spirits rose a tad. There was a chance she could snag some of them as new clients.

After they unloaded the contents of the van and brought them to their booth, Pearl surveyed the other vendors setting up. Florists, bakers, DJs, entertainers, and caterers showcased their wares under white tents and arches. They decorated their spaces with flowers—both fake and real—and set out chocolate, treats, and samples in an attempt to lure expo-goers.

Pearl spied on the competition: other event planners.

"Check them out, Ate." Pearl shifted her eyes to the right while pretending to look through their boxes. "Two o'clock. Heartfully Yours?"

Mari tipped her to-go cup of coffee to her lips. "Yeah?"

"They're an up-and-coming shop, and a future rival."

Located ten miles away from Rings & Roses, Heartfully Yours had blown up in the last couple of years because of their exceptional social media game. "Not that there aren't enough clients to go around. But see that color scheme they have? The total business branding? We need to keep working on that. Our website's not exactly the way I want it to be. It lacks feeling and personalization."

"Don't get too excited. We don't have the money right now."

She handed her sister a box of swag to spread over their tables. "I know, but it shouldn't be the last thing on our checklist. The Rings and Roses logo, the way the shop's decorated, the website—it's all a hodgepodge. All I've done is put a Band-Aid on it. I'm proud we now have at least an online base, but we could do more. I mean, look at that video playing in their booth. It's even got other vendors to mill around their space."

"What's wrong with the shop? There's nothing wrong with the way Mommy and I decorated it." Mari hugged the box to her chest.

Pearl clucked under her breath. Of course that was what Mari focused on out of everything she'd said. "We have to ask ourselves: How will a passing bride remember us? There are over three hundred vendors here. How are we going to get people to stop? Just because we're wearing matching shirts? As it is, our booth swag isn't enough."

Mari spread out their brochures, pens, stickers, magnets, and chocolates on a long table. Pearl unrolled an inexpensive bright turquoise rug to its twelve-foot-by-ten-foot size and set up their tall bistro-style round tables for potential customers to congregate around. They hung a vinyl banner behind their table.

Pearl sighed. Their booth felt empty. It needed something with oomph. Lights, or a blinged-out backdrop, maybe.

"I heard that," Mari said.

"Heard what?"

She mimicked Pearl's sigh, except she threw in a pathetic, downtrodden expression.

"Nice. That's nice." Pearl half laughed despite feeling the complete opposite of pleased.

"I just think you should focus on what we do have instead of what we don't. You keep shooting for more, wanting more, when the priority should be maximizing what you've got."

"That makes no sense, Ate Mari." She crossed her arms, then

uncrossed them. They were in public. She lowered her voice. "There's nothing wrong with raising the bar."

"Sure, if you can navigate the one at the current level."

The insult hit Pearl square in the eyes. Stunned, she opened her mouth, then closed it. It was a fair statement, right? Her weddings weren't always executed smoothly. This week's slipup could have broken Mari and Hazel's professional relationship. But when was enough enough?

A tidal pool of emotions swirled in Pearl's chest, and she hurriedly tidied up the rest of the display to take down her heart rate. Thank God, an announcement blared that the doors would open in five minutes.

An idea formed in her head, chasing away her current anger. She'd only posted photos on Facebook to date. Heartfully Yours might've had video playing in their booth, but Rings & Roses could stream their attendance. "I'm going to do a live feed."

"What? Why?"

"Why not?" She grabbed her purse from under the table and touched up her lipstick, feeling her sister's gaze on her face. When Pearl met Mari's eyes, she caught a hint of regret in them. Mari's way had always been the tough-love, no-holds-barred sort of criticism that acted as a double-edged sword. There were no games with this woman, no minced words, no passive-aggressive actions, but damn did she say the most hurtful and truthful things. "If you could move a little to the right, you're blocking the banner."

Mari did as she was asked, silently.

Pearl pressed the Record button. "Welcome, Northern Virginia and DC brides and grooms! It's Pearl from Rings and Roses. Today, we're at the Perfect Weddings Expo with hundreds of other vendors. I know that some of you are out here today, and if you are, please stop by and say hi. We can do a free quick consult about your current plans and see where we can get involved. We're in booth one seventy-five, at the northeast corner of the building." Pearl flipped the camera view and scanned the area in front of her. "We're right next to Chocolatiers and Company, and Party Limos R Us." When she flipped it back, viewers had logged into the stream. She called them out by name. "Molly, hello! Reagan, hi! Are you all here? Hi, Lacy, I know, it is overwhelming, but we're here and we're going to take care of you. If nothing else, we have candy and lots of it."

She ended the livestream just as the doors opened and the line of customers entered. Pearl stepped out in front of their display, a candy bar in hand, along with their promotional flyers. Throughout the day, she lured would-be clients into their booth to flip through photo albums. She wrote up sample proposals, and with some, she discussed the investment of having a wedding planner on retainer.

At day's end, Pearl had three solid clients to follow up with. Each had verbalized that they wanted her. Not Rings & Roses, but her: Pearl's ideas, Pearl's enthusiasm.

Yes, she *did* know what the hell she was talking about. In fact, she'd established the bar with marketing and publicity. Today, she'd give Mari a pass for her insult, but never again would she allow her big sister to undermine her talent.

Pearl probably should've cancelled her dinner plans after her long day at the expo, but being in the same building with Mari had seemed far more irritating than trying to beat the dating game. But she had been wrong, because Winston Katz—her date, courtesy of the Love Unlimited gift certificate she'd received on her birthday—was truly a dud.

"I'm almost done here." Winston didn't bother to look up as he texted. The glow of his phone cast a dim spotlight on his face, accentuating his high and round cheekbones.

Pearl pushed the food around her plate with a fork as he answered yet another email. Winston—preppy, perfect on the page—picked from a twenty-five-point compatibility list, was supposedly a good match. *An arrow right in the middle of the target*, the email from Love Unlimited had said.

More like an arrow to my eye. The guy must have lied on the survey where it asked him about the importance of face-to-face conversation versus social media and text, because he'd broken her big first-date rule: no phones at the dinner table unless it was urgent. And his current Cheshire grin did not indicate this email was urgent.

Despite the nature of her work, Pearl did not leash herself to her phone, especially on dates. Okay, once, she took a call in the middle of lunch tapas while on a blind date a couple of months ago because Jane rang in. Resourceful Jane never asked for help, didn't call *just because*. Sure enough, that day, Pio had gotten himself stuck on the highest branch on one of the fifty-year-old oak trees at the elementary school. No one could climb a tree as well as Pearl, and she'd spider-monkeyed up that tree to coax him down.

Barring that, though, the first date was sacred. Winston, who'd started with a rating of seven—he was well dressed, had a firm but not overbearing handshake, and pulled her chair out for her—plummeted to a four.

Still, Pearl would power through. Maybe he was on the phone ordering her flowers and they were going to show up any minute. Maybe his sister had gone into labor, and he had to make sure both mom and babe were safe. Maybe a client—he was a litigator on Capitol Hill—had emailed regarding some crisis. She'd give him the benefit of the doubt.

He'd, after all, taken her to Küche, the best German restaurant in Northern Virginia.

Point, Winston.

But as the seconds passed with him still thumbing through his phone, the moment became rife with boredom.

"My sauerbraten was delicious." Pearl rambled on purpose. "The marinade had a tang to it, but the meat was perfectly tender. My spätzle was perfect. Did you like it, too? Did it pair well with your *Jägerschnitzel*? I don't know about you, but I'm craving a Black Forest cake. With a cappuccino. In Munich. I wonder how much a direct flight from Reagan would cost me."

Winston mumbled an answer.

Pearl sighed and rolled her eyes. Winston's rating tumbled another rung to a three. Well, two could play at this game. Pearl took out her phone, which was—by etiquette—on silent and scrolled through her notifications. It could get hairy at times with her professional and personal accounts all mixed up in one tiny phone. She had caught herself more than once a tweet away from responding to a Rings & Roses tag using her personal account.

She swiped up to the family group text that had run amok. Their parents had gotten an international iPhone, and her mother still didn't press Return for a new paragraph of text. Instead, she sent messages by the sentence. There were at least ten from her, all with the explanation that she and her husband were heading to an island called Mindoro to vacation and would have limited internet access for three weeks.

Next. Mrs. Gonzalez, the bride of a fortieth wedding anniversary event and a close friend of her mother, thereby "family" in title: Is it too late for us to change from buffet to sit down service? I hate buffet! I only agreed because your Tito David insists on his way.

Pearl groaned aloud. Tita Imelda, I will call you tomorrow to discuss this with you. ☺

Onward. Pearl scrolled down to Kayla's last text, to where she wrote: I miss you! Not fair my bro sees you more than I do.

Pearl: But it's you I love!

Kayla: All right, you pass. Seriously. Belated bday dinner?

Pearl: Yes! Ne—

In the middle of her text, another flashed on the screen. Mari: You know what to do if the guy is no good.

Pearl's fingers flew on the touchscreen, somewhat wary after today's interaction. Then, she remembered: this text was personal, not business. This was Ate Mari, the oldest sister, not the CEO. At the end of the day, Mari would've done anything in Pearl's defense, as she'd done before. Pearl texted back: Food is magnificent. Location is perfect. He's on his phone.

The text dots appeared immediately. You're on your phone.

Pearl: He started it! Okay I'm ditching him. Maybe I'll go to the bathroom and never come back.

Mari: Check in when you're done!

Pearl: OK.

She scrolled to the next notification. An email from Daphne Brown:

Hi Pearl,

Loved our convo yesterday. Could you send over your contract for us to review? No promises yet, but you said all the right things.

xxx, D

She pressed her lips together to keep herself from squealing. Daphne was almost hers. Her plan had worked like a charm. She imagined the months ahead, picking out linens, trying on wedding dresses, and tasting cake.

"Where were we?" Winston's tenor disrupted Pearl's thoughts.

She tore her eyes from the screen. *Focus.* Placing the phone screen-side down on the table, she cleared her throat. "I'm not sure, to be honest. Is everything okay?"

"What do you mean?"

"Your emails just now." Pearl glanced at his phone, which coincidentally flashed another notification.

"Oh, yeah. Just stuff I'm dealing with . . . you know how it goes."

Pearl waited for more. An explanation, maybe. If anything, a jump back into some random conversation. Instead, he turned his attention down to the last patty of his undoubtedly cold *Jägerschnitzel* and cut into it.

She placed her plate to the side and brought her wineglass forward, scanning the restaurant for the waiter.

"Wow. You took that dish out," Winston said, being garish and loud.

"It was delicious. It's my favorite dish here." She jumped into the cauldron of facts stored in her head. When she took on the social media position at Rings & Roses, she created a "Friday Fact Day" on Facebook and #FridayFacts on Twitter. Since then, her research had her providing interesting tidbits about local area venues and wedding statistics. "Did you know this restaurant is one of the oldest here in the area? It was built in—"

"I mean, that was a huge helping." Winston spoke with his mouth open, and when he bit down on his French fries, the crunch of his jaw sent nasty shivers through Pearl, though she wasn't misophonic. "With the spätzle and the white asparagus. Plus our appetizers. I mean, wow."

She willed herself to ignore the chewing. "I was hungry."

"Obviously." He chuckled. "Should we order you a second meal?"

Okay, he was officially being rude now. "Is there something wrong with having a healthy appetite?"

"Nope." Amusement flashed in his eyes. "I mean, I've just never seen anyone eat like *that*."

Pearl clasped her hands on her lap under the table. *You're hovering at a two, dear Winston.* "Like what?"

"Like some zombie out of *The Walking Dead*."

Pearl's heart beat in her ears. Her blood pressure rose as the insult seeped into her skin.

Why? Why did her appetite warrant a comment? What an eye-opener it would've been for him to sit among her sisters, food aficionados, who dug into food with wild abandon, who could've discussed a meal's play-by-play like it was a World Series game.

"Don't get upset! I'm just teasing you."

Teasing, my ass. She sucked in a breath at his gaslighting attempt. Her mind clamored for peace. It wasn't just this date. This date was a representation of the time she was wasting, in her personal life and in her career. Her emotions began to spin like a top, but she caught herself. She envisioned herself in *Tadasana*, or mountain pose, though she was sitting: eyes ahead, back straight, and shoulders back. Relax the shoulders and breathe.

As she got into the pose, she felt her power return.

She took her napkin from her lap and placed it on the table. Leaning to the right, she retrieved her purse hanging from her seat back and pulled out her wallet. In front of her, Winston halted mid-chew, utensils pointed up in the air. Another faux pas that she wouldn't have even noticed in a good man, but him? He was a caveman, with a mouth to match.

Pearl had enough good examples of men in her life. Her father. Her uncles. Trenton.

Had Mari been right? Had Pearl set the bar too high, even in her personal life? Maybe her expectations were skewed. Perhaps only a percentage of good men existed, and they were all married or committed.

She shook her head.

Even so.

She wouldn't lower her bar. Not in work or in relationships. Especially not for Winston.

"You are officially off my chart. As in, below it." She slipped three twenty-dollar bills on the table and stood. "I would say thank you for the night, but the only thing I'm thankful for is that I'm going home with a full stomach."

"You're leaving?"

She laughed. "Duh." She tugged her jacket from the back of her chair, jazz-handed her goodbye, then headed to the front of the restaurant.

Upon passing the hostess stand, a tap on the shoulder gave her pause. She heaved a sigh and turned. "Look, Winst—"

Her words seized in her throat, because the person she turned to was Trenton, wrapped oh-so-perfectly in a double-breasted wool coat. It had been a day since their last yoga class and impromptu late dinner with Daphne and Carter, but his warm smile was a sight for sore eyes. "Oh, hey."

"Where are you going in a rush?" He glanced over her shoulder.

"I was just leaving this ass—" She did her own reconnaissance. Behind him was a woman with straight posture. "I mean, I had a date. You?"

"Me, too. I mean, I'm on one. Now," he said, then, as if remembering, pointed at the woman. "Pearl, this is Leighann. Leighann, this is my childhood friend, Pearl."

Childhood friend. Right, not girlfriend, real or fake.

Pearl shook the woman's hand and appraised her. Firm grip. On-point golden brown and blond highlights. Confident smile. Hazel eyes that sparkled. "It's nice to meet you."

"Same here."

"Well." She inhaled a deep breath with this double blow to her ego and pasted on a smile. "I had the sauerbraten. I highly recommend it."

"And your date?"

"Him, I would stay away from." She laughed. "I've got to run. Have a great night, you two."

Pearl spun on her heel. She ducked through the revolving door of the restaurant, and into the cold night air. It woke her resolve.

Her personal life might be a mess, but it was time to improve her career.

In the Uber back, Pearl had gone over her words in her head. She had developed a strategy: First, she would praise the business. Next, she'd glorify Marisol, and then she was going to make her announcement—that she had Daphne and Carter practically in the bag.

But when Mari opened her apartment door in pajamas, hair held back in a wide headband and face covered in a charcoal mask, Pearl lost all thoughts of shop talk.

"Hey. So how did it go?" Mari grinned—or it looked like a grin to Pearl—and stepped aside. "Hungry?"

"I'm still full from dinner. And yeah, the date sucked." Pearl kicked off her shoes and followed her sister into her kitchen. Mari flipped the lights on, threw the freezer door open, and stuck her head in it.

"I picked up *ube* ice cream at Barrio Fiesta while you were at dinner. I know you love it."

Pearl thought twice. *Purple yam* anything was her favorite, and she would need the sugar reinforcement for what she was going to propose. She nodded, and Mari set about scooping them each a bowlful.

"Pearl, I was thinking a lot about today." Her sister recovered the ice cream carton and licked the side of her palm and passed Pearl her bowl. "I shouldn't have said what I did. About the bar thing. I didn't mean it that way. At all. Because you're damn good at what you do. You were amazing at the expo—you clearly know what you're doing. The livestream was an excellent idea."

"Thanks." Pearl melted onto the barstool and smiled. "I appreciate that. And I'm kind of relieved because I've got some news."

"What's going on?" Concern rang through Mari's tone.

"It's nothing bad." She half laughed to ease the moment.

Mari responded with a hesitant smile. "Then why do you look like you're going to drop a bomb right now?"

"Well, because it is one." She stabbed at her ice cream in the bowl. "I mean, not really. The metaphor isn't right. It's more like if someone shot a flower cannon and roses were raining on us right now. Scratch that, a dollar-bills cannon."

Mari slipped onto a barstool and started on her ice cream. "You've got my attention. Pray tell."

When it was only the two of them, Pearl felt the heavy truth of their birth order. Without Jane to buffer the space, to fill in their six-year gap, their differences were magnified so Mari was the knowledgeable one, the mature one, the successful one. An incredible temptation existed within Pearl to succumb, to defer to her oldest sister's wisdom.

Mari had paved the way for all of them, and Pearl, if she'd chosen it, could have followed in this shadow, could have lived comfortably, and could, truthfully, have had all the advantages without the struggle.

But she didn't want easy. She wanted to tear down Mari's pedestal so they could be on equal ground.

Though if someone were to ask her how it felt to be under her sister's appraising gaze, she would have described it in one word: intimidating.

"Daphne Brown and Carter Ling nuptials. Henceforth known as 'Bling.'"

An eyebrow shot up.

Pearl ran with it. "Four hundred guests. Thatched Roof Winery. Full-service from day one to the big day."

"They're looking for full-service?"

"Better. They have our service."

"You're kidding. You landed them? When? I want all the details. Is the venue already locked in? After the Glynn wedding, I will be absolutely free, though I may need to get Carli to help me until that time. Oh, did you already have her sign the contract—"

"*Ate*." Pearl burst through the barrage of words exiting her sister's mouth. Her heart had begun to beat the dreadful song, like a civil war drum line leading soldiers to their sure deaths.

"What?"

"Bling is mine. Remember? Last week? At Hazel's dress fitting? You agreed I would keep them if I got them to sign on the bottom line. And well, though it's not official, yet, I have a verbal. I forwarded her our contract, and she said she would get back to me soon."

"Okay, so it's not completely official yet—let's hold off on discussing the details. You know these brides, they'll do their due diligence and research before actually saying yes. Tell me though, how did you do it?"

Pearl frowned. "What do you mean?"

"I mean, how did you make contact? Did Kayla do the introductions?"

"Not exactly. We spoke at couples' yoga. Her wedding came up and I told her I was a wedding planner and I pitched her a theme." Pride welled up insider her. "I had a little help from Trenton, who instantly bonded with Carter. We had a late dinner last night—like a double date."

Mari's spoon was halfway to her lips. "Couples' yoga? Trenton, as in Trenton Young?"

"He was actually filling in for Kayla, but long story short—yes."

"So . . ." She narrowed her eyes. "She thinks you and Trenton are a couple."

"Yeah, I guess." Pearl shoved the *ube* ice cream in her mouth. It was delicious. Her sister's shoulders sagged, a sure sign of what Pearl had been afraid of. Her body tensed. "What is it?"

"It's just that we touched on this after the pregnancy spill with Hazel. The relationship between a wedding planner and their client must be built on trust, Pearl. You made contact under false pretenses. It seems like it's a tiny detail—that you and Trenton are a couple—but you used that to create this bond with her."

"It's not a big deal. I know what I'm doing." Suddenly her ice cream turned sour on her taste buds. She set down her spoon.

"Do you, Pearl? Because sometimes I think you totally gloss over the basics. You think you're above doing what the rules dictate."

Pearl's core shook as anger bubbled up like lava in a volcano. "You're not going to say that I'm not ready for this. Because I am—you just said so. And I've been assisting for years."

"And then you do something like this that makes me question where your head is at." As if detecting Pearl was about to blow, Mari put a hand up. "I don't want us to fight—I'm bringing up a valid point; it's something you'll have to tackle if she comes on board. You have to tell her the truth eventually."

It was a cork that stopped Pearl from bursting with frustrated words. Her sister was right in all her points, but it was in the way she said it, in the way she had control over Pearl's future career. "Just as a point. I've done over two dozen coordinated functions on my own. And it's not easy to come in at the last minute either. My relationship skills are spot-on. I mean, if social media doesn't test my ability to interact with people on a daily basis, I don't know what would." She put up a finger. "I can talk people down from a ledge. I know I'm a little frazzled at times, but in the end, I come through. And I know I messed up with Hazel. I get it. Lesson learned. It won't happen again. Finally, if Daphne signs with us, she'll know the truth about me and Trenton."

Mari bit her lip. Pearl jumped in with a plea. "I am perfect for this client. In fact, I'm going to leave now, and we'll go on with the week and do our thing, and you can tell me yes if and when the contract comes in."

"Pearl."

"Ate Mari." Pearl's voice shook. She hated herself for it, but she'd run out of tangible arguments, and the only thing left was her honest-to-God feelings. "You cannot keep holding me back. I want to fly. On my own." Then, at the surge of emotions from deep inside her, emotions that she'd had to overcome through yoga, she begged, "So don't make the decision right now, okay?"

Finally, Mari nodded. "Okay."

part three

There is no rose without thorns.

—Pam Muñoz Ryan

eleven

Mood: "Heart of Glass" by Blondie

When a top gets married, it is all hands on deck, especially during a spring snowmageddon.

Mari crossed her arms and shivered at the sight of the snow that had begun to blanket the tops of buildings. Forecasters had predicted a twenty-four-hour snowfall that would end with four to eight inches of accumulation. While the inside of Studio 1900, the penthouse restaurant and event space in an upscale historic hotel in Arlington, was cozy and warm, this didn't bode well for a smooth wedding afternoon for Jane's couple, "Rhockenzie." Maggie Rhodes and Gabriella Mackenzie expected to take the bulk of their photographs outside after the ceremony. Worse, most of their guests were coming from out of town, notably from Florida.

Jane, next to her, shook her head. "It's literally freaking March thirty-first—Mother Nature is killing me right now."

Mari shook her head, dismayed. "Do you know the status of your couple's guests, and what's plan B for the photographs?"

"Most of their out-of-town guests are staying at this hotel, and a majority of them got here last night for the rehearsal dinner, so we should still expect generally the same number of attendees. I'm more worried about the serving staff not getting here. The DJ has yet to arrive." She glanced at her iPad. "Pearl had an idea to propose regarding the photographs and she should be back soon. Snowfall on Easter weekend. What a mess."

"We can only do what we can, right?"

Jane nodded and heaved a breath. "Right. T-minus an hour before start time. Let's keep going." She scrolled up on her iPad. "Follow me to do the final walk-through of the ceremony spaces? Help calm me?"

"I'm at your disposal. And we can chat while Pearl isn't here."

"Okay?" Jane's tone lifted at the end of her question. "Is this about giving her a top?"

Mari hummed a "yes" and followed Jane through the ceremony room. With walls of exposed brick, a large antique fireplace, and floor-to-ceiling windows that brought the outside in, the view of the snowfall would surely be a topic of conversation for days to come.

The decor the couple had chosen had an old-world aesthetic with a modern twist: hammered copper Moscow mule mugs, rose gold cutlery, contrasted by classic bright white plates and dainty, romantic orchid centerpieces. The jaw-dropping star was the two-tier square cake with white icing, hand-painted with rose gold luster dust. Mari had met the couple briefly months ago. On paper, the vision seemed mismatched. Now, with all the details, it was a masterpiece. And it was all Jane's doing.

Mari and Jane were built for this kind of business. Both were mega-focused and uncompromising. Detail oriented. Early. Jane was more gifted in the budget arena, while Mari saw the big picture. They had both become assistants as each graduated from high school, working side by side and absorbing their mother's lessons when Rings & Roses was a one-woman show, when Regina de la Rosa worked morning till night, seven days a week. When each young woman turned twenty, they'd been promoted to day-of coordinators. At twenty-one, after Jane and Mari graduated from Georgetown and George Washington University respectively, when each had shown the drive and promise, and when Mari was over the hump of her short-term rebellion, they'd been promoted to full-time wedding planners, the business doubling and then tripling in size by the time Jane came on board.

And Pearl . . .

Her baby sister was convinced she wanted this job, but she hadn't a clue what it entailed. Pearl gravitated to her whims with such fervor but lost interest in a hot minute, except for yoga.

And that was partly Mari's fault. Because of that night, that one incident, with *him*, the whole family guarded Pearl, too much she was realizing now. Their mother had demanded the same kind of perfection she did from her eldest two, but Pearl was allowed to "seek," to "explore." What the hell did that mean, anyway? After graduating from William & Mary, changing her major twice in the process, Pearl had jumped into dabbling in different interests—radio journalism and blog writing—while working at Rings & Roses. What guaranteed that she wouldn't lose interest in working with a top halfway to the finish line?

For Mari, it had only taken that one night to understand that passive action was foolhardy, that results occurred through decision and action.

As if the universe had read her thoughts, Pearl stepped out of the building's renovated birdcage elevator, carrying a bundle in her arms so only her eyes could be seen.

"What the heck?" Jane jogged toward her, and Mari paced close behind.

Pearl's chest heaved as if she'd run the entire fourteen flights up. Her beanie cap was covered in droplets. "There's a vintage specialty store three blocks down—and I happen to know the owner. And guess what she had in her stock?" She gestured to the bundle with her lips. "Go ahead. Take it off."

Jane peeled off the damp sheet, revealing fur. Brown, gray, white. "What is this?"

"Faux fur stoles and there's even a caplet in there. In exchange for a shout-out online, our wedding party can use them. We have to return them before the night is over." Pearl's gaze darted from Jane to Mari and back. "I mean, it's worth a try, right? Snow-bridesmaids? A quick shoot outside if the wind lets up?"

Mari let out a smile. "That is a freaking fantastic idea. I swear, Pearl, you can turn things around. Great work."

Jane took her sister's cheeks in her hands. "I owe you one. I'm going to tell the ladies after the ceremony. Cross your fingers that it all works. Do you mind finding hangers—one of the hotel staff can help you, and could you hang them in coat check?"

"Of course." She spun and headed in the opposite direction.

Jane snapped to. "What were we doing? Oh right—to the waiting rooms."

Mari, too, picked up on her last thought. "When Pearl does things like that, I want to give her the world. But giving her a top? I'd consider another client who's lower profile, less risk. Let her get her feet wet without compromising our financial future with a potential mistake."

Jane sniffed a rebuttal as she took off to an anteroom, passing a catering cart and picking up a navy blue table cover. "I don't agree. She's ready."

Mari followed a step behind. "She's scatterbrained. She spends half the time at yoga, and the events she coordinates always feel a little messy. Remember the Orbinson wedding? She didn't follow the standard checklist. That's planning 101. Mommy would have tricep-pinched us if we made the same mistakes. And did you know she faked a relationship with Trenton to get to Daphne? Deception from the jump. What am I supposed to think?"

"Her mind is everywhere because she's been too busy making us look good on the internet. And anyway, we can't expect others to be like us, just as we are not like our mother, who isn't perfect herself. Must I remind you that she and Daddy are the ones who left us with such messy books and missing inventory? Which, by the way, you need to address."

"I know I do. But they're on vacation now, so . . ."

They arrived in one bride's anteroom, cozy and sparse except for leather couches pushed up against the exposed brick walls. A table was set up in the middle. Jane parked herself on one side of the table, while Mari stood at the opposite end. Jane tossed a hem of the tablecloth across it.

"I call bullshit. You're avoiding approaching Mommy because we've been taught that questioning authority is a sin that will take us straight to hell or get us struck from the will. But that's your job as a CEO. See? Not everyone is perfect." Jane continued. "Pearl has her own process, but you can't deny she gets it done. Feedback from her clients tells us that they love her spirit. What you call messy, they call exciting and flexible. And I know our sister's heart. It's not malicious. She needs direction, not a stop sign."

"I'm not denying anything." Mari smoothed out the linen on her side. "You're making it sound like I personally don't want her to succeed."

"Don't kill the messenger, but if it quacks like a duck . . ."

The hair on the back of Mari's neck stood; the statement prickled down her spine. These were familiar words. Mari had accused her mother of the same thing when she'd wanted to move away from home. And where did that get her except in a bad relationship that almost broke their family apart? "I'm trying to protect her."

"From what?" Jane moved the couch back so it was perfectly parallel to the wall, then ran a finger against the leather to check for dust. Mari trailed behind her as she walked out of the room. "*I'm* grateful Pearl schmoozed a potential top. Finding another one was the first 'to do' item on our Save Rings and Roses Checklist. When did she send out the contract?"

"Sunday."

"So . . . a week ago. Do you expect an answer soon?"

"Anytime now." Mari bit her lip.

"If you're asking my opinion, I don't see the problem."

They'd reached the other bride's anteroom. The table was already covered, with a similar orchid centerpiece. Right on time, the catering manager entered the room and delivered French pastries, two champagne flutes, and a copper ice bucket with the neck of a bottle of Cristal sticking up from the ice.

Mari couldn't concentrate on the details with the pros and the cons list materializing in the air in front of her. It was a risk either way: a monetary risk if Pearl didn't do a good job, a personal risk if Mari didn't let her try.

"Checking in," a man's voice said from the doorway.

Mari jolted at the sight of the six-footer at the door. He had a shock of black hair that swooped to the back and wore a short-sleeve shirt open over a white tank. She flashed back to a decade ago, to a similarly dressed man—Saul—who used to unbutton his shirts during the hot Virginia summers.

"Oh, I'm so glad you're here. Mari, this is Peter of Good Vibrations, our DJ," Jane said.

Mari blinked, swallowed the image away. *Right. Not Saul.* "Hi."

"The roads weren't too bad. I'll go ahead and set up." Peter grinned, then stepped away.

Jane brushed a hand over the linen to straighten it. "You didn't answer my question. What are you trying to protect her from?"

"From failing." The words fell from her lips, mind still reeling at the slip to the past.

Jane frowned, reflecting back the sadness that had crept into Mari's conscience. "We all have failed at one time or another. And we're always there for each other, aren't we? We'll be there for her," Jane said.

"It's not that." The unease grew. Protectiveness was only one part of it, though she couldn't put words to the dreadful knot in her belly.

"This is not Saul," Jane reminded her. "This is not a repeat of history."

Or was it? It was, after all, Pearl pushing her way in once again. Of her possibly being exposed in a space where she was not prepared. History didn't have to replay itself in its entirety. History sometimes came back in snippets to teach the same old lessons foolish people didn't learn the first time around.

"Ate Mari." Jane was at the front door now, pulling her from her thoughts. "Time to go. It's showtime."

Mari shuffled out. From afar she watched a bride enter the anteroom, beautiful and hopeful. Today was her day, her day when the future forecasted an infinite number of possibilities.

For Mari, there would only be two choices if Daphne and Carter were to sign with Rings & Roses: keep the client under her control, or let Pearl take the reins to appease her and risk a less than perfect outcome.

With the success of Rings & Roses on Mari's shoulders, there was only one right choice.

———

Mari had awakened on her secondhand microfiber couch. At first, she was discombobulated. The air was smoky with the sweet smell of weed. Bodies milled above her in zombielike movements. Had she been taken in her sleep and transported to some party house? Was she dreaming? But with the leftover taste of alcohol on her tongue, she remembered the three solo cups of a sweet cocktail Saul had magically concocted, which she'd downed after a long day at Rings & Roses.

Mari's vision was wavy and fuzzed at the edges; she stood carefully. Where was that boyfriend of hers? Annoyance pricked through her in between the thumping beats of music. Someone in her apartment had changed out the playlist and an unrecognizable nineties new wave song filtered through her speakers. She squinted at the dozen bodies in her living room and at the couple making out in the corner and winced. The neighbors would surely complain. She'd moved in less than two weeks ago.

Her thoughts tumbled into the abyss of what would come next. Her parents would find out about this somehow since they cosigned the lease. They'd find out she'd gotten back together with Saul.

She had tried to stay away from him. For a bit she'd even resisted his calls, his texts, his unannounced visits. But oh, he was convincing. His lips, his body, the way he'd begged her to give him another chance. She'd taken him back after he'd vowed for the hundredth time that they would be equals, that this time he would keep his temper in check.

"Where's Saul?" Mari yelled above the music to Brendan, Saul's buddy, who currently had one hand hooked around his boyfriend's neck. They were staggering to her U-shaped kitchen, tiny and tucked into the back of the third-floor apartment. A woman was sitting on the kitchen countertop, legs wrapped around her partner.

"Dunno." A cigarette dangled from Brendan's lips and it bobbed up as he spoke. "Somewhere around this dump."

"Hey. Respect," she snapped back, showing him her palm, and walked toward the bedroom. She passed another couple, and said to no one in particular, "You all need to go soon."

Annoyance turned to guilt as she surveyed the accuracy of Brendan's words. Her place *was* a dump. How long had she been sleeping? Tomorrow was Saturday. A Wedding Day. She'd have to see her parents face-to-face, and they'd know. They'd know that she'd been partying, that she'd been with Saul, that she'd gone back on her word.

He isn't good for you, her mother had insisted. Saul was different; he was older. Yes, he partied. Yes, he sometimes asked for too much. Yes, he yelled. He'd insisted on his way. But her mother hadn't seen his good side, hadn't witnessed how he'd known exactly what to say, how he really was sorry for his terse words. That when they'd made up, it was heaven on earth.

But this party—this party was a bad call. And this time, she couldn't help but think that maybe her mother was right. This pressing feeling of all of these people around her—she wanted out from under it.

The buzzing in her head permeated throughout the rest of her body.

Oh, her phone.

She reached into her back jean pocket, pulled out the bright

screen, and saw Jane's face staring back at her. Shit. One rule between her sisters—they always picked up. They might've
screened their mother's calls, but never each other's.

Mari cleared her throat and willed a steady, lucid voice.
"Hey."

"Where the fuck have you been, Mari?"

Mari pulled the phone away from her ear, confused. She
looked at Jane's smiling picture once again. Goody Two-Shoes
Jane who did everything perfectly. In their home, it was Jane
who was the perfect one, who kept to the straight and narrow.
The eldest wasn't revered, not in that way. Pearl looked up to
Mari because she rocked the boat, but Jane was the golden child
because she didn't.

"What's wrong with you?" Mari snapped.

"Where's Pearl?"

She frowned. "How the hell should I know? You're the one
who lives at home."

"Because she was headed to you."

"What?" Mari's apartment was clear across Falls Church,
miles from Duchess Street in Old Town. "How is that even possible?"

"She left a note in her room. She had a fight with Daddy,
and you know that never goes well. Is she there?"

"No!" Was her first answer, though worry eclipsed her
drunkenness, because it was a lie. "I . . . I don't know."

"What do you mean, you don't know. You're at your apartment, aren't you?"

Her fingers found their way to her forehead. It was slick. "I
am . . . I mean." She scanned the living room again. No, none of
those women were her sister. None were fifteen years old, with
her baby face or her innocence. Someone came out of the bath-

room, snatching Mari's gaze. Scratch that, it was a couple, holding hands, passing her closed bedroom door.

"What's all the noise in the background?"

She lowered the phone from her ear, not wanting to hear her sister's demands, and her legs took her to her bedroom. She turned the knob and opened the door.

What she saw froze her in place: Saul and another woman, a woman Mari recognized from the bar down the street, standing next to the bed. Saul with a blunt between his lips, unbuttoning her shirt. His face lazily scanning the room when the door creaked. Confusion materializing on his face when he caught Mari's eyes.

He stepped back from the woman. "This isn't—"

Mari, overcome by a violence unrecognizable to her, with an anger beyond any she'd ever experienced, pulled this woman away from Saul. She battered him with her fists, cursing his betrayal and her own foolishness.

It all became fuzzy after that. Saul seemed to transform. His features turned into a monster's. His voice escalated to a roar, and his hands fell to the front of Mari's shirt, tearing her away from him. She staggered toward her windows and she clawed hopelessly at the mini blinds for purchase before falling on the floor. Back against the wall, she looked up at Saul's ominous figure. His hand rose. Mari's anger flipped to fear; she shut her eyes in the anticipation of pain. Cowered. In the past, he'd only struck with words, but she knew this would be more, like she had been slowly preparing for this inevitability.

But Saul paused; he grunted. Mari opened her eyes, seeing him turn to someone behind him. From between his legs, Mari glimpsed Pearl standing at the doorway, frightened. Shame rained over her. She was Marisol de la Rosa, raised proud and independent, now under the thumb of a man who liked to hurt her.

Shame, until Saul turned to Pearl with fury in his face, sputtering with rage. In that split second, shame became ferocity.

She clambered to her feet, grabbed the first thing within reach, a wooden candlestick she'd picked up for a client, and held it like a bat. As Saul snatched the front of Pearl's flannel shirt with both hands and hefted her off her Vans-clad feet, Mari swung the candlestick at Saul's skull.

Mari jolted up in bed, face covered with sweat. Her chest heaved. Her eyes adjusted to the dim light, to her neat, sparse bedroom, to the empty space on her queen-sized bed. Her surroundings told her she wasn't back at that apartment with Saul, but the images had been vivid. Too real.

After the burst of adrenaline, she wanted to be outside, to reassure herself that that was all in the past. She shuffled out of her room and unlocked the French doors that led to her snow-covered patio.

The forecasters had overshot their estimated snow total. Only two inches had fallen since the Rhockenzie wedding, and the band of the storm had headed north and east. Luckily for them, there had been just enough snow to create the snow-bride photos Pearl had suggested but not enough to deter the rest of the party.

Mari slipped on her rain boots and walked outside; the floodlights turned on. She raised her face to the dark sky, shut her eyes, and breathed in the frigid night air.

It was just a dream.

A chunk of snow fell from above. She turned in the direction it came from; another chunk flew toward her and she stepped aside just in time. "Hey!"

Soft snowballs were being lobbed in her direction. From 2402. Her face warmed despite the weather. *Reid.*

"Those monkey pajamas aren't the proper outerwear for this kind of cold, Ms. de la Rosa. Even a southerner like myself knows that."

Mari wasn't sure if she was more embarrassed or thrilled. She hiked her hands on her hips, squinted at his shadow on the balcony. "Haven't you realized? They make us hardy up here."

"Oh, I know how hardy you are. Like a rose. With thorns and everything." His voice was light, flirtatious.

"I'm proud to be prickly, Mr. Quaid. If you can't take the thorns, you don't deserve the bloom."

"Well, if that isn't an invitation, I don't know what is."

She felt her grin widen at his cool attitude, happy that he could dish it right back. "Welcome back to Northern Virginia."

"Got in before the snow started."

"Lucky for you. What are you doing out here?"

"Chilling."

"Literally." She laughed. The hint of smoke reached Mari's nose. "I smell differently."

"You caught me. Bad habit, occasional now."

"No judgment." At the lull, she pointed at her lit kitchen. "I'm headed in. I might be hardy, but I've got nothing on under this and—" She halted, realizing what she'd said.

He laughed. "Wait. Why are *you* outside?"

"Wouldn't you like to know." Though, admittedly, since seeing the man, the memory of her nightmare had fallen away. What replaced it was giddiness. It was a silly, almost innocent emotion.

It gave her an idea. "If you come down here, I'll tell you all about it."

"I'll be there in two."

Her heart leapt. She leaned down and scooped snow from the ground. With the help of the excess length of her pajama top sleeves, she rounded it into a ball and hid it behind her as he came out of his sliding glass door.

Reid was in sweats and an Emory University sweatshirt. He took a step toward her with an expectant smile. Mari felt a momentary pang of guilt but pushed it away. He'd had two shots at her. It wasn't her fault he'd missed.

Mari drew her arm back and let the snowball fly, hitting Reid square in the chest. He halted, stunned. Then, a playful growl escaped his lips. "You didn't."

"Not only am I thorny, but I'm a good shot. Goodnight, Reid."

"Night, Marisol."

Mari entered her kitchen and kicked her shoes off. There was no way she'd be able to sleep tonight. Might as well start the prep for Easter brunch.

twelve

Mood: "Chasing Cars" by Snow Patrol

"Easter, the time for egg hunts, church, chocolate bunnies, and speed dating. My, how times have changed." Jane had not stopped whispering into Pearl's ear for the last half hour. Sitting with a group of women across a room from a group of men at the Wheelbarrow Bar and Grill for part two of her Love Unlimited gift certificate, Pearl guzzled her white wine like water on a sunny day.

Her sister was right, of course. It was the Monday after Easter. With the rise in temperature that melted the snow into a slushy mess, the previously stranded single people came out to play. The Wheelbarrow was packed.

"You owe me big-time." Jane, white-knuckled, gripped her wineglass. Her gaze darted around the room. "Two, heck, three babysitting days. Four, damn it."

"You said you wanted to get to know more guys." Pearl infused confidence into her voice as she overtly scanned her sister from head to toe. Jane was dressed to the nines tonight: a short black dress with capped sleeves, two-inch heels, and sexy smoky eyes that impressed the hell out of her. "Besides, you are hot."

"Quit kissing up."

"I swear I'm not."

Her gaze faltered briefly. "Well, thanks. But this wasn't what I meant about meeting guys. I was thinking of more like getting to know the single dads at the next PTA meeting. This feels so . . . fake. Not to mention anxiety producing. Five minutes. Is that enough time to get to know someone?" She gestured at the banner hanging above them: Love Unlimited Spring Speed Dating Extravaganza.

"Well, no. But we're here now, so . . ." Pearl tipped the wineglass to her lips to keep her own nerves in check.

Admittedly, she hadn't expected so many people. Across the room, men of all skin shades, hair styles, builds, and postures milled about like animals stalking their prey.

Even for a major extravert this was . . . overwhelming. "And," Pearl added. "You are one-half responsible for my gift certificate. You had to know I wasn't going to do this alone."

A bell rang from the front of the room, bringing their attention to the grand bar and the stunning view of the Washington Monument through it's tall windows. Chrome cone-shaped light fixtures hung over scratched and roughed-out tables and stools, the dichotomy of old and new, city and country.

A woman in a fitted pantsuit with a plunging neckline and sky-high silver heels stood in front of the bar. Hair up in a chignon, Davina Petrovich, Love Unlimited's owner, was attractive and intimidating.

"Here we go. I can't believe you convinced me to do this. I can't believe I said yes. I'm way too nice for my own good. At least Ate Mari was around—I didn't have to pay a sitter." Jane babbled.

"Shh." Pearl listened as Davina explained the rules: ladies moved counterclockwise, timed five-minute sessions, no skipping, no backtracking, no exchanging numbers at the table, requests for contact information must be made after the event through the planners.

"Gentlemen, please go to your assigned tables," Davina announced. Men weaved through the crowd and sat at their seats. Pearl snuck a look at her sister, grabbed for her hand, squeezing it.

Jane's smile was thankful, if not wary. Her last date had been Pio's dad.

"Ladies, head to a table," Davina said.

"See you soon," Pearl mouthed.

Jane nodded, then walked across the room.

Pearl headed to Table Twenty-Five with a rehearsed smile and braced herself for the disappointment. What was it they said? Expect the worst but hope for the best?

She turned on her professional persona when she sat at the table. She was courteous and reached for the man's hand to shake it. She listened to the man boast about his credentials. She answered questions. She smiled. Davina rang the cowbell at the end of five minutes, then off she went to Table Twenty-Six. Then Twenty-Seven, and then Twenty-Eight.

The men she met were handsome enough, pleasant enough. Interesting enough. And yet nothing sparked. No one shone. Twenty-Nine was a jerk. Thirty mentioned being a perpetual day drinker. Thirty-One asked her where she was from. "No, but where are you *from*?"

As she transitioned to Table Thirty-Two, Pearl's hopes for a match declined. She peeked across the room to Jane. She gave Pearl a thumbs-up and a toothy smile.

At least one of them was having good luck. Pearl's night

would have been better spent planning out the Bling wedding, if Daphne ever signed the contract.

She admonished herself. *When, not if.*

Pearl picked up another glass of wine from one of the waiters, eager to drown her worry about the Bling account.

"Pearl?"

Her wits returned to her; she was the only woman still standing. She turned to her spoken name, to the man at Table Thirty-Two.

She plopped down on her chair with a stunned expression.

Trenton's dazzling smile greeted her. "Well, well, well."

"Well, yourself. What are you doing here?" She shook her head, laughing. "I mean, I know what you're doing here, of course."

"Apparently, the same thing as you." A pause, and his eyes widened. "So your date at Küche was . . ."

"Level one." She finished his sentence.

"As was Leighann."

"Oh . . ." She bit the side of her cheek.

"Any luck? Today, I mean."

"Some prospects," she lied, assessing his reaction to her answer. "You?"

"Honestly? Nope." He shrugged. "I dunno. Starting to think that maybe this whole matchmaking thing isn't for me. I might be more old-fashioned than I thought."

She looked into his eyes. "Is that old-fashioned, though?"

"You're right. Not old-fashioned. It's an excuse to cover up the fact that I'm failing even when I'm being professionally set up."

"Same." She looked away for a beat, but dared to make the next statement. What the hell, right? She was done holding back, in work and in play. "I want this, but it doesn't seem to be happening. It's not as if I'm not putting in the effort, you know? Then again, should I be trying so hard? Shouldn't that person— love, whatever—have some responsibility to come to me?" She met his gaze, and understanding flickered through his face.

"And yet here we are," he mused.

"Tortured by speed dating."

"But the beer, the view."

She sighed, gazing upon the smile that had grown on his face. A smile that she'd known all her life. "The view indeed."

He narrowed his eyes, playfully. "Are you flirting with me right now, Pearly-Pearl?"

Warmth flooded her cheeks, but she pressed on despite the flutter in her chest. The bell rang. "Guess you'll have to wonder, since our time's up."

"Luckily, I already know your number. And your yoga sched- ule. Speaking of. Still on for Friday night?"

Another woman had come up on Pearl's side, waiting her turn, her presence overbearing. Pearl stood and dared him with a coy expression. "No, I've got a wedding on Saturday I have to prep for, but since you know my number, why don't you call me?"

"You've got it."

The rest of the night was a haze, with Pearl's thoughts occu- pied alternately by Trenton and Mari. In the Uber, as Pearl watched DC fall away to the beltway, she laughed with Jane at the luck of seeing Trenton at the event. Jane chatted on about her favorites: Fourteen who had the handsomest smile, and Twenty-One who made her laugh. As the car turned down to bulb-lighted Burg Street, two blocks past the shop, Mari glimpsed a banner hanging in front of Light Up, a specialty lighting shop.

"Did you see that?" Pearl interrupted Jane.

"See what?"

Pearl tapped the Uber driver's shoulder. "Excuse me, can you do a quick U-turn?"

The car flipped around. It pulled over to the side at Pearl's signal.

Jane scooted next to Pearl, eyes on the banner hanging from the inside of the shop's windows. "No freaking way."

Heartfully Yours, a wedding shop. Opening this summer.

———

Pearl's eyes were closed but sleep was miles away. She tossed and turned, and her tummy did flips. It was partly from the white wine and the hors d'oeuvres she'd consumed during the two-hour speed-dating event, partly Trenton's presence and what seemed to be an alternate path they were taking in their friendship. Mostly, it was because competition was setting up shop a mere two blocks away.

When she and Jane had arrived home three hours ago, they'd gone straight to Mari, who was Pio-sitting for Jane in her apartment. Pio was sound asleep in his bedroom, but the news brought Mari's voice up to its third octave and woke their nephew. They'd decided to table the discussion until later on this week—they'd all needed to process whether Heartfully Yours's presence would be beneficial, a hindrance, or simply inconsequential. Nothing could be done about it at eleven at night.

But Pearl knew her sisters, understood their inner workings sometimes better than her own self. While Jane was able to compartmentalize, categorize, and place each problem into a box and lock it up for safe keeping until it was time to tackle it, her oldest sister was probably up. Cooking, maybe. Or sifting through recipes while strategizing in her head.

The sound of a man's voice nudged Pearl from her thoughts. Their backyard faced the backyards of town houses the next street over, and it wasn't uncommon to hear their neighbors' conversations. But when the man's voice was followed by a woman's distinct cackle, Pearl's eyes flew open.

She sat up in bed on her elbows. Was that Mari? Who was she speaking to? All at once, Reid came to mind, the teasing the sisters had done, and the way Mari couldn't hold their gaze when she talked about him.

Pearl snuck out of bed like she wasn't in her own apartment, went into her kitchen, and popped open her balcony door as quietly as she could. From below, she smelled cigarettes. She got on her hands and knees and peeked through the slats of her balcony. Reid sat in a chair next to her sister; each had a cigarette in their hand. He laughed at something she'd said. A giggle burst from her lips.

Well, well, well. Looks like her sister did, in fact, have insomnia, but for an entirely different reason.

thirteen

Mood: "Salted Wound" by Sia

As Mari looked at herself through bleary eyes in her office bathroom mirror, she remembered why she usually put herself to bed before eleven at night. There were real consequences from lack of sleep. One was that she couldn't think straight, and the other was the appearance of bags under her eyes. Correction: not bags, but oversized steamer trunks.

But the more Mari dabbed concealer on the swollen areas under her eyes, the worse they looked. The perfect shades of concealer and foundation were already unicorns; she'd suffered for years looking either slightly pasty or too tan. Despite the highlights and contouring she added as per the instructions from her makeovers at Sephora, the fine lines that had cropped up and the blue hue that had taken permanent residence below her eyes were a beast to manage. And those were the days when she'd managed enough sleep.

"Damn it." She peered into the mirror.

The shop's front door jostled open, followed by the sound of humming. Amelia.

"Marisol, it's me. I see your coat. Are you here?" Her footsteps sounded on the stairs.

Mari popped out of the bathroom. "I'm here, second floor." When Amelia materialized from the staircase, Mari kissed the older woman on the cheek—she smelled reliably of makeup and mint. "How was your long weekend?"

"Good. Glad now that the sun's out. Hoping it's the last snow so the cherry blossoms can do their thing. Don't you have a wedding at the Tidal Basin this weekend?"

"It's actually Pearl's. But I got word that the snow didn't do the current blossoms too much damage."

"Cross our fingers." Amelia did a double take. "But you're here early."

"Brunch with my top. And . . . I have a lot on my mind."

"Ah—I can tell." She rubbed a thumb just above Mari's cheekbone. "There. Glob eliminated. Are they good things on the brain or bad? Because you're smiling."

"Both?" Mari honestly was on the fence. Last night, her sisters had come home with disconcerting news, news that could affect the shop. But she'd also had her first cigarette in almost ten years—she didn't finish it because it turned her stomach—and more importantly, she'd spent the night chatting with Reid, discussed things that had nothing to do with work and everything to do with her as a woman, a person separate from Rings & Roses, individual of her sisters. She and Reid had taken breaks in her kitchen, refilled their tea and coffee until the sky turned pink, until he'd departed with a simple goodbye. He'd left this morning for Atlanta and wouldn't be back until next weekend.

"Okay, that sounds promising."

She shook her head, jostling her brain to work properly. "No, not really promising." She brought Amelia up to speed about

Heartfully Yours but refrained from discussing their finances in general. Her mother and Amelia were close, but she couldn't assume her mother had shared that kind of information.

"Seems to me you're going to have to be like the restaurants, clothing shops, and gift shops in the area," Amelia said. "Level up. Actually compete."

"We do that now."

"Not in the same way the Whistling Pig or even Ohm does," she said of their neighboring businesses. "It's never been this in your face. Luckily, you have the best team in the business." At Mari's questioning look, Amelia laughed. "Oh, come on. You don't think seamstresses talk? Just because we're in the back room doesn't mean our ears aren't perked. We have our own whisper network. You have the most established, the most experienced, and the most connected team in the area. You might be worried about Heartfully Yours, but they are equally worried about the three of you."

———

Amelia's words rang in Mari's head through brunch with Hazel and Brad. She'd said them like a kind of warning, as if Amelia had known about the ever-present conflict between her and Pearl, about the rough couple of weeks they'd had.

Ultimately, Amelia was right about one thing, it was teamwork that businesses were built on. And it was up to Mari to find the key to unlock her team's potential.

"C'mon babe, do you really want to carry such a big bouquet? And with all the flowers up the aisle—orchids are for funerals and offices, aren't they?" Brad's voice nudged Mari back to the present. He was holding Hazel's hand above the table. Behind him was the view of the Potomac through the windows of Brunch!, a restaurant in Foggy Bottom.

"No, not really—" Hazel said.

He droned on, ignoring her. He called the table settings "gaudy" and "over the top," and remarked that gifts to visiting wedding guests were a waste of money.

The tension at their table had gotten thick despite the cheerful ambiance of the restaurant. More disturbing: Hazel had little to say back. The woman who had been so expressive in the past had been reduced to nods and shrugs.

Oh, did Mari miss Reid at this moment. He had been replaced by Brad and his negative personality.

In short: Brad was pissing Mari off.

Why should he care what kind of flowers the flower girl was carrying? Except for the fact that, maybe, Brad himself was a control freak.

"And now that I'm seeing the invitation." He passed the intricately designed cardstock back to Mari, face scrunched in disgust. "I don't know if I like this calligraphy after all."

"But we decided on it, together." Hazel's voice choked.

His expression was dubious. "Eh, technically I made the decision from the pictures you sent. Now that it's in front of me, I'm finding it too feminine."

Mari interrupted—this was getting out of hand. "We're two months away from the wedding, and to have it hand lettered—"

"Is there a rush service?"

"Well, yes—"

"Then let's rush. We didn't hire you all to take a back seat. This is the time to show me you're worth the money I've spent on you. Or, we could simply postpone the wedding."

His words were so smooth, so sly, his mood so even that the ultimatum stunned Mari. Did he just threaten to put the actual wedding on the line, over invitations? In the pause, Hazel's eyes glassed over with tears. "Of course they can do it. Won't you, Mari?"

"Yes, of course." Rattled, Mari's voice shook. "I'll contact the calligrapher straightaway."

She typed out an email to Lily Mai, her favorite calligrapher, on her iPad, heart thudding in her chest, mind only on Hazel and protecting her interests.

Below this instinctual emotion, something else clawed through. Tension. Fear. Part of Mari rebelled against it, tried to ignore it. Hazel chose Brad. For better or for worse, he was the love of her life.

Yet, if Mari had a say, if she had the opportunity to verbalize her feelings freely, Mari would admit she had seen this kind of man before. Brad was a brand of a sly, slick jerk who didn't have to raise his voice. Passive-aggressive at first.

Her conscience whispered a sad phrase: *It would only get worse.*

She pressed the Send button with force. *No.* She wouldn't transfer her experience to Hazel, because it was hers alone. Hazel wasn't Mari, and Brad wasn't Saul.

But the suspicion she held close to her heart rooted itself in her belly. From here on out, she would watch this Brad closely.

"What is this, a noon party?" Mari arrived at Rings & Roses after her brunch with Brad and Hazel, surprised to find her family in the foyer. Mari ruffled Pio's hair. "Hey, buddy, what's going on? Why aren't you in school?"

Jane held a tissue up to Pio's nose as he blew into it. The boy's eyes were swollen and red. "I'm sick," he croaked.

She glanced up at Jane, who, too, looked worse for wear in her favorite oversized and worn Georgetown sweatshirt. "You okay? You're a little green."

"I think I'm coming down with something, too. It was probably from all those hands I shook last night." Jane rolled her eyes at Pearl.

"You know you loved it." Pearl laughed. "Number Fourteen already texted you. He might be your Prince Charming."

Jane covered Pio's ears. "Hush."

Pearl's eyes widened. "Sorry."

Mari took a step back from the group; she couldn't afford to get sick. "Why didn't you all stay at home?"

"Crisis with the Johns." Jane looked over her shoulder toward the shop's reception area as she took Pio's coat off. "Carli, do you mind heading to Barrio Fiesta for some *arroz caldo*?"

"Of course." Carli picked up the phone to preorder.

The thought of chicken and rice porridge sent Mari's taste buds into full salivation mode, but it was eclipsed by her concern. "Crisis already? Their wedding is over a year out." Grooms John Kolb and John Avant had just been signed a month ago, and their wedding wasn't until next August. "That doesn't bode well."

"I think we need to have a sit-down about expectations and what is a crisis and what isn't a crisis. Over chat obviously, because my lungs got a workout coughing last night, and I'm a hot mess. After I take care of this issue, I promise we'll head home."

"There's my boy," Amelia said to Pio as she floated down the stairwell. "I have a chocolate bunny for you. Keep me company while your mommy works."

Pio clasped his hands under his chin. "Please, Mommy?"

Jane's expression softened. She nudged him. "Go. He's sick, Amelia. You've been forewarned."

"I'm a tough old lady. C'mon, buddy."

Pio bounded up the stairs, leaving the three in the foyer.

"All right," Mari said to Jane warily. "If you need backup, let me know."

"I might take you up on it. My mind's a little fuzzy from cold medicine." She sniffed.

Mari did a double take at Jane's shoes—she was still wearing her house loafers.

Jane's health was always, for lack of a better word, *susceptible*. She was born a preemie. Sick more often than the rest of the sisters, she'd caught the flu every other year despite the vaccine. Her seasonal allergies had required allergy shots until she was nineteen years old. She'd lost a lot of blood when she gave birth to Pio and had to be transfused.

"Before we go our separate ways, can we have a quick meeting in my office?" Pearl asked. Only then did Mari notice that she had a bundle of magazines in her arms.

"Okay. Sure." Dread bloomed in Mari's gut. She ascended the stairs after her sisters, but called back down to the main floor. "Carli, give me a few minutes, and I'll be back and relieve you so you can go to Barrio Fiesta."

"Got it!" she answered back.

Mari had just entered Pearl's office when she announced, "Read it and rejoice!" From in between the pile of magazines, she pulled out a stapled packet, which she tossed on her desk. A triumphant grin spanned the width of her face. "I'm still in major shock. I did it—I have my own top client."

"What the hell, really?" Mari blurted out, but at Jane's pointed look, the one that said, *Let her speak*, she regrouped. She picked up the packet and scrolled through the electronically signed document. Sure enough, Daphne's initials were next to their policies and one large signature was on the last page. "I mean, wow!"

"Estimated four hundred guests for a late-August affair, with a six-figure budget. No expense spared—Daphne wants the full experience, from engagement announcements to honeymoon planning."

Mari swallowed at the written numbers on the page. "I see."

"I already jotted down some notes." Pearl lifted her iPhone for emphasis. "There's so much potential, and the great thing is that she's open to suggestions. As soon as we're done here, I'll start my phone calls . . ."

Her sister continued to speak and all Mari envisioned was a waterfall of potential issues showering upon them. "Pearl—"

"Don't worry. I'm planning to use your checklist. To a T."

"Good." Mari's train of thought twisted into a pretzel. She should've practiced what she was going to say, but she hadn't expected the contract this quickly. Or, if she was being honest with herself, she had avoided thinking about it. "How would you feel about partnering with me or Jane?"

"No. Can't do it." Both their gazes swung to Jane. "The Johns wedding is late summer. They're my top for the season."

"And I don't need a partner. I'm ready to go solo."

"It's a big client, Pearl. You should have someone around to help in case you mess up." Mari jerked at her own words, instantly regretful.

Stunned, Pearl reared back.

"That came out all wrong."

"Yeah, it did. Especially coming from someone who's screwed up herself. And more than once." Pearl walked out of the office, a fierce expression on her face. Unlike Mari, Pearl had meant what she said.

Ouch. "Okay, I deserved that, and it's true, I did screw up." She swallowed her pride and followed Pearl to the hallway, aware of the presence of other people in the building. The hairs on the back of her neck tingled with discomfort at their history launched into the open. But she refocused. This was about Rings & Roses, and she had to deescalate the conversation. "But I wasn't given my first big client until I straightened myself out."

Pearl laughed, sardonically. "That. That is funny."

She raised an eyebrow at the comment, chest thudding. "Why is that funny?"

"It's nothing, okay?" Pearl pressed her fingers to her temple. Her voice softened. "Ate Mari, I'm ready. So ready I can taste it. So ready it's all I've thought of since I spoke with Daphne."

Movement to the right alerted Mari to Amelia, who'd come down from the third floor. She rested a hand on Jane's wrist as if preventing her from interfering. "Ladies." Her voice was firm. "Maybe take this elsewhere? Like in a room, with a closed door. We have a building full of customers."

This was when business and personal got messy, when Mari herself didn't know what kind of a meeting this was. Was she speaking to Pearl as a business partner, or as a big sister? Was the torn emotion inside her because Pearl was a less experienced planner, or was it from this indescribable need to keep everything the way it was?

No matter what, Mari would look like the bad cop. So she fortified her logic, which had begun to waffle. "Managing a client this big is less about feelings and more about skill. And you're a novice."

Pearl placed her hands on her hips, and her head lolled forward. "So that's it? You're saying no."

Relieved and wary at her level tone, Mari nodded.

"You're saying no—you, who's claiming to be better than me because you've straightened up? Because you're an expert and you've had more years under your belt? Someone who's *so responsible* but hanging out in secret with your top's brother."

Mari's breath caught in her belly. "I . . . it's not what you think . . ." Yet, despite her poor excuse of a rebuttal, Mari understood that Pearl was right. Mari had been wrong. And foolish.

"As usual, you are the biggest hypocrite I know. Classic Ate Mari: do as I tell you not as I show you. Well, I'm done doing what you tell me to do."

Mari's eyebrows scrunched down. "I don't understand."

"I want out of Rings and Roses. Obviously my third share doesn't get me a damn thing when it comes to my thoughts on client assignments. I'm giving you my notice. I'll speak to Daphne and give her the option to sign with me or to sign with you all. I'll finish out my summer commitments. That will give you guys time to buy me out."

"What? No. Absolutely not." Mari chased the tail end of her sister's words as if yelling for a bus that had left her at the stop. Astonished at the trajectory, blindsided by the turn of the conversation. "You're not allowed to leave us. We are a family business."

"The good that has done for me. I haven't advanced at all. I have stalled."

"What are you talking about? You became the director of social media two years ago."

"Because I thought it was a stepping stone. And quite frankly because it was pathetic how deep in the dark ages the shop was. It was Mommy's idea, not yours, to even do that." She met Mari's eyes. "I've worked really hard."

"I know you have."

"Then give me Bling."

No! Mari's heart yelled. It screamed from her chest, from the insult Pearl had thrown her way, from their history that spurned fear and anger, from her need for stability. But her brain. Her brain reeled her back. She had to pull Pearl off the ledge. "This is not about working hard. Working hard doesn't mean entitlement. And I don't get why this has to be black or white. You can take the lead, but I can mentor you throughout. We need you for social media, more than ever. You're amazing at it, and now with Heartfully Yours coming up around the corner, it only makes sense to put our talent to its max use."

"No. Nope." Again, Pearl laughed Mari off. It was a move that pushed Mari's buttons, but she kept calm. Pearl crossed her arms. "First of all, this isn't about entitlement. This is about you giving me a well-deserved and well-earned chance. Secondly, everyone in this building knows that you are incapable of being a partner. You'll end up taking over. It's me alone, or I'm out. And third—"

Incapable of being a partner. Those were fighting words. Hurtful words. And underlying the meaning of that phrase was the absolute truth that Pearl was right. Mari had been unable to be a partner, find a partner, keep a partner without hurting others. Without hurting herself.

The underhanded insult stung. Instantly, the sting grew to anger, and pain spread through her nerve endings, rendering her limbs weak. Pearl's argument was indecipherable from the overload of emotions. "You want Bling? Fine, you can have her, but not under our banner. You want out? Then you've got it." Mari took two steps toward her office, tight-lipped, then decided she had one thing left to say. She turned. "I hope you have thought long and hard about this, because once this is all said and done, nothing will ever be the same."

Jane and Amelia launched into the conversation; they rushed at the two of them.

Pearl pushed past the crowd and voices, and went into her office and shut the door, leaving Mari to deal with the fallout of their fight.

fourteen

Mood: "This Is How We Do It" by Montell Jordan

Pearl entered her office and shook her body out like she was coming down from a prize-winning fight. Finally, she'd said her piece. She'd revealed what she'd harbored in her heart since their mother had announced her retirement. Hadn't Pearl given her sisters enough of herself? What more could she have shown to Mari? The hours she'd clocked at work exceeded full time. Her effort was reflected in the satisfaction of her clients. Damn—she brought Rings & Roses to the twenty-first century. And she procured a top client. *A top.*

Jane walked in after her. She must've been right at Pearl's back. Of course, per the de la Rosa style, no one left their feelings in cliff-hanger status, nor was anyone allowed to walk away.

Jane closed the door and spun around, arms crossed. "You've got to be joking."

"Do I look like I'm joking?"

"How could you have made this decision without speaking to me first? I could have helped you. Guided you on how to approach this. Maybe I could've fixed it for you."

"That." Pearl pointed a finger up in the air, because she was taught that it was rude to point at a person, despite her desperate need to accentuate her point. "That right there is why I need to go. Are you even listening to yourself? You're talking about guiding *me* and helping *me* and fixing it *for me*. What I need is support. Support because we are all equals. Support because you respect me."

Jane's shoulders slouched. As if defeated, she sank into Pearl's upholstered wine-colored wingback chair. "Of course we respect you."

"Conditionally."

"No." Jane shook her head. "Always. But we're talking about something else entirely here, something tangible, involving experience and—"

"I can't right now." Pearl put both hands up, resigned. Out of the two, Jane was supposed to come to her aid. "You of all people should know how hard it is to be under a shadow."

Jane's face darkened at the dig—she had been perfect because she had to be. When Mari had decided to be a teenage rebel, all their parents' worry and attention naturally shifted toward her. Jane and Pearl had no choice but to stay the course and fly under the radar, with Jane scooping up the big sister role and squaring it on her own shoulders. Protection from parents? Jane. Who Pearl went to when she lost her phone and needed to pay back her parents? Jane. The person she called to sneak her into the house when she got drunk for the first time at a party? Jane.

Guilt overcame Pearl, but she pushed it aside. "I'm sorry, but I have tried. God, this morning I gave her the benefit of the doubt that she was going to say yes. I was hopeful that bringing Bling to the shop was enough."

Jane sighed. "For what it's worth, I weighed in that you should take Bling."

"But you don't really think I can handle it."

"That's not it. I think you need help."

A maniacal giggle bubbled through her lips. "You can't play both sides."

"I obviously am. I'm being logical. What Ate Mari says is true. This is a big client to go at alone. You read the contract—the budget is six figures, her guest list expansive. I trust your skill, but it hasn't been tested like this client will test it. Understand?"

"Yes. I understand Ate Mari wants to take over a client's wedding, a client that I brought into the shop, a client that she doubted I could sign." Pearl's neck heated with impatience at this convoluted conversation. She needed space to think. "It will be up to Daphne and Carter to make the decision. Until then, my ultimatum stands. But please. I need some time to myself. I've got a full day—a full week prepping for the 'Kento' wedding at the Tidal Basin this Saturday. Oh, and I even scored an interview with Northern Virginia News to discuss weddings at national monuments. Cool, right? I'm so damn awesome, but no one wants to give me any credit for it. Anyway, I have to get my shit together." She turned away from her sister and went around to her desk.

"Fine." Jane's voice softened. "One last thing: Did you tell our mother this was on your mind?"

"Why, does she have pull in the situation?" With the slight twitch in her sister's eyebrows, Pearl knew she had her. "Exactly. Our mother has no say in this. I tried my best. You know I've felt trapped for a long time."

"So why not fight Ate Mari?"

"I'm tired of fighting. I'm a third owner. If she isn't going to budge on something I deserve now, she's never going to give me what I want in the future."

Pearl pressed her laptop's spacebar just to do something. Her screensaver popped up and the de la Rosa sisters appeared on the screen, from a recent photo shoot for their web presence. They'd all decided to wear a version of a white outfit, and their interpretation reflected their distinct styles. Mari's, an ivory pantsuit, was by far the most conservative. Jane had donned a short-sleeve sheath dress, and Pearl posed in a sleeveless romper. Collectively they were a triple threat. Under the supervision of their mother, their clients got the mix of passion, precision, and energy. Now, left on their own, their differences clashed and brought out the worst in each of them.

One would have never known it from the photo, but once upon a time, Mari would have worn the sleeveless romper, too. She might not want to admit it now, but Mari had been like Pearl once.

Which pissed Pearl off to kingdom come. Their mother had given Mari another chance. Who was she to not give Pearl a first?

Jane stood and put a hand on the doorknob. "Well, don't get too comfortable designing your logo. I'm not down with this."

Pearl nodded and watched her sister walk out. From downstairs, the door jingled with another customer. If she could've, she would've run home, jumped into her workout clothes, and spent the afternoon at Ohm. But, right now, she had a wedding to work on.

It probably wasn't a good idea to schedule a wedding at the height of cherry blossom season, but Pearl's clients had been undeterred. Tonia Nguyen and Ken Akingtola, or Kento, had their elaborate plan to marry at the National Mall already laid out by the time they'd hired Pearl four months ago. And despite her warnings that their ceremony could be interrupted and photobombed by the tourists who flooded the Tidal Basin to take pictures of the lush blooming pink and white cherry blossoms, they were optimistic and hell-bent on their decision.

Because of the chaotic tourist-laden outdoor venue, that Saturday, Pearl had donned her headset and two-way radio with direct connection to Carli. Jane's cold kept her from assisting today, and while Pearl had the option to call Mari for help, her pride prevented her from reaching out. The week had passed without any communication between them at home or at work, and Pearl refused to take the first step to reconciliation. Too much had been said, and her intention now was to show her eldest sister she could execute a wedding perfectly.

This decision, however, was now biting her in the butt. Pearl had quickly realized Carli just didn't have the experience or the foresight to manage the moving parts of an outdoor, public wedding. Pearl ran around, flustered, keeping the ceremony space clear as the limos with the wedding party circled the parking lots to find a nearby appropriate place to stop among the tour buses that lined the streets.

The couple's permit only allowed two hours' time on the west lawn of the Jefferson Memorial, and they would need every second. Unlike a dedicated space where the background was ceremony and picture ready, a tourist spot begged to be prepped. The bulk of Pearl and Carli's job today was crowd control. Most tourists were empathetic and understanding. Others? It spurred them to act inappropriately.

Finally, the wedding party arrived; the bride's party ahead of the groom's. To Pearl's horror, Tonia was in tears, in contrast to her festive crystal-encrusted sleeveless trumpet-style dress, and flanked by her bridesmaids. Ken and his groomsmen milled in the background, among their parents and close friends, wary and worried. Tonia held up her shoes. One was missing a heel.

Pearl took the shoes from the bride. The maid of honor handed her the broken heel. "Holy shit." She winced. "Excuse my language. I'm sorry."

"No worries, I cursed way more coming out of the limo. What are we going to do? I refuse to go barefoot."

"Superglue?" Carli offered.

"Nope. Too dangerous." Pearl chewed on her cheek, thinking, looking out onto the droves of people around the Tidal Basin. What would the chances be that someone out there had an extra shoe? Then, a thought came to her. "Extra shoes. Carli!"

"I'm right behind you."

"Grab my tote," she said, then called over all the women in the group. Eight came forward. "Let's go down the line and tell me what your shoe sizes are."

Each woman called out their size. None were the bride's 8½. But Pearl didn't dismay—this had happened once when she and her sisters took a trip to Vegas. Jane had forgotten another cocktail dress for their final night. They'd switched dresses until something fit *just enough*.

Carli handed off Pearl's tote, where she retrieved ballet flats. Pearl grinned. "A must for every wedding planner who can't handle heels for too long. To be honest, I'd rather run around barefoot." She took off her chunky-heeled pumps. After slipping on the ballet flats, she raised her shoes in the air. "So what I'm going to ask is unconventional but necessary for this next hour. You don't have to participate if you don't want to. No pressure. But who here has a size 7½ they'd be willing to trade with my black size 7 shoe?"

Beats passed. Just when Mari started to lose hope, Ken's grandma raised her hand. "Me. I'm dying to get out of these heels. I'm closer to a 7 than I am to a 7½ anyway." She removed her beige size 7½ heels.

"Great. Step one is complete. Now I need someone who's a size 8 who's willing to wear a 7½ heel."

"Oh, that's easy. Me." A bridesmaid raised her hand. "I got this shoe online and the size is completely off. I didn't have time to return it. But is it okay for me to wear beige and not this pale pink like everyone else?"

"Absolutely." She exchanged shoes with the bridesmaid. "Your dresses are long enough to cover them during pictures. Now is there anyone with a size 9?"

The maid of honor raised her hand. "I have a 9. I'm willing to wear that 8, though, if necessary."

"Okay. Let's see if this size 8 will do first." Pearl took a knee in front of Tonia. "Care to try it on?"

With a face full of hope, Tonia tucked her foot into the shoe. Pearl could have heard a pin drop as she worked the shoe around the back, to her heel. And like Cinderella's glass slipper, the shoe fit like a glove, albeit a snug one.

~

"Now *that* is a happily ever after if I ever heard one." Kayla bumped her hot chocolate to-go cup against Pearl's as they walked down Burg Street. It was 8:00 p.m., but the sun was still out—the only good thing about daylight savings. They'd shared a lasagna for two at Leonardo's and thought to do a lap up and down the street to walk off their full bellies.

"If only the rest of the day had gone more smoothly." Pearl took a sip and hissed when the hot chocolate scalded her tongue.

"It was a bear getting everyone back to the reception, and catering wasn't ready for us. They scrambled at the last minute to get hors d'oeuvres out on time. Luckily I'd earned enough props at the wedding that my couple wasn't too bothered by it."

"Because you're magic. I just don't get why Mari's so against you getting a top."

"It's not just Mari; it's Jane, too. They think Bling is too big of a client. They think I need a mentor."

"Did they have mentors?"

Pearl thought about it. "I mean, yeah. My mom. But that was different. My mother is my mother, and there's no arguing with that . . . that authority. And when my sisters got into full-time planning, they were younger than me, early twenties. I'm officially over the quarter-life mark. My resume is way more extensive." She looked askance at her friend. "Why? Do you think I need mentoring, too?"

A group of teenagers gaggled in their direction, coming between Pearl and Kayla. Once they were back side by side, Kayla said, "Look, I'm not one to give you that kind of advice or suggestion. I'm not in your business. But in medicine? Even the most skilled surgeons are accompanied during an extensive case. It's not about being alone and being the best. It's about the health of the patient, or in your case, the happily ever after, right?"

"I guess."

"Have you told Daphne and Carter?"

"No, because my sister and I kind of left things hanging. But I need to, soon."

Kayla clucked. "What a mess."

"Yeah." She sipped her drink. "Enough about me. How are you?"

"Same stuff, different day. Work, sleep, rinse, repeat. Waiting for Trenton to move out so that sleep part can include a certain man named Calvin. This having him go home after every date is for the birds."

Bringing up Trenton sent tingles through Pearl, but she steadied her voice. "He won't let you have your man over?"

She shook her head. "I'm the one not allowing it. I can't handle the idea of my boyfriend walking around in his underwear with my twin in the next room. No way. No how. Anyway, I've missed you." She linked her arm with Pearl's. "I still think it's hilarious that you and my brother are fake dating."

There went another delicious twinge traveling through her body. "I credit him for this big account. Carter loves him."

"I mean, have you had to hold his hand?" She held a palm up. "Never mind. I don't want to know. Gross!"

"What, you don't think your brother is dateable?"

"Pearl. Seriously? The man farts, okay? And he spills globs of toothpaste in my sink and doesn't wipe it up, ever. But anyway, you guys are like siblings. That's just weird." She sighed, pushing a stray curly bang out of her face. "This adulting business is for the birds, too—my social life is the pits."

Grateful for the change of subject, Pearl said, "Yeah, if only we didn't have to make money to eat."

"Or drink hot chocolate."

"Or buy shoes." Pearl laughed and came upon the corner building that would soon become Heartfully Yours. Pearl paused at the window, curiosity drawing her closer. She hiked a hand over her eyes to block out the sun and leaned in. Shelving and racks were bunched in the middle of the room.

"I wonder how they're going to set it up. Will they have dresses, too?" Pearl said, more to herself.

The shop's green front door swung open and Pearl jumped

back from the window. A blond woman stepped out wearing an apron; she had her hair up in a bun. "Why, hello!"

Pearl recognized her from the expo, and the need to get out of there tugged at her ear. This was traitorous for them to be speaking to Heartfully Yours, so she murmured a haphazard, "Hi," and tried to speed past.

"You're Pearl de la Rosa, right?" the woman said, tucking her hands in her apron pocket.

"She is." Kayla stepped in because she was way more fearless than Pearl ever was.

"Great work today at the Tidal Basin."

Kayla shot Pearl a look. Pearl found her voice. "Oh?"

"Yeah, the video circulated around. A tourist caught you while you all were switching out your shoes." She pulled out a business card. "I'm Wendy Salazar, the owner of Heartfully Yours. We're a small shop. Just me, an assistant planner, and a part-time manager. I know it's a long shot, and it's probably totally unethical, but what the hell, you're right here. I heard you might be up to freelance."

Pearl's face went hot. "Wh . . . where'd you hear that?"

"You know . . . word gets around." She grinned. "Actually, it was from the mouth of a potential customer—she said she heard it while at your shop."

Pearl froze, unable to form words or thoughts.

"Well, thank you, and nice to meet you, Wendy." Kayla took her card and guided Pearl by the elbow down the street, toward home. "We're going to look for that video online. Holy shit, Pearl. What the hell was that?"

Pearl said the first thing that came to her mind. "That was someone who wants me."

fifteen

Mood: "You Dropped a Bomb on Me"
by The Gap Band

Mari turned the key to lock up Rings & Roses and jingled the doorknob for good measure. It was an early Saturday night for her—the shop, usually closed on Saturdays, was especially quiet without the crew. Pearl had wrapped up her wedding and was out with Kayla, and Jane had called it a sick day and didn't step into the office. It had given Mari the time to catch up on administrative work. And it allowed her some alone time to think.

She and Pearl had to make up. It was necessary. Their fight on Tuesday had gone too far. She'd decided: tonight she would apologize and somehow find the middle ground in their negotiation. Compromise was the bedrock of weddings, of marriages, of every relationship, and the de la Rosa sisters only had each other. She'd missed Pearl during their last four days of radio silence.

As usual, she took her time on her walk and enjoyed the sixty-degree day. The sidewalks were especially crowded. Locals had donned their shorts and T-shirts—it was a heat wave compared to last weekend.

A text pinged, and Mari viewed a message from Jane: Click on this video!

The link went straight to someone's Facebook page. The caption: *J.Lo move over, this is the real wedding planner.*

The still was of Pearl across from a line of women: a bride, three bridesmaids, and their wedding party. Behind them was a large, blooming cherry tree.

"What the heck?" Mari clicked on the Play button, and the video came to life. The scene played out with Pearl switching shoes, one for the other until the bride had a pair to wear. The conclusion brought the bridal party to a rip-roaring cheer, including the person who took the video.

"Yessss," Mari heard herself say. *Way to go.* She was going to tackle her sister to the ground with a hug. Not only for her creativity, but because she'd given them some publicity. She texted Jane back: OMG! Did we boost this on social media?

Jane: Not yet, and I feel too gross to act chipper online. Post it. Don't think Pearl has seen it.

Sure enough, after Mari found a sidewalk bench to park herself on and clicked on their Facebook page, she discovered Pearl hadn't yet posted.

No time like the present. While Pearl had been meticulous about curating their social media schedule, message, and branding, she'd never ruled that the other sisters couldn't help out. And really, as much as it had been an ordeal to set up their page, the rest was easy, in Mari's opinion.

Mari copied the link of the video and pasted it into the Facebook page, then added a caption: *One of our own solving a crisis. #switchinghoes.* She tapped on Post.

There. That was sure to bring in some attention.

But as she stood and crossed over to Mary Street, passing a family who'd taken up the whole sidewalk, something else caught her attention: her baby sister speaking to someone in a Heartfully Yours apron.

⁓

Bright and early the next morning, Mari spun a red light bulb into the Rings & Roses front porch light fixture. On the way down the ladder, she pressed a palm-sized Washington Nationals static cling on the window.

"Thought I'd find you here," Jane said, then coughed and sneezed. Correction, that sound was no mere cough or sneeze, it was a monster's howl that had Mari cackling. "Not funny. I can't seem to kick this illness."

"Did you take your meds?"

She nodded, clearing her throat. "I've been. Both the steroids and the antibiotics." She promptly squeezed a dollop of hand sanitizer on her palms, the prepared mom she was. "You're changing the subject. I knocked on your door last night but you didn't answer. What are you up to?"

"Nothing. Thought I'd spend today doing some building maintenance, and supporting our Nationals, of course." Mari wiped her hands on the front of her apron, then tucked them into the pockets of her zip-up hoodie all to avoid Jane's appraisal. What she'd wanted was out of the building, to avoid running into Pearl. "Which reminds me. We have to make sure we grab tickets for the home game against the Cubs."

"I've already told Pio's teachers that he won't be at school that day. Although, we're all going together, right?" *All* meaning the sisters and Pio. They had been season ticket holders the last eight years or so. But since her parents had left, collectively, the sisters had decided a home game against Pio's favorite team, the Cubs—though it was a mystery as to why—would suffice.

"Of course we are. Why wouldn't we?" Mari collapsed the

ladder and, with Jane following behind, maneuvered it into the shop and to the back storage room. The metal was unwieldy, and it clanged against the doorway. She hoped the sound camouflaged the doubt screaming within her.

Would they still hang as a family? Pearl hadn't exactly been speaking to Mari. And with the new development of seeing her with the Heartfully Yours owner—she didn't know what to surmise. Last night, her mind had run the gamut of reasons, all the way to the assumption that Pearl would leave Rings & Roses for their competition. Which was a preposterous idea. Right?

Pushing it out of her brain, Mari asked, "So why did you need me last night?"

Jane laughed, shaking her head. "Did you even check back on your post last night on Facebook?"

"Nope. Why?"

"Because! Oh my God." Jane pulled out her phone. "I took a screenshot."

Mari glanced at the screen. "I don't get it. I posted the video." She shook the phone. "Look at the hashtag."

"Switching shoes."

"No, you wrote"—her voice dropped to a whisper—"switching . . ."

"What?"

She whispered it a second time. Then, exasperated at Mari's confused expression yelled, "Switching hoes!"

Mari's hand flew to her neck. "No I didn't." She grabbed the phone, reread her post, her stomach bottoming out at her obvious typo. "Oh God, I did."

Pearl put a hand on her arm. "No worries. Pearl caught it and changed it just as the first of the comments came in."

"Why didn't she text me?" When Jane didn't respond, Mari

raised her eyes to her. Handed her the phone. "Of course she wouldn't."

"See why I'm worried about the two of you not making up? This isn't right, this fight. Anyway, this morning I had to get some sun and air. Luckily our sister took Pio for some auntie time."

"It's not as if I want us to be fighting, Jane." Mari grabbed a screwdriver, and while passing her planner, she flipped it from Seasonal Checklist to the To-Fix Checklist. She went to the front door and screwed the hinges in until they were nice and tight. "She wants to go. And honestly, I'm insulted."

She nodded. "I admit I'm still pretty shocked."

"Yeah." Mari bit her lip at the memory of the escalation of their discussion. It went from what she thought was a negotiation to a full-on ultimatum. Were the sisters so unimportant to Pearl that she hadn't cared to warn them of her unhappiness? And then her interaction with Heartfully Yours . . . "It came out of left field." She thought about telling Jane what she'd witnessed, but decided to wait.

She'd confront Pearl first. It was foolish to jump to conclusions with something as neutral as Pearl speaking to the competition. There was no law about communication; there was no standing rule about their boundaries.

Jane's attention zipped away to the front window, to a child holding his father's hand. "I should keep walking, get my sun in." She hacked a protracted cough. "To be honest, I've been on edge lately. Pio is at a . . . tricky age."

Mari nodded. Pio was having a bit of a time without his grandparents. He looked to his lolo as a father figure.

"And with his party next Sunday . . . well, he keeps asking for his father as his birthday present."

Mari choked out a laugh. "What? What do you tell him?"

"As little as possible. I try to weasel my way out of the conversation by bribing him with a toy or ice cream. How do you explain his sperm donor doesn't want anything to do with him? Daddy not being here makes it worse. Pio has no one else to distract him."

Jane's ex had earned the Lifetime Jerk award. Marco Padilla had been her college love affair. Their meet-cute had been all too romantic: two hearts brought together while working at a theater production company. He was a theater major; she the finance major brought on to do the production's accounting. It was their last year of school. They'd all thought it'd been love. But he'd ghosted her before she found out she was pregnant right before graduation, only for him to emerge as an off-Broadway actor. Jane had tried to connect with him, to no avail. She still carried the heartache. It didn't help that Pio was the spitting image of his father.

Mari and Pearl did what all devoted aunties did in these situations—they spoiled her kid. "Maybe Pearl and I have to step up our auntie game, distract him that way."

"You guys do so much for him already." Jane coughed. A pedestrian passing their front door jumped from what sounded like a seal's bark. Jane rubbed her chest.

"Maybe you need a follow up with your doctor."

"*Yes, Mom.*" Jane rolled her eyes.

Mari waved a hand in the air and laughed. "Whatever, don't listen. Go for your walk."

"All right." Jane walked out the front door, then turned. She tucked herself into her light sweater. "We're going to be okay, right? Rings and Roses, I mean. We can't split up, Mari. We're de la Rosas."

"We're going to be okay," Mari reassured her.

Jane stepped off the sidewalk and dodged across Burg Street. But as Mari looked at her sister's back, something else weighed heavy. She was failing in the one thing she swore to herself that she would do, and that was to keep her sisters and the business together.

Could she live with that?

—⁓—

A text from an unknown number beeped through Mari's phone at 11:00 p.m. that night, rousing her from bed: What I wouldn't give for some time out on your patio right now.

It took a second for Mari to get her bearings: Reid?

Reid: Yes. Was there anyone else hanging out on your patio?

Her lips wiggled into a smile. It wouldn't be any of your business, would it?

Reid: You're absolutely right about that. Sorry.

Mari: It's okay. Really. How's it going?

Reid: I was just thinking. You and I should take our patio talk elsewhere when I get back this weekend.

Mari stared at the words on her phone, gauged what to type. *Yes* would have been the easy answer. But it would be the wrong one. I don't think it's a good idea right now.

No dots appeared on the screen, and after a while Mari tucked herself back into bed, though this time, she took the phone with her. The phone beeped another text.

Reid: Okay. I respect that.

part four

She who loves roses must be patient and not cry out when she is pierced by thorns.

—Sappho

sixteen

Mood: "Unforgettable" by Nat King Cole

Absolutely not, her mother had said that night during Pearl's sophomore year a decade ago. *Absolutely not*.

Being the third de la Rosa to attend Alexandria High School, there had been expectations of her. Mari had been a wicked leader; Jane was the quiet and studious one. And then came Pearl, who muddled through her freshman year searching for a way to make her mark in the world.

She made her mark, all right. She became the most social. She'd thrown herself into her extracurricular activities and built her own resume: Founder of the pep club. Student representative. School newspaper reporter. Varsity tennis player. With her wit and humor and her ability to move from one crowd to the next, by her sophomore year, Pearl had been invited to upperclassman parties.

And finally, she'd felt untouchable.

That night, her parents had refused to let Pearl go to a senior party. She'd been out too much, they'd said; she was hanging with the wrong crowd. Her parents were already worried about Mari—*We don't like her boyfriend*. They'd thrown this statement around ferociously; they disapproved when Mari moved out.

We don't want to have to worry about you, too, Pearl.

Pearl had hated her parents at that moment; they were punishing her for Mari's sins. They'd stood like towers despite their same five-foot-four-inch heights, two pillars of pure will against her wishes.

She'd thrown a tantrum then, especially unbecoming of a fifteen-year-old, considered shameful in Filipino culture, where she was supposed to hang her head and accept the verdict. But she felt she was too old, too modern, too American. Her parents didn't have a clue what it was like to live in the twenty-first century in the United States, where teenagers had opinions. Where teenagers had a voice.

So, that night, she had done what any self-respecting teen would do. She snuck out. Not that she had to try too hard. Their town house on Duchess Street creaked and moaned. Its drafty windows whistled during windy days. And with so many people in the house, it wasn't unusual to hear somebody up in the middle of the night. Their parents had learned to sleep through the chaos of a large family.

Pearl had simply walked out of the house. Then, she stole the Volvo and drove to the only person who'd understand her plight—Mari.

Mari's apartment was stuffy and full of smoke. Bodies were lined up in the living room. Her sister wasn't to be found, so she settled herself in Mari's kitchen.

A keg was situated on the floor, and various bottles of liquor decorated the countertop. Red and blue Solo cups littered it. A punch bowl was filled hallway with a foamy drink. Dipping her nose down, Pearl whiffed something fruity—she decided it was the safest thing to drink. She tipped an empty cup into its froth and brought the drink to her lips.

No one batted an eye.

This wasn't her first taste of liquor. The de la Rosa girls had grown up with alcohol in the home. On New Year's Eve, they were allowed a taste of champagne. Her parents had thought the less they'd treated it as taboo, the more their girls would approach it moderately as they became adults.

Their theory worked for the most part. Pearl hadn't been lured into friend's parents' liquor cabinets. During sleepovers, while her girlfriends oohed and aahed over what they could drink, Pearl passed on the opportunity.

But right now, in the depths of this party where she was anonymous, she felt older. Even if she had gotten caught, what would her sister have said? She would have surely just taken the drink and admonished her. Anyway, Mari was too cool; she would understand what Pearl was going through—she'd lived with the same parents, after all.

The first taste of the drink was sweet. The next, bitter. Then the sour aftertaste made the sides of her cheeks wince and tears leapt to her eyes. God, it was disgusting. But she kept a straight face, wanting so much to be older than she really was, and more like her sisters.

But a thought snuck into her head—what if she couldn't be? What if the talent that her parents had kept saying each of them had—*the gold star*, they'd called it, the thing that every person possessed that made them uniquely stellar—didn't apply to her? Maybe she was just ordinary.

Before Pearl knew it, she'd drank the entire cup. The buzz took over. It fizzled in her veins, made her warm. It compelled her to go ahead and pour another scoop of the drink in her cup.

A guy and a girl walked into the kitchen, lips locked. They didn't pay her any mind. Her gaze darted away from them, only to slide back. Their hands roamed each other's bodies. He lifted her onto the countertop; she wrapped her legs around his waist.

She'd watched enough R-rated movies—she'd seen this before. But up close, this 3-D experience brought heat to her cheeks.

Panic flooded her. She shouldn't be there. She looked at the drink in her hand and realized she'd polished off the second cup. Her vision waved; her eyes crossed. She padded out of the kitchen feeling disjointed—where was Mari?

Halfway across the living room, Pearl heard her sister's voice. It was at its third octave, which meant she was pissed. Pearl followed its trail, leading her to the hallway, where Mari's bedroom was. A woman came out of the room and pushed past her, the door slamming shut. Pearl fought against this wave, finally coming to Mari's bedroom door.

Her hand settled on the door handle. One push, and the door clicked open.

Her sister had always kept a meticulous space. That was where she and Pearl had differed. While Pearl never did get the point of making one's bed, Mari squared her corners and folded down the top so it was a perfect rectangle across.

But right now, Mari's bed was a mess. Pearl's gaze swung as the door opened to its full breadth to reveal someone's back. A man; his voice rumbled. Although his words were indecipherable, his tone was . . . scary. Pearl stepped in, now with Mari on her mind.

That was when she saw them . . . the bottoms of her sister's shoes staggered in between the guy's stance. Mari had this thing with pointy shoes. It was her vice. While everyone was wearing

Doc Martens or round-toed ballerina flats, Mari liked her toes sharp. *It gives me an edge*, she'd said. *It makes me feel fierce.*

Mari had been sitting on the ground, legs straight in front of her.

"Ate Mari?" Pearl's voice was a squeak. In that room, Pearl had felt smothered, powerless.

The bodies halted. Her sister's face appeared from the guy's shadow. He towered over her with a hand up in the air.

"Pearl? Pearl, what are you doing here?"

It was her voice—Mari's, unlike Pearl had ever heard it.

Mari was a force. Mari was in charge. No one messed with Mari. This voice coming out of her sister's mouth was one laced with fear.

The guy—Saul—turned. Pearl hadn't ever met him, but she knew it was him from Mari's description. The square of his jaw, the slicked-back hair. Mari had once yammered on, describing him in delicious and enamored detail.

But this version of Saul wore a snarl; his massive stature was threatening.

The boom of his voice followed. "Get the fuck out of here." He took a step toward Pearl. More words spilled out of his mouth, but Pearl didn't hear them, she was so focused on the expression on Mari's face.

"No," Pearl heard herself say. She was a de la Rosa—she was supposed to be invincible, too.

"I said, get the fuck out of here!"

"No." Stubbornness fueled her.

Saul charged toward her. His paws landed on her shoulders, shocking her body like a bolt of electricity. His hands caught her neckline and he began to lift her off the floor.

The next second, she heard her sister scream. A thump and

Saul fell toward Pearl, a yell escaping his lips. Pearl stepped aside in time, aghast, as he crashed onto the floor. She looked up; Mari held a candlestick in her hand. Her chest was heaving, and it was only then Pearl saw the full extent of Saul's doing: Mari's shirt torn right down the middle. Face wet with tears.

Someone else barged into the room and cursed. "Call 911."

"Hello. Did the screen freeze? Can you hear us, Pearl?"

The sound of her name snapped Pearl out of her vivid daydream, and her eyes focused on the figures in front of her on the screen. Carter and Daphne, seen from a slightly distorted view, each with an earbud in their ear. Around them was the busy atmosphere of a restaurant with the sounds of laughter, the clinking of silverware, and the faraway beat of a pop song.

"Yes, I'm here." Her voice kicked in. She swallowed, though her throat was dry, as if in the middle of the fight-or-flight acute-stress response. She glanced down at the Post-it note with some scribbled words, a couple with a check mark next to them. Right.

They were discussing the Thatched Roof Winery.

"I'd just said that yes, we're definitely available tomorrow to do a quick tour. We're so excited," Daphne said.

"Great! I'll call them and confirm the appointment. Tuesday, April tenth, at ten a.m."

"Will Trenton be there?" Carter asked.

"Honey!" Daphne frowned and shot him a glare. "Trenton is not our wedding planner."

"Hey, you can't blame a guy for trying." He turned to Pearl. "No pressure. But you know, if he's available, we can kind of make it a double date."

Daphne all but shoved her fiancé out of the screen's view. "I'm so sorry about that. Don't even listen to him." To Carter, she said, "Make yourself useful and get me a vanilla affogato."

Pearl laughed. "I'll ask Trenton, though I can't make any promises. He's right, though, it's worth a try, and if it gets you what you want—" she implied with a wink.

"Ha! I like how you think. I knew I hired the right woman."

Pearl drew in a breath. The mention of being chosen out of many increased the weight on her shoulders. When Daphne had hired Pearl, it was under the banner of Rings & Roses, a well-known company, time-tested and reliable, with a Santa Claus list of satisfied customers. But today, she would offer herself as an individual. Just one person to manage Daphne and Carter's happily ever after.

For a second, she felt like fifteen-year-old Pearl, a girl who obviously did not belong at a college party and almost got hurt because of it. Then again, if she hadn't been there, a lot worse could have happened.

"But there was also another reason why I wanted to video chat, Daphne." Pearl's fingers had a life of their own and began to tear at the corners of the Post-its.

"What's up?"

She infused optimism and confidence into her voice. "I'm in a great time in my career right now. After five years at Rings and Roses, it's time for me to move on. I'm jumping at this opportunity to take on my own clients for my own business."

Daphne's jaw slackened. "Wow."

Pearl pushed on. "It's not happening right away. These things take time, and I have clients with Rings and Roses through the summer. It won't change the way you and I do business. That is, unless you want it to. Because your contract is with Rings and

Roses, you have the option to stay with them, and the planning will be done by either one of my sisters. Both are capable, remarkable, and exact planners. If you love working with me, you will love working with them. I do hope, though, that you'll stay with me."

Daphne seemed to recover from her shock. "This is a lot to take in. I mean, we love you, Pearl, no doubt, but leaving this event all up to one person feels . . . risky. What if you get sick? Or have a fender bender. Who else can step in?"

Pearl felt every cell in her body slacken from what she could only describe as sadness. Yes, she would be the sole person in her business—she wouldn't have backup. She'd relinquished the camaraderie that she'd grown to rely on. "I completely understand this worry. I do plan to hire an assistant."

"I know, but . . . we're expecting four hundred people, Pearl." She bit her lip. "Can we . . . can we think about it?"

"Absolutely. Of course."

"I'm sorry—"

"Don't you dare be sorry." She smiled for good measure despite her disappointment. It was a good sign that Daphne wasn't upset. "This is business. It doesn't change us. And I don't want us to cancel this appointment with the Thatched Roof. If you choose to stay with Rings and Roses, you'll continue to work with me until I transition out."

"Okay." A relieved grin appeared on her face.

"But there's one more thing . . . about Trenton." Pearl swallowed her nervousness. "He's my one and only, but not how you think." She grinned into the screen, and hoped that her honesty would be enough for Daphne. "He and I are just friends. We have been friends for decades, and while he came to couples' yoga with me, we're not technically a romantic couple. But there's more. We went to couple's yoga to make contact . . . with you."

"You guys were faking it?"

Pearl nodded, wincing on the inside. She waited for a negative response: anger, shock, disappointment. Instead, Daphne went silent, frowned, then a smile bloomed on her face. "Damn. That was one good hustle."

"You're not mad?"

"I mean, I should be, right? But I'm not. I'm impressed. The both of you were convincing. The two of you together are . . . great."

"Honestly, I think it's one-sided, on my end." Pearl exhaled, feeling like she'd been unshackled. "I still plan to ask him to come to the winery. I know he has a ball with Carter."

"Okay. Great." Except her face did not indicate she thought the conversation was going great. "Sorry, this is just a lot of information. I don't know what to think."

"I know. Well . . ." Awkwardness filled her, and with nothing left to unveil, she said, "I look forward to seeing you tomorrow."

"See you tomorrow."

The screen switched to black. Pearl leaned back in her chair, looked up at her ceiling. What did she do? What had she done? She'd placed her eggs in one basket without reinforcing the bottom.

Think.

With her memories still hovering in the periphery, and now with the uncertainty of Daphne's business, Pearl's thoughts were like cards thrown up in the air, fluttering down aimlessly around her. She couldn't grasp at a solid comforting idea. Her belly turned in nausea, a sure sign that she had to get to her happy place or else the rest of her day would be an unfocused mess.

She raised her left hand, tapped on her watch's face.

She'd have to play hooky, but she could still get to the 11:00 a.m. class at Ohm.

But first, she texted Trenton.

You wouldn't happen to be free tomorrow, would you? No pressure. 10 a.m. winery tour with Daphne and Carter. Thatched Roof.

Trenton: Is this a double date, Pearly-Pearl?

Pearl: Yes. Carter has summoned you.

Trenton: I must answer the call, then. Just got word my new apartment's ready for me, so was calling out of work anyway. I'm in.

Sixty minutes. Something always happened to Pearl in those sixty minutes. Focusing on her breath smoothed the rough edges of her perspective. Her lungs seemed to hold more oxygen; her muscles, limber and loose, felt like they could take on the weight of the world.

So when she glanced at her phone on the way out of Ohm's front doors and found Mari's text with a request to speak, she didn't answer right away. Her knee-jerk reaction had taken a back seat—she would speak to her sister in person after she changed out of her sweaty clothes. And when she passed Heartfully Yours on the way to Duchess Street and saw its owner, Wendy Salazar, wiping down her windows, she homed in on exactly what her parents had said over the years. *When one door closes* . . .

Pearl, now with both heart and mind opened, decided that maybe Wendy had something interesting to offer.

Wendy waved to her from the opposite side of the glass, then opened the front door to let her into the building.

"I'm so glad you came by." Wendy stretched her arms to present the space and flashed a kilowatt smile. "What do you think? Coming along, right?"

"It is. You took down the mirrors."

"I don't think we'll need them. Since we're a corner shop, we'll have enough light. And my hope is that we won't clutter this first floor. I want it to be bright, airy, which I think will be a challenge. Sadly, unlike Rings and Roses, we don't have a renovated attic, so no third floor for us. We'll have to try to fit the different parts of our shop onto two floors."

"Different parts?"

She put her hands in her apron pockets. "Pearl, my goal is for Heartfully Yours to be a one-stop shop."

Pearl stood straighter, compelled. "One-stop?"

"Yep: wedding planning, invitations, and photography to start."

She shook her head. "Wait, so you're proposing—"

"Well, I'm not proposing, yet." She grinned. "Ideally I would like to sit down for a date interview. Maybe two, where I can get a feel of what kind of planner you are. And if that all works out, I'd *then* propose for you to join the team. The photographer coming on board is Amy Marie Weddings."

"I know Amy. She's fantastic."

"And talented. I already have a calligrapher in mind—not mentioning who that is yet so I don't jinx it. The total concept is this: I want our clients to come in, sign us all in one sitting if they choose to. Vendor choices are vast in this area, and what I've found from my clients is that many don't want the stress of making those choices. They want quality work, of course. But bringing together a few select vendors, I think, and offering them in one package is a good risk. Where you would come in is as our bread and butter, the planning. Currently I have an assistant planner, but she only wants a part-time position. I want to manage this shop, advertise and market it. As you know, that alone is a full-time job."

"I do." Pearl swallowed the information in chunks, and all the energy she'd spent at yoga returned. Heartfully Yours was competition, but not really. Not exactly.

"I know I probably gave my spiel already, but if you're interested, I'd like to treat you to a proper date interview."

"I'm interested." Pearl's mind reeled with the possibility of being *the* planner of this shop, though still a part of a group identity. This was what she'd wanted: autonomy within a support system.

"Great. Are you free tonight? Over coffee or tea, at the Kafehaus at the end of Burg. Eight p.m.? I'd love to have a copy of your CV or resume."

It had been years since she'd written a CV, but feeling the bottom of her once soggy plan solidify, Pearl answered, "It's a date."

seventeen

Mood: "Turn the Beat Around" by Vicki Sue Robinson

Mari tapped her Apple Watch for the millionth time to silence the texts coming through. They were all from her mother: Finally back in Manila from vacation.

I missed you all.

I'm uploading my pictures to Facebook.

Update me on R&R soon!

And despite the lump forming in her throat, Mari focused on her current task: managing Brad Gill's needs.

This would be her first appointment of many with the Glynn couple over the coming three days; Brad had insisted on front-loading all of their wedding planning while he was in town *So Hazel doesn't have to worry her pretty little head about it.*

God, if he said that phrase one more time.

Currently, Mari was playing mediator between the couple and Lauren Goshen of Goshen Photography, their future photographer. From the window side table of the Bar, an upscale burger joint two blocks from Rings & Roses, with her iPad in front of her and her planner opened up to a page of notes she had scribbled throughout the meeting, Mari lamented the passing time. She wanted her mother on the line to discuss their business structure. And where was Pearl? She'd texted her hours ago, and with every moment spent in this limbo, her suspicion rose.

Mari needed to remedy her family situation ASAP, whether or not Pearl was ready to talk.

"I'm not sure I'm down with these formal pictures," Brad said, breaking up Mari's thoughts like a sledgehammer. He scrolled through Lauren Goshen's online portfolio on her iPad while Hazel turned the pages of a wedding album. "Us with every family who came to the wedding? It's unnecessary."

Hazel harrumphed next to him. Her thinning patience showed in her rigid posture. One hand clutched the stem of her empty water glass, knuckles white. Up to this point, she'd acquiesced to all of his changes. "It's important to me for memory's sake," she said, voice clipped. "And I'd love to give a print to each of the families who traveled as part of their thank-you note."

"Thank-you note?"

"And presents. A gift basket sent later on, with some specialty teas and desserts from the area and, of course, a framed picture to my matron of honor and to your best man, your parents, my mother."

At the thought of tea and dessert, then of food in general, or the lack thereof, Mari's tummy grumbled. Upon their arrival this afternoon at four, they'd ordered happy hour drinks, and Mari had chosen an exceptional tiramisu that was the perfect blend of crunch and sweet cream. The dessert had given her a quick jolt of energy and enthusiasm, though momentarily. An hour had passed and so had the sugar high.

"What do you think I am, made of money? We're feeding

them, giving them a party. Two, if you count the rehearsal dinner. We should stop at a web package and then get one single print done for us." He snorted, taking a swig of his beer. He casually pointed at Mari. "Let me guess. This was your idea, right? Always trying to upsell—the two cakes, and I saw how much you all charged for the rush service. That fee was almost as expensive as the invitations themselves."

Mari gripped her pen and pursed her lips so the anger that threatened to escape her lips was kept at bay. How dare he imply she was nickel-and-diming them?

Hazel, mortified and doe-eyed, fussed. "Brad, that's not necessary."

Lauren cleared her throat, a tight smile frozen on her face. "We can definitely start with the web package—I keep all your proofs for a year after your wedding, and you can reorder as you need to. And, instead of a picture with every household, Ms. Flynn, we can have you do a group picture with each table and it will cut down on the time."

"See. I like that idea." He leered at Laura, who didn't hold his gaze. He met Mari's eyes. "Enough with the photographs. My lovely bride-to-be and I have been at odds about the wedding theme. What are your thoughts, Ms. Wedding Planner?"

Mari treaded carefully considering the table's vibe: Hazel's nervousness, Brad's aggressive posture, the restaurant's upscale but relaxed flair. The fact that they were window side and people were on the other side of the glass, sometimes peering through while waiting at the trolley stop.

"I propose 'Leather and Lace' now that I've spent time with the both of you." She kept her facial expression neutral. "A bit of old school, bit of vintage, but classic through and through. Leather strips made into ribbons instead of grosgrain or silk. The

menu hand-lettered onto leather for each table. Lace table run-
ners, Primrose-style goblets, cutlery with wooden handles, antique silver chargers."

After a beat, he pointed at her. "That's good. I like that." He
sighed as if satisfied. Next to him, Hazel seemed to fold in relief.
"See, it's coming together, babe. You were worried for nothing."
He took a swig of his beer and snorted out a laugh. "The only
thing that would ruin this is if my future wife walked down the
aisle looking like a tramp. I mean, you are knocked up, Haz.
Can't give anyone the wrong impression."

Mari sucked in a breath. And as if the reel changed to an old-
school movie, in a blip, she was back in Saul's apartment kitchen
one Sunday. It had been an unusually hot and humid summer,
and his AC was out. She'd retrieved a tube popsicle from the
freezer, brought it to the counter to cut the top open with scissors
when a hand snuck out and tried to swipe it from her grasp. Mari
had gasped but held on to the popsicle, until she was met with
Saul's look of authority. It said that what he took was his.

He hadn't laid a hand on her. He hadn't said a word. It had
been the way he'd looked at her.

It was exactly the way Brad looked at Hazel.

"No . . . of course not." Hazel spoke up. Her body was rigid,
because yes, the dress she'd picked was sexy. It was perfectly sexy
and gorgeous and classic and exactly what Hazel wanted to wear
on their day.

Pain pierced Mari's heart and she yearned to deliver a clap
back to put Brad in his place. This was the time to resist. This
was the time to stand up for her client. But Hazel's panicked
expression—a plea for silence—held Mari's rebuttal at bay.

Reid wasn't due back in the area until this weekend, but Mari still couldn't help but look up at his town house windows. Thrill buzzed through her each time she thought of him jiggling the door open, of him gesturing her inside. Especially today, when all she wanted was to unload the weight off her shoulders. The idea that it was lonely at the top? It was 100 percent true for her. To get here, she'd sacrificed a social life, and when she finally needed a friend, she found not one to turn to.

The look in Hazel's eyes haunted her. There was nothing tangible to report to anyone, but there was so much negative potential between Brad and Hazel.

She stuck her key in the front door harder than usual to snap herself out of her thoughts. She was allowing her memories to cloud her views about Hazel and Brad's relationship, when it was none of her business. Besides, a couple's relationship was based on more than what they let others see. Like the iceberg effect of a foundation under the water, she wasn't privy to their lives behind closed doors. Brad could've been the sweetest man. Perhaps today was another off day. Maybe they'd had a fight before their appointment.

Mari stepped into the doorway and ran into a body.

"Holy shit. Sorry," Pearl said, dropping her purse and a folder on the floor. She smelled fresh from the shower. The damp tips of her hair brushed against Mari as they both knelt to pick up the spilled contents: lipstick, a pen, her iPhone, receipts.

Mari reached for the folder; papers fanned out of its pockets. "You didn't text me back. I wanted us to talk, for real, to fix th—" The rest of her sentence never made it out of her mouth, her brain focused on a word at the top of one page. *Resume.*

Pearl stood, straightening her clothes. She wore high-waisted slacks, a tank, and a cropped blazer. Definitely business casual.

"Headed out?" Mari asked.

"Sort of."

Mari cocked her head and waited for the rest of the answer. Her face heated with the start of anger, because she already knew. She'd known it when she saw Heartfully Yours's owner speak to Pearl.

Pearl rolled her eyes and laughed under her breath. "Don't even."

"*Don't even* what?"

"Lecture me. Because you're about to, right? Because of the resume? You can't have it both ways. You can't tell me I'm not good enough to work for you and then expect me to sit here when an opportunity arises. Wait, let me clarify that: when someone who knows what I can offer chases after my talent." Pearl waved Mari away, shutting her eyes as if she couldn't bear to look at her. "Forget it."

Oh no, Mari wasn't going to let her get away that easily. "First of all, you can't start and end a conversation and walk away. Secondly, you're the one who's lecturing me. You're the one putting words in my mouth. Thirdly, if there's anyone who should be mad right now, it's me."

"You? Whatever."

From behind her, Jane's door opened. She stepped out in her robe, eyes bleary. "*Shhhh.* Pio is asleep, and I feel like shit, if you all didn't remember."

"I'm on my way out anyway." Pearl barely glanced at Mari.

"Pearl." Mari gritted her teeth. "We have to talk."

She cocked her head back to laugh before stepping outside. "Definitely not now. I'm busy."

After the door slammed, Jane raised her arms in exasperation. "You are . . ." She shook her head and growled. "Are you just going to let her go?"

"I'm not going to chase her down Duchess Street. She has her mind made up. Do you know what she had in her hands? A resume—she's probably dropping it off right now at Heartfully Yours."

"It takes one sorry, Ate Mari. One. True. Sorry."

"Why should I be sorry? I didn't do a damned thing."

"I can't with you." Jane shot Mari a glare and interlaced her hands on top of her head. "I am disappointed. In all of us." She turned and walked into her apartment, shutting the door with a whoosh.

Mari looked up at the ceiling and said to no one in particular. "This is not my fault!"

Jane yelled from inside her apartment. "But what are you going to do to fix it?"

eighteen

Mood: "More" by Bobby Darin

The nerve. The absolute nerve of her to think she has any say over my life." Pearl stepped on the gas as she sped through Alexandria the next day. Red lights flashed as cars crawled to a stop from morning-commute traffic. She slammed her foot on the brake.

In the passenger seat, Trenton hooked a hand on the oh-shit handle. "Okay, Ms. Fast and the Furious. You actually have to share this road with the rest of the city."

"Ugh, we're already ten minutes behind schedule. I was so focused on looking over the contract for Heartfully Yours last night, and then I was so pissed about the whole thing that I couldn't sleep, and then I didn't hear my alarm."

Trenton sighed dramatically. Pearl glanced over; a grin pulled at the sides of his mouth.

"What?" Pearl gave him the side-eye. The traffic started its slow roll so she inched forward, pressuring the car in front of her. The person had practically a full car's length in front of it. "Seriously."

"I've seen you and Mari fight like this more than a handful of times."

"And you think she's stubborn, completely inflexible, and infuriating, too, right?"

At his silence, Pearl caught his knowing glance, reminding her that he'd been there from the beginning, and like Jane, he had remained objective through every de la Rosa family crisis. "I was thinking that you two are so much alike."

Never mind. Trenton didn't know what he was talking about. "Not true. And this isn't a normal fight, not something stupid like me borrowing her clothes."

"It's still about who's the boss of whom."

"Exactly my point. We're both equal partners in the business now."

"And yet neither one of you is compromising. It's always Mari acting protective, and you resisting any of her suggestions. You both want the same things but don't listen to one another."

"I've listened to that woman all my life. She's the one who has yet to see me." Pearl took a right onto Interstate 495, where traffic was miraculously free flowing.

"Do you know why our mothers got along so well?" he asked.

"Because they both could close down a restaurant?"

"Besides that." Trenton grinned. Their mothers had met up once a month at a restaurant for a girls' night, and took up a table until they were the last customers, sharing a dish from every course. "It's because our families are the same. Lots of drama, but close nonetheless. Nothing could come between us siblings."

Pearl's heart hollowed out. "I'm not sure about that this time around."

The warmth of Trenton's hand enclosed hers where it rested on the gear shift. They'd held hands in front of Daphne and

Carter as part of their ruse, but nothing about this moment was fake. "You and Mari have come back from worse."

She nodded, acknowledging that he was, in fact, present for the weeks and months the entire family recovered from Saul.

She and Mari hadn't gone to counseling immediately. At first they'd thought they could simply "get over it." Their family grounded themselves in each other and their faith, foolishly thinking it was enough. But the threat of violence broke through the usual de la Rosa optimism. It ate away behind the facade of the family. Mari had nightmares; Pearl's insomnia became debilitating.

When Pearl finally had gone to counseling, she put a name to her feeling: anger. Anger at Mari for keeping an asshole boyfriend around. Anger at herself, at how helpless she felt. It took months to properly assign that anger to the correct person: Saul. With the introduction of yoga, she'd transferred her anger to her breath.

"You have to talk to her," Trenton said, after miles of silence.

"That's the thing. I don't want to. I want to stay mad. And now with Wendy offering me a spot with them, I don't even know where to start. I mean, how do I tell Jane?"

"Have you decided what to do?"

"No. I took the interview because it was timely. And to be honest, it felt nice to have someone want and value me. Wait a minute." His words had caught up to her, and she narrowed her eyes. "Did you imply that I'm stubborn and completely inflexible and infuriating like my sister?"

"Maybe." With an amused grin, he let go of her hand.

The mood veered to one of quiet anticipation as they exited the highway, listening to the sound of the car's blinker and the rumble of the tires over gravel and dirt. As they rocked along the unpaved path up to the Thatched Roof Winery, Pearl thought about the other thing she had in common with her sister. How their heart remained tightly closed to everyone except for the people who had their backs.

Trenton was one of those people.

Pearl sloshed through the grass in her red calf-length Hunter boots. They'd had an April shower overnight, and the ground was soft, though green and lush. Around her was a cacophony of birds who seemed to be announcing their group's arrival onto the plateau where the Thatched Roof Winery was situated.

"You'll have to imagine an abundance of red, gold, and yellow leaves." Rene McDaniel, the general manager of the winery, spread his arms out and presented the view of the Potomac like a prize. "But look at that vista. There isn't anything like it."

"I do love it. Don't you, honey?" Daphne, next to Pearl, spun around, only to find her fiancé far up the hill, speaking with Trenton with exaggerated hand gestures. Trenton clutched his stomach, doubled over in laughter. "Babe, really?" she yelled.

Pearl and Rene laughed.

"Seriously. Maybe they should be the ones to get married. Talk about a bromance," Daphne said.

But whatever annoyance Daphne had felt seemed to disappear once Carter stomped toward them and slung his arms around her. She tipped her face upward, the wind catching the loose hairs that had fallen from her messy topknot. He nuzzled his chin into her Burberry scarf. "It's beautiful and perfect. If you love it, it's a yes from me, too," he said.

Pearl hung back and allowed the couple to make their final decision. She met up with Trenton at the crest of the hill. She took out her phone and captured the panoramic view and uploaded it to the Rings & Roses social media platform. The caption: *A future wedding spot? We'll see.*

"This is gorgeous." He stuffed his hands in his pockets, inhaled deeply. "The air, the view. Would you want to get married here?" He stumbled over his words. "Someday, in a place like this? I remember how you were, Pearly-Pearl. Always cutting up those Martha Stewart magazines, watching *Say Yes to the Dress* on repeat."

"Market research, even way back then."

"It did you well. So, is this your style?"

She turned her face away as a gust of wind swept her hair into her face. Instead of the usual nervousness, what came over her was a feeling of comfort. The comfort of talking to a friend, of confiding in someone she trusted, someone who didn't judge her.

"No." A grin burst from her lips. "Is that weird? With all the wedding scrapbooks I put together and all that talk about having the red carpet and the ball gown dress"—all with Trenton in mind, though she would have never said—"honestly? After all this drama with my sisters, I think I want a destination wedding. Someplace tropical. I would say the Philippines, but that would be impossible for many to go to—the flight alone is astronomical. But I'd love to marry someplace warm, with sand in between my toes. No makeup that will render me unrecognizable, without the stress that will turn me into a crying mess. Anyway." She snapped herself out of the dream, looked up at Trenton.

He pushed the hair out of her face, tucked it behind her ears. It was innocent, evergreen, and sincere. "I hope you get it." But there was more in his eyes. Something she couldn't decipher.

"Okay, lovebirds." Rene approached them.

Pearl's high crashed back down to earth—time to be a professional. "Thank you, Rene, for squeezing us in."

"Not a problem. Anything for Rings and Roses."

Pearl's heart dipped in her chest. Technically, she hadn't been bought out yet, and she was still part of the business. Technically, she was still under the store's banner. But soon, she wouldn't be. "I think you might have yourself another couple booked for next fall." She motioned to Daphne and Carter, who were now taking a selfie using the red barn with the metal roof, the reception area, as the backdrop.

"Next summer and fall is booking up quickly."

"I'll have an answer for you ASAP."

After their final goodbyes, Pearl walked Daphne back to the couple's car, parked on the side of the road. Trenton hung back with Carter. Keeping her voice neutral, Pearl asked, "What do you think?"

"It's a yes," Daphne said.

"Great. I can submit the paperwork tonight."

She tugged on Pearl's elbow. "Now the big question is—will *you* say yes?"

Pearl smiled hesitantly. "What do you mean?"

She gestured to the men behind them. "I know you said the crush is one-sided, but it's so obvious that Trenton is actually in love with you."

"What?" Pearl heard the woman loud and clear but couldn't believe what she'd said.

"Ah, you're still in denial. That's cool. Carter and I are patient. We'll wait. By the way, not sure if it's clear, but we are going to stay with you. With or without Rings and Roses. Besides, I don't think I can split those two up." She gestured to the guys.

Pearl halted in her tracks. "Really?"

"Really." She nodded and leaned in, arms out for a hug. "You get all my props for your hustle."

Carter walked up. "I guess you told her the news?"

"Yep," Daphne answered.

"I'm biased but I agree with this decision." Trenton wrapped an arm around Pearl's waist. "But do you mind if I ride with them since they're headed straight to Arlington? I'm due back at the apartment to meet the movers. My stuff from my last duty station is being delivered today."

"Yeah, of course," Pearl said.

Trenton walked her to her car. He opened the driver's-side door, and as she climbed in, he bent down, leaned in close. "Would you consider having dinner with me, tonight?"

Dumbfounded, she blubbered the first thing in her head. "Dinner?"

"You know? Food?"

"I was gonna order pizza," she heard herself say, because that was truly her plan and she was still processing the words *dinner with me.*

"Pizza then. My place."

"Um. Sure." She pushed the shake in her voice away.

"Text me when you're done? I can swing by and grab you."

"Yeah, okay." Pizza was simple enough. But as he planted a kiss on her cheek, Pearl had an inkling that dinner at his place might end up a little more complicated.

———

That night on Trenton's apartment balcony, Pearl gasped at his view. Against the black sky, the imposing, brightly lit figure of the Pentagon and the spiky sculpture of the Air Force Memorial broke the horizon's line.

But that wasn't the only reason her heart thumped at a sprinter's pace. She was with Trenton, alone, and not on a fake-date premise. This was a date-date.

She followed Trenton back through a sliding glass door that lead to the living room. It was decorated simply, with a leather couch and a coffee table. To the left was a bar island and behind it, a small range and a stainless steel refrigerator. Above the island hung pendant lights, casting a glow over Trenton's head. Boxes lined the walls from today's household goods delivery.

"I got lucky. The soldier who lived here before me had to break his lease. And my roommate is never around—he's also a government civilian but travels often. He's on a trip the next couple of weeks. It's like having the whole place to myself." He lifted two plates onto the bar, each with two slices of pizza on it. Pearl's favorite: Hawaiian. His: Everything.

"Thanks." Pearl took their plates and brought them to his round kitchen table, big enough to seat two. She grabbed a napkin from a stack on the bar and set one down at his place setting, one at hers, and naturally began setting a third. For Kayla. Who wasn't there.

She took back the napkin and perched on the chair. "Does Kayla—"

"Know you're here?" He stuck his thumb in his mouth to lick off pizza sauce, then came around the counter. He'd kicked off his shoes at the door. "She doesn't." His voice was gravelly as he sat, forearms on the table, as if preparing to launch into an explanation. Instead, he picked up a slice of pizza. "I'm starving. Aren't you?"

"Hangry," she said, though she'd lost her appetite. Kayla had known all about their fake dates, and she'd encouraged it.

But this wasn't fake, and this was in secret.

She wiped off her fingers with her napkin though they weren't dirty.

"I sense something serious coming," he said after swallowing a bite.

She tore her eyes away from his face. The tops of her cheeks were coal hot. "You asked me to dinner. And Kayla doesn't know about this."

"Are you saying you don't want to be here?"

She shook her head. Then did it so forcefully that it brought a grin to his face.

"Is that a no you don't want to be here?"

"You're going to make me say it out loud?" She huffed exaggeratedly when he nodded. "I do want to be here."

"Then we'll figure it out, okay? But for now, enjoy this magnificent pizza. Man, I missed Filippo's. The sauce. The herb crust. And they deliver. It's the trifecta of pizza." He stuffed half the slice in his mouth, chewing heartily.

Pearl, satisfied with his answer for now, took a bite of her pizza. She fed her belly and devoured Trenton with her eyes. She tried to imagine him in uniform in real life. His fancy dress blues had been impressive in pictures, sure. But now she took it to another level. She thought of him shaving without a shirt on, dressing in his camouflaged uniform, flexing, and lacing up his boots. A different pose for every calendar month.

"Pearl. You okay?"

"Mmm? Yeah. Um, I'm relishing the moment. The food, I mean."

He grinned, and a devilish look came across his face. "I'm gonna grab another slice. And start up a movie. You want another?"

"No . . . I think I'm good." She stuffed her mouth, ravenous now, then wiped the bottom of her chin when she got sauce on it. She shut her eyes. This pizza *was* good. Perfect melty cheese. Crunchy, thick-cut, fatty Canadian bacon. And a crust that had herbs packed into its core.

"Sure? I know how you are with bacon." He stood and went to the kitchen.

She grinned. "Well, maybe another slice."

"You got it." Trenton's face was in the fridge, and he popped out with two soda cans, one stacked on the other. He dragged two pizza slices from the box and brought them to the coffee table, where Pearl met him and sank into the leather couch.

"Aw, you remembered." She accepted a can of orange Fanta. Pearl wasn't a big soda drinker, not after all the talk of artificial sugars and excess sugar in them, but the thought was too sweet to decline. Orange Fanta had been her obsession in high school.

"You *are* talking to Triple-Threat Trent. I know the ladies."

"Whatever!" She bopped him on the arm with a couch pillow.

He popped his root beer can open. He sank to the floor, back against the couch. With a few pushes of the buttons of his remote control, the TV menu screen appeared. Then he cocked a head at her, inviting her down to the floor. "What do you feel like watching?"

She conceded, heart pounding now. It felt so much more intimate with them side by side, legs straightened out in front of them. "Um. How about a classic? *The Matrix*?"

"You've got it." He picked it from the TV's menu. He pressed another remote and the lights dimmed above them. Pearl's heart shot to her throat. She nestled back against the couch, the moment straight out of every angst-filled John Hughes movie she'd watched on Netflix—rife with too much thinking on her end. Did he lean in closer? Should she? What should she do with her hands?

Pearl's phone buzzed in her pocket, as if answering her, and it broke apart her neurotic thoughts. "Sorry," she whispered as she read a text from Jane. Family, not business, meeting, tomorrow 8 a.m. before the shop opens. Ate Mari's apartment.

Pearl pursed her lips.

"What's up?"

"Looks like Jane's going to be the one to mediate, yet again." She showed him the phone, then lowered it facedown on the carpet. "But this is good. I'm going to tell them about Heartfully Yours."

"And what about it?"

"I still have no idea." She slumped her shoulders. "Can I ask your opinion?"

He put the movie on pause. "Course."

"Do you think I was right to ask to leave Rings and Roses?"

He looked briefly at the glowing screen, his profile contemplative. "My opinion on this is that my opinion counts for nothing. Only you can decide. But I don't think you *want* to leave. Look, when you are hell-bent on doing something, Pearl, God bless anyone who tells you otherwise." He laughed. "Seriously— you have always marched to your own drum. So, no, I don't think you want to walk away from your family like this. But I think you feel that you have to, and that is something else entirely."

Pearl let his words settle into her head as her gaze dropped to the space between them, to the fluffy carpet. She ran her fingers through it, feeling the fibers, and focused her intention back to her breath, the base of her entire existence. "Things are a mess right now. What if I made the wrong decision, putting my foot down like that? Especially now that Daphne has said yes. Isn't that just stupid? I wanted a top and now that I have it, I'm scared as hell I won't be able to do it alone. I'm afraid I burned the bridge to the most important people in my life, personally and professionally."

The leather gave as Trenton turned. His fingers wrapped around a loose strand of hair and he tucked it in behind her ear. "There's nothing that says you and your sister can't fix this. You're both still here, right?" He lifted her chin with a finger. "Which means whatever you choose to do, you can. It's not too late."

Now that she had enough food in her belly and semi-good calories working through her, she digested his words. "With the way you say it, it should be easy. But when you have someone like Mari—"

"Who is someone like you. Someone who has a strong opinion and isn't afraid to stand up for herself. Which aren't bad traits."

"—it's hard to come together."

He shrugged, a small protest to her comment. "You can let superficial stuff get in the way, and believe me, I know that our differences are ninety percent superficial. Or you can focus on the ten percent of similarity. I hate to put it this way, but when the shit hits the fan, when things start blowing up around you, that ten percent is what's going to matter. That's when camaraderie— brotherhood, sisterhood, humanhood, whatever—kicks in." His Adam's apple bobbed as he swallowed. "I have full confidence in you and in Mari. At the end of the day, you have each other's backs."

Pearl searched the depth of his stare. His arm now rested around her against the couch, but the intimacy of his touch lingered. The subject of Rings & Roses fell to the rear of her thoughts. "What are we doing here?"

A shy smile graced his lips. "I forgot to add 'can't get anything past you' to your list of traits." He paused. "I guess I wanted for us to be in another space, a place we'd never been to before. I wanted to see how it would feel to be truly alone with you, to see if what I was feeling was all in my head."

And there went her breath. "How . . . how are you feeling?"

"Now *you're* going to make me say it." He scooted closer by a smidgen. As if magnetized, Pearl leaned in. Though humor laced his tone, the moment was so serious, so unlike what they usually were. "I like you."

"I like you, too." She squeaked out the words despite herself. Like she'd been pining for a Christmas present and finally, finally, she was tearing the package open.

"Oh, good. I wasn't sure, with the yoga and Daphne and Carter." His face broke in relief, surprising her.

How could this man be so confident and shy at once? To Pearl, he was larger than life, with his feet firmly planted on the ground. "I felt it at the Coronation," he said. "I pushed it away at first. I didn't want to misstep because of our friendship. After spending time together, I now believe it's so natural because of our friendship."

His words fell like cool raindrops on a hot summer day. It created steam between them.

"And your matchmaker experience?" she joked, though her voice cracked.

"Yeah, that was a flop. How about you?"

"Total flop."

"What's on your mind right now?" Worry flashed through his expression.

Pearl swallowed. She was as much an open book with her emotions as she was protective over her vulnerabilities. She fought her first instinct—to clamp down and dig in her heels—and blew out the words she'd ached to say since they were kids. "That I've wanted you to say that for forever. I think since we were eight."

"I seem to remember you calling me a stinky jerk at my ninth birthday."

"It was probably for good reason."

The crevices on the sides of his cheeks caved in. "You're probably right."

"So, what now?" she whispered. She usually flew by the seat of her pants, taking leaps and bounds. But Trenton was a man who planned. He'd known he wanted to be a soldier the moment their elementary school had taken a field trip to the Pentagon. Since then he'd methodically laid out his future, from then onward.

"It means we do this. Us." His fingers grazed her cheek. She leaned into his touch. "If that's okay."

The answer that came from her was the most instinctual thing she'd done in a long time. She didn't question his intentions, or hers. This was Trenton, and he wasn't just her present. He was her past, her childhood. And maybe her future.

She scooted closer. He placed his left hand on her waist, then her hip. Her leg crossed over and she straddled him. From above, she looked down upon him, at the beautiful face she'd seen change over the years. "Yes, that's okay."

She lowered her face as his hands rose. His fingers embedded themselves in her hair. Their lips touched, and like a match against a firecracker, they sparked. The heat between them grew, encompassing them in the fire Pearl vaguely understood would either grow into a roaring flame or burn her magnificently.

nineteen

Mood: "Shake It Off" by Taylor Swift

The link to Reid's Facebook profile was one click away. Hazel had friended Mari last week, and when Mari had accepted hesitatingly—she'd always intended to keep customers closed to that kind of access—the Flynn and Quaid family opened up to her. Now the temptation was too great; her heart clamored to catch a glimpse of him.

After her meeting with Brad and Hazel two nights ago, and then after her fight with Pearl, a fight that had gotten out of control within half a second, Mari had begun to experience something like loneliness. She needed Reid, his friendship. She wanted to speak to someone who wasn't her family, someone who could give her an objective point of view. Even Amelia was too close.

To distract herself, Mari scrolled past the engagement pictures Hazel had posted on her wall. Liked and commented on by dozens of people, the staged, smiling photographs were deceptive.

Online personas were a smidgen of reality, if that. For many, it only showed the optimism and joy of one's life. For some, it was a projection of the life they sought. It was a vicious cycle—this perception-reality conundrum. Did one beget the other? Were humans simply torturing themselves by subscribing to it? Here's what Mari knew: while others around her, like Pearl, were comfortable baring their truths to just about anyone, she held on to hers tight. She protected her faults, her secrets, and her mistakes ferociously, and it spilled over so she didn't share her positive news online either.

She knew this kind of introversion was costing her relationships—Pearl was one of them. But she wasn't willing to be vulnerable to scrutiny.

As it was, despite adoring Hazel, Mari scanned her engagement photos with a critical eye. In person, the woman smiled less around her fiancé; the light in her eyes had dimmed since these photos were taken a few months ago.

Was it her responsibility to tell somebody about her impressions—to tell Reid?

But what would you say?

It isn't any of your business.

You'll push Hazel away.

Mari stood from her stool, breaking her warring thoughts. Focus would be the name of the game today. This morning was about Pearl.

She took plates from the cupboard, scooped three sets of forks and spoons from the drawer below it, and set it on her kitchen island buffet-style. Then, to the warming oven, where she extricated platters filled with Pearl's favorite brunch foods: *tortang talong*, a Filipino-style eggplant omelet; biscuits with sausage gravy; and maple sausage. From the refrigerator, she pulled out sliced sweet mangoes, but kept her secret dessert-weapon hidden. She turned on her electric kettle.

Was Mari sucking up? Yes, she was.

When Jane had texted Pearl last night and set this morning's meeting, Mari had been against it. Their fight two nights ago was not any of her doing; she wasn't the one who instigated it. But, as usual, Jane was right—their sisterhood had to come first, despite their disagreements. The last time she and Pearl had a decent personal conversation rather than a business one was . . . she couldn't even remember.

Mari wasn't sure what that meant in terms of the business, but if Pearl was willing to meet her halfway, then she was all for talking about it, civilly.

After the counter was set, Mari checked the time. Ten minutes till eight. She milled about, tidying up. She threw dirty laundry into the washer, then cleaned out her sink.

Yet her laptop and Reid's profile tempted her.

"Damn it." She wiped her hands on a kitchen towel, admitting defeat. After taking a breath, she clicked on Reid's profile page, which only showed public posts, meaning his profile was locked down tight.

Mari gritted her teeth and scrolled down anyway. The man had been tagged recently by several people during social events. There were always women with him. Gorgeous, fabulous women with flawless faces, hair in beach waves or tight ponytails. Mari closed the laptop. Her hand stilled on the cover, and she shut her eyes, willing her curiosity away.

"You okay?" Jane flew in with a bag of tortilla chips, one hand deep inside of it. Oh, this was no good. Her sister had a thing for all foods crunchy, and when she was stressed, chips were her go-to therapy.

"Um, are you?" Mari eyed the way her sister noshed on the chips, lips dotted with salt.

"No."

"What's up?"

"Last night, I wasn't just pissed about you and Pearl." Her tongue darted out and she licked her lips. "I . . . I reached out to Marco. Yesterday afternoon. After some sleuthing through his social media, I found his personal email address."

"Wait. Sleuthing, as in stalking?" Mari's eyes widened, shocked.

"It's not stalking if all his info is out there for the world to see." She stuffed a chip into her mouth, and while crunching, said, "Anyway, I might have emailed a rant, like, all my emotions in one long letter. *Gah.*"

"And?"

"And nothing. Yet. I've refreshed my inbox about a million times today."

Mari bit her lip, inched her fingers along the counter, and pried the bag of chips from her sister's hand. She had a feeling future Jane would want Mari to steer her in the right direction. She rolled the top of the bag down and handed her sister a napkin. "What are you going to say if he writes you back?"

"I don't know." Her voice was far away as she methodically wiped her fingers. "I don't even know what I want from him."

"This is a big deal." Mari stuffed the bag of chips in the cupboard for safekeeping.

"I had to do it for Pio. One more try."

Mari reached out for Jane's hand and squeezed it. "Then I support you. But if he says one stupid thing, I will lay it on him, Jane. I won't be able to keep my mouth shut about it. I'll sneak into one of his shows and give him hell."

"I know." She squeezed back. "I love you for that."

Mari's phone beeped with a calendar notification for this morning's meeting. She frowned. "Have you seen Pearl this morning?"

"No, I haven't."

Ten minutes later, Pearl still hadn't arrived. Fifteen minutes after that, Mari called Jane to the table. As she scooped food onto her plate, Mari raised her eyes to her sister. Her voice shook. "This. This is why I can't deal with how she does business."

⁓

Pearl finally showed up a half hour later, in the middle of dessert. Her plate was cold; Mari had portioned a little bit of each dish and wrapped it in cling wrap. She and Jane were on their third round of coffee.

Mari had somehow survived the meal without speaking ill of the youngest de la Rosa. She and Jane passed the time by discussing how they were going to sit their parents down for a business meeting over Skype, Pio's parent-teacher conference, and their spring container gardening plans.

The eggplant omelet had come out perfectly, and Mari's biscuits had been fluffy and perfectly light, if she said so herself. Had Jane not stopped her, she would have eaten Pearl's share. The rule had always been "you snooze, you lose," but Mari conceded that it wouldn't have boded well for their attempt to make up if she'd eaten Pearl's helping.

Mari's irritation had reached a boiling point by the time the outline of—was that Trenton's car?—idled in front of her windows. By then, Mari was ready to give Pearl a piece of her mind.

"Oh my God, I'm so sorry." Pearl was already apologizing as she walked in, kicking the shoes off her feet, and she came to a full stop ten feet away from the kitchen island. "Oh . . . banana pudding."

That was right. Banana pudding, the worst dessert, ever. Mari had cringed the entire time she made it. It was sacrilegious to desecrate a good banana in this manner. Banana bread, sure. *Turon*—sugared sliced plantain and jackfruit wrapped in an egg roll wrapper—oh, heck yes. But bananas and pudding and Nilla wafers?

Mari's tone was curt. "Your favorite."

"We . . . I . . . slept in. I . . ." Her eyes darted around the room. "And is that?" The usual smile in her eyes dimmed.

"*Tortang talong* and shit on a shingle and *where were you?*" This time, to Mari's surprise, it was Jane who spoke.

"You should have told me we were having breakfast."

Mari didn't raise her voice. "It was a family meeting."

"You're totally making me look bad here." Pearl sported a crooked smile.

As if that was going to work. "Me?" Mari stood, taking her plate to the sink. She turned on the water, intending to rinse the dish and to wash her irritation down the drain, then promptly shut it off. She spun to face her. "You don't need me to do that."

"That's just unfair."

Mari barked out a laugh. "Welcome to our wonderful world, where fair isn't a criteria. But if you really wanted to pursue that line of thinking—how fair was it that you wanted us to trust you with a huge client when you can't seem to come through when we ask you to? Or that you decided all on your own to throw down a life-changing decision and simply expected us to roll with it? Or wait, no. Also that you didn't give us a chance to remedy our conflict before starting to look for another job?"

"This wasn't a work meeting. This was a family meeting. If

you had been clear—" She walked up to the counter and put her hand on it. "And if you're asking why I want to walk away, it's because of this. No one can make a mistake around you. The job is never good enough. I'm never good enough."

"Not true. And quit trying to twist this conversation on me."

"Because it's all wrapped up together." Pearl pressed her fingers against her temple. "A job isn't good enough unless you do it yourself. You have to control every little thing. *You* can make mistakes, but others can't. *You* can be whatever and whoever you want to be, but you don't let anyone else grow up. *You* can fuck up and be forgiven, but you can't seem to do that for others."

The words that came out of Pearl struck Mari right in the gut. Pain ratcheted through her system. It burned in her veins. It pushed her to the edge. "I'm better off trying to control things, trying to change things rather than burying my head in the sand. At least I'm taking responsibility. At least I've taken responsibility."

It was a low blow, a blow lower than she'd ever reached.

She and Pearl had talked about the situation with Saul. They'd gone to counseling. She'd gone to church. She'd prayed about it for days and days, until the event had worn itself thin in her head. While they'd resolved that it was no one's fault, that the entire situation was a series of unfortunate events, Mari knew that if she hadn't set the stage, it would have never happened. If she hadn't fallen into the arms of a man who controlled her, who convinced her that her life belonged to him, she might have noticed. She might have paid more attention that Pearl was getting into trouble herself.

But yes, a tiny bit of her wished Pearl hadn't been at her apartment, that she hadn't been there to protect. She wished Pearl hadn't been there to witness her at her lowest. And now,

Mari would forever hold the guilt of what Pearl had seen, and she would always be responsible for scarring her so badly.

Mari had tried to turn the page. She'd filed a police report and a restraining order; Saul had taken off to the Midwest, to start anew. She'd resolved to be a different woman, to be a more focused woman, with all her efforts placed on Rings & Roses, on the happiness the business brought to other people. She'd buried herself in the stress of planning her clients' special days and in the—sometimes manufactured—joy of the happily ever after. *I dos* became her penance. They were payback for the black spot in her past.

But the past had repercussions. It still cast shadows. It was still ever present between her and Pearl.

Pearl's face changed from indignation to pain.

"I—" Mari clamped her mouth shut as she saw what her words had achieved.

"I . . . I'm gonna go." Pearl spun and walked out Mari's door. Jane chased after her.

Alone now, Mari went into her bedroom, closed the door, and sat on her bed as realization set in. Less than two months after assuming control of Rings & Roses, everything had officially gone to shit.

Business had to go on. Mari followed the opening checklist to the line later that morning; she pretended life was perfect with the customers who'd arrived early to browse through the shop. As soon as Carli checked in for her morning shift, Mari retreated to the third floor, to the alterations area, where she took her stool out and plopped on it.

Amelia hadn't yet made it in for the day, and the room was

empty and silent, the lights dimmed. Mari stared at a framed picture on Amelia's wall. It was of the de la Rosa girls when they were much younger—Mari looked to be about twelve or thirteen. She had been heads taller than the other two, at the cusp of puberty and her one and only growth spurt. In the photo, she had an arm around each of her sisters. They were tucked into her like baby birds under their mother's wing.

Both her parents were the firstborn, overachievers, and impeccably resilient, and they'd passed on the impression that Mari would somehow be invincible despite the pressure thrown at her.

Mari wore this layer of invulnerability like an armor. She articulated it with her no-nonsense expression, her straight posture, her lists that would protect her from the unexpected.

But the armor was a deterrent as much as it was a shield, for if one got past what she chose to show the world, one might wonder if they were dealing with an entirely different woman altogether. Mari was far from invincible. She felt everything.

And in the quest to keep herself safe, she had hurt the ones she loved.

The room grew brighter. "I thought I'd find you here."

Mari's vision focused. Amelia was at the doorway with a hand on the light switch. Mari wiped her tears and sniffed in her emotions. "Did Jane call you?"

"Pearl did."

"Ah."

"Do you want to talk about it?"

"And rehash how everything has gone completely upside down? Wasn't I sitting here a couple of months ago worrying about the other shoe dropping?"

"One didn't have anything to do with the other, I promise you that. The worry might have taken away some of your joy, but it didn't cause what happened between you all. Anyway, it's now that matters—it's now and what your next step will be."

"I don't know, Amelia. I don't even know where to start. Our problems are coming from someplace deep, a place I can't fix."

"I don't think anyone is asking you to fix something from a decade ago, Marisol. That's a big expectation to put on yourself. But I think I know someone who can help you sort this out."

"I can't." Mari shook her head, defensive, knowing exactly who Amelia was talking about. "I can't deal with her disappointment."

Amelia walked to Mari and knelt in front of her. "Oh, sweetheart." She clasped her hands. "I'm not old enough to be your grandmother, but I love you like one. I'm also objective enough to understand how you de la Rosas work. Your pride shouldn't stop you from getting the good advice and love you need. You should call your mother, sooner rather than later."

Mari nodded, shutting her eyes briefly. Then she took her phone out of her pocket and clicked on Regina de la Rosa's phone number.

⁓

Regina's face on Mari's phone screen didn't have on a bit of makeup. It wasn't covered in foundation, concealer, eyeliner, and lipstick. She rarely wore makeup in the Philippines, citing the humidity. Mari knew the real reason: the Philippines relaxed her mother. There, her parents were away from the hustle and bustle of the business. Now truly free from it, her mother had not a care in the world. The usual crease in the middle of her forehead now lay flat, replaced by laugh lines on the sides of her mouth and eyes. "Marisol?"

"Did I wake you, Mommy?"

"I wasn't asleep, just reading here in the living room." Her body straightened. "But you can wake me and call me anytime, *iha*."

At the Tagalog word for daughter, and hearing her mother's comforting voice, Mari relaxed a tad. "We have to talk about the business, Mommy. We're kind of at each other's throats here."

"Let me guess who it's between." She peered at Mari, and the examination jolted her back to when she was a teenager, when half of her mother's time consisted of dissecting truth from fiction. "You and Pearl."

Mari tore off the Band-Aid. "She wants to leave Rings and Roses."

Her mother's face froze. It was as if the connection stilled. Then, finally, she spoke. "Why?"

"Because." Mari held her breath, then blurted, "She said she needed to branch out on her own, to start her own business."

"But she already has a business, iha. It's called Rings and Roses, in partnership with her sisters."

"Well, she decided to move on."

Her mother's voice steadied. "Marisol?"

After steeling herself, Mari revealed the history of the last two months to the stunned face on the screen. As she spoke, the braver she felt to discuss not only Pearl but the state of Rings & Roses. "We were surprised at what we saw in the finances. Mommy, why didn't you tell me? It wouldn't have changed my decision to take over. This is my dream. But I would have been better prepared if I had known about the finances. I would have made better plans. We could have tried to remedy or enact changes while you were still here."

A slew of words left Regina's mouth, most in Tagalog, her reaction spanning the first stages of grief: denial, bargaining, anger, and depression. Mari listened and rode out the roller coaster as her mother recounted the business's history, the struggle of making ends meet, the twenty years of ups and downs.

Finally, what came was what Mari recognized as acceptance. "I was the head of Rings and Roses for twenty years, Marisol, so all the good and bad you inherited was ultimately my responsibility. But I swear to you, I didn't realize the state of the business when I left it. Thinking back, I really should have had an accountant, but when we started out, I was a one-woman show handling maybe one wedding every two months. I'm sorry."

The hurt in her mother's eyes was evident, and Mari said, "I know you are, and we're going to do our best to make everything right. To be honest, though, we are going to need help. Pearl wants to leave, and I can't lose another wedding planner. She is essential to this business, and I don't know what to do. We can't speak to each other without jumping down each other's throats."

Her words caught up to her, causing her eyes to water. *She is essential.*

Pearl was essential.

"The three of you belong to me no matter how far away I am and no matter how old you are, and what I'm about to say is from me, your mom." She pinched the bridge of her nose and collected herself. "There should never be a question: A business can be rebuilt. A business can be restructured. But your family must come first. Marisol, what have I always said should be your priority?"

"To take care of the top."

"Right now, the top is Pearl." Regina sighed. "Remember back then? I tried a million ways to keep you under my wing. Found all the reasons why you needed to be watched over and guided. All the while, you desperately tried to pry yourself away from me. The more I pushed, the harder you did, too. I didn't consider how important it was for you to *want* to stay."

"What are you saying?"

"I let you go, Marisol. I let you go with a world full of pain and hurt and trust. You have to do the same with Pearl. And then, the hard part begins."

"And that is?"

"You have to forgive yourself."

Business meeting, tomorrow, 10 a.m. in my office. Mandatory and please don't be late.

Mari sent the text and waited until two text bubbles appeared below it, acknowledging receipt.

"Mari?" A knock sounded from her office door.

Mari set the phone facedown on her desk. "Yes?"

Carli stepped in with a long, thin box. "A package."

"Thanks." The box was labeled with the 1-800-FlwrsRUs logo, and she peeled the tape off the sides. It wasn't uncommon for Rings & Roses to receive thank-you notes and gifts from their clients, and she expected sunflowers or tulips that she would display in the foyer.

Instead, what she uncovered was a single red rose. A card was attached to the package: *The bloom is worth the prick of the thorn. Hope to see you on your patio this weekend.*

She put the rose up to her nose, inhaled its sweet scent. Her heart stretched at the thought of Reid's gesture. She imagined something more with Reid, something that might be lasting and real. But as she slid her finger up the stem, her skin snagged on a small thorn missed by the flower shop's garden shears. Mari brought her thumb to her mouth. She had to laugh.

Back to reality.

twenty

Mood: "One Call Away" by Charlie Puth

We've been summoned." Pearl looked up from Mari's text to Jane, who sat next to her on a park bench at the end of Burg Street. They both clutched clear cups of bubble tea they'd picked up at Superior Tea on their walk, thirsty from the uncharacteristically warm spring day. And yet Pearl still tasted the bitterness from the low blows she and Mari had slung at each other. "She wants to go another round, I guess."

"That kind of thinking doesn't solve this problem," Jane said, slurping her tea. The tapioca balls made shadows as they shimmied up the straw, and her sister chewed, still eyeing her. "I think the text shows she wants to meet you halfway."

"Humph." It had been two hours since Pearl's fight with Mari, when she had walked out of 2404 Duchess Street, and she hadn't been back there or at work since. Jane had insisted on tagging along, managing her clients on the go. "Won't believe it till I see it."

Jane reached over and squeezed Pearl's hand. As beats of silence passed, Pearl attempted to calm her nerves by people watching.

They were interrupted by Jane's calendar notification. "That's my cue. I wish I could stay out here in this gorgeous weather with you, but I unfortunately have to go," Jane said softly. "I have to get some work done before Pio's home from school. The pollen is also giving me a headache—damn allergies. Are you going to be okay the rest of the day?"

"Yeah, I'll be fine." Pearl nodded, and gave her best smile, despite feeling anything but happy. "What do you think Ate Mari will say at this meeting?"

"I believe she's going to give you what you asked for, Pearl, like, for real and concrete." Her forehead wrinkled as she frowned. "Is this really what you want? Because it's definitely not what I want. At the heart of it, the idea of you leaving is killing Ate Mari."

"I have to think about what's best for me. I've asked myself time and again: What do I contribute that makes me indispensable? What will I take away from the team if I leave? As it is, Ate Mari's and my relationship is . . . not doing so well. I don't want to get to the point that I can't even stand seeing her at home."

"Pearl, you leaving would render our team incomplete. Each of us brings something special to the table. What you forget, we pick up on and vice versa. Different doesn't mean unsatisfactory or unacceptable—"

"Yeah, you should say that to our sister."

"—but being different under an overarching set of rules is reality, Pearl. Opening a business on your own, and even jumping into someone else's business model, doesn't change the fact that there are standards, rules. Some are going to be hard no-gos. Like your fake relationship with Trenton." She put both hands up in peace. "I've got nothing against Trenton. I love the guy. But the guise of this relationship to further yours with Daphne and Carter? It was borderline unethical, right? I'm just saying. It's not just our sister who's a hard nut to crack. You are, too."

Pearl looked into her sister's eyes, which were full of love. Mari had said a version of these words before, but coming from Jane, it was digestible.

"When do you have to give Heartfully Yours an answer?" Jane asked.

Pearl touched her temples. "I don't have a deadline, really. But if I accept, I would have Wendy Salazar as backup, so I wouldn't have to do the Bling wedding on my own."

"Just consider all of your options before joining Heartfully Yours, okay?"

"Okay. I'll think about it. I promise."

*

"So, that's it?" Pearl leveled Mari with a gaze from across the table. At their meeting the next day, Mari had laid out a contract in bullet points that only could have come from Jane's logical mind. True to her eldest sister's word, the meeting was strictly business, with no other pleasantries or apologies or discussion about their personal differences. It was a relief that a cease-fire had been called but a disappointment that their separation would be official.

"That's it. We'll pool our resources and buy you out. But we need time. September at the earliest so we can wrap up our summer weddings, if you don't mind." Mari's gaze slid to Jane at her right, who wrung her hands. "We're cutting down the shop's hours to several days a week, and will readjust after that. I just . . . want for us to move on."

Pearl nodded. "Me, too."

"It will be fuzzy during the transition. I'd prefer we don't announce the change until we've signed the paperwork in the next couple of weeks. Until then, we'd prefer you still work under the Rings and Roses banner."

"That's fine." Everything seemed fair and straightforward, but Pearl's heart ached at what this all meant. Then she admonished herself. *You wanted this. You asked for this.*

"I've already set up an appointment with our lawyer to draw up the contracts. Until then, we can figure out stipulations like a no-compete clause and the like."

Pearl started, and she shot a look to Jane.

Jane nodded. "We have our vendors and our contacts, and ideally, we'd like those to stay with us."

"You're saying I can't partner with them?"

"Not necessarily. But we developed those relationships as Rings and Roses, and we'd prefer that you make your own connections with your own vendors."

Mari jumped in. "You do understand, right? Every business creates their own processes and contacts. You'll need to start your accounts under your own name. Meaning, you can't use our name in your conversations with them. We obviously can't police that; we trust you'll uphold that request. But it's especially important to us if you're working under another shop, especially one close by."

"For the record, I haven't given Heartfully Yours an answer. I'm not doing this for them. I'm doing this for me." Pearl waved a hand, annoyance zinging through her. She hadn't thought of this. Vendors had given her the best deals and catered to her clients because of the shop she represented. "But fine, fine."

Mari stood from her chair and stretched a hand across the table. "Okay. It's a deal, then."

Pearl returned her firm handshake with a smile. The moment was still formal and there would be the details to hash out, but she forced her body to relax. She'd done it, and Mari was letting her go.

Mari stepped around the table. She hugged Pearl and said, "I love you."

"Love you," Pearl said into her neck, patting Mari's back. The words felt like the first shovel of dirt to fill the chasm between them, forced and seemingly futile. Jane stood and they huddled together into a group hug, anticlimactic, but necessary, until Mari let up, and their bubble broke.

"Time for work," Pearl said, ready to get on with it. She wanted her office to herself, needed the space to breathe and to understand what had just transpired.

"It never ends, am I right?" Jane gathered her purse.

"No rest for the ambitious," Mari said.

A knock on the door interrupted them. Carli spoke over their heads. "Jane? I'm sorry to interrupt, but I have someone here for you."

"Who is it?" Jane collected the papers on the table and stacked them.

"Janelyn?"

The sisters spun at the sound of a man's voice.

"Holy shit," Pearl said, reaching out instinctively to a hand, any hand. She was met by Mari's. In sync, they took their free hands and reached out to Jane. Now linked, they created a force field around their sister.

The man who entered the room was formidable and handsome. Full, wavy dark brown hair, golden brown skin. And his eyes, his eyes were like Pio's: round, smiling, soulful. "It's me—"

Mari sliced through the man's introduction, voice unwavering. "We know who you are, Marco. What the hell are you doing here? Because you were not invited."

Pearl tightened her hold on Mari's hand as a sign of support as well as to draw strength from the woman. The time-lapse of Jane's child-rearing played in her head: The hard nights when Pio suffered from croup. When the only way he'd get to bed was for her sister to drive him around Old Town in the Volvo. The years she'd given up in her career because she didn't have a dedicated partner. For even if Jane had her sisters, she hadn't taken advantage of them; she'd often declined help. That's how Jane was: she put others before herself.

"I asked him to come." Jane said.

Pearl did a double take. "What?"

"I said, I asked him to come. Sort of."

The link broke. Mari frowned. "What do you mean, 'sort of'?"

"I said"—she tilted her head at Marco—"that if you want to know your son, this is your very last chance."

Marco spoke. "I didn't know, Jane. I didn't know about my . . . our . . . boy."

Pearl had had enough of this. This was ridiculous. "No. Absolutely not. You're not going to come in here and spread some bullshit that you didn't know. I was there when she sent you emails. She even sent you a Facebook message."

"I swear." His eyes glistened. By God, he looked like he was going to cry.

Mari snorted. "He's an actor. He's paid to shed tears."

"Just stop it." Jane shook her hands free as if she was being held against her will. She spun around. "I'm going to handle this. Okay? Ate Mari, can we stay in your office?"

"No. Not allowed," Pearl declared. "You're not allowed to be alone with him."

"As far as I remember, I'm an adult and I'm older than you. Leave, please."

Pearl shot a gaze to Mari, who was tight-lipped. Mari dipped her head, hesitantly, then pulled Pearl by the arm toward the door. As Mari passed Marco, she whispered, "We are right outside. One squeak, one tear, and we'll be so far up your butt . . ."

"Ate Mari," Jane pleaded.

Pearl followed her big sister out the door, which she shut behind her. In the second-floor hallway, still holding hands, they stared at each other, bewildered. "What does this mean?" she asked.

"I don't know," Mari said. "But we have to be here when it all shakes out."

"I'm always going to be here."

part five

A rose is a rose is a rose is a rose.

—Gertrude Stein

twenty-one

Mood: "Push It" by Salt-N-Pepa

Pearl howled and bent down to grab her toe. "*Youch!*" She cursed the culprit that had tripped her: a basket of sample favors Daphne had sifted through earlier today. Placed next to her desk, they were just one of a million things on her once clear floor.

The perils of working from home—there wasn't a separation between work and play. Her desk overflowed with paperwork, contracts, and stuff that came with planning a wedding and managing a start-up. Propped on her kitchen buffet was a corkboard covered with pictures and receipts, and a whiteboard scribbled with notes rested against the couch on the floor. Spread upon her kitchen countertops were wedding magazines of all sorts—her research—turned to specific pages.

"Are you okay, Pearl?" the gentle voice of Pastor Denise Pfieffer said through her phone.

"Yes, I'm so sorry. Um, where were we?" She hobbled to the whiteboard and hooked a dry erase marker in between her fingers.

"August twenty-eighth for Daphne Brown and Carter Ling's

wedding. I cannot officiate it, unfortunately. I'm already booked for another ceremony."

Pearl winced. She was afraid that was what she'd said. Pastor Pfeiffer, a semiretired celebrity television evangelist, traveled all over the country to deliver deep sermons on love and commitment. "Will you be anywhere in the area? My couple and venue have some flexibility in the timing. We can do an earlier morning ceremony or even a late afternoon."

The woman hummed in thought. "Ummm. I can't. I hate declining, but I can't make it from Philadelphia."

"Can you suggest"—she paused and bit her lip, not wanting to sound desperate—"any other pastors who . . ."

"No, unfortunately."

"No one at all?"

"If anything changes, Pearl, I'll give you a buzz, okay?" The pastor's speech sped up. "All right. Thank you for inquiring and I wish you luck."

The click of the phone was swift.

"Great work, Pearl." She tapped her phone to her forehead, then drew a line across Pastor Pfeiffer's name on the whiteboard. What would she do now? She didn't have the contacts or the reach to acquire a high-profile officiant. She could technically ask Mari for help since she was still under the Rings & Roses banner. But she was in a weird limbo with the shop. She'd moved out of her office two days ago, after their last business meeting. Two days of confusion, of sorting out Jane's drama with Marco, of cluttering her apartment with business stuff, of buying her web domain and cobbling together a beginner website for her brand-new business, perfectly called Pearls of Joy, Inc.

Since then, she'd had bouts of loneliness. She couldn't simply walk out of her office and commiserate with a sister. Her group text with her sisters had dwindled, too—she'd passed on her social media responsibilities to Mari and her only responsibilities were to her last two clients. She was no longer included in business chatter. In moments like these, when work seemed insurmountable, she'd realized that in this wedding business world, she was a baby planner. And while she was an expert in social media and in customer relations, her relationships with vendors were essentially nonexistent.

But damn it, despite currently feeling the opposite of her business name, she was going to "suck it up"—Trenton's words—and charge forward. She had to prove to her sisters that the decision to break away was the right one.

At this moment, Pearl literally did that; she took a deep, cleansing breath, hobbled to her computer, and plopped gingerly on her yoga ball, but not before she cleared the top of her keyboard of paperwork. In her Google browser, she searched "Television evangelists."

She clicked and clicked and took down names on a Post-it. When she filled one, she stuck it on her screen and wrote on another page.

Then, her phone whistled an email notification. In her inbox, she clicked on her most recent received email. A triumphant smile grew on her face. Finally—a win. After downloading the email attachment, she pressed Control-P, and with a protracted whine, her printer across the room spit out two pieces of paper.

With a hop, skip, a jump, and an accidental step on a pushpin (luckily on its side!), Pearl managed to cross the room to pull the papers from the printer. It was her mother's *leche flan* recipe. Yes, the coveted Filipino flan recipe her sisters had begged for but had been denied—until today. After much groveling and talk of legacy from Pearl, her mother passed down the too-complicated recipe.

She was going to make the dessert for Pio's birthday party

this afternoon, come hell or high water. Who cared if she hadn't made a flan before? Showing up with the dessert, rather than her usual contribution of chips or soda, would be a statement that she was independent, grown, and reliable.

Yes, it was a ridiculous notion if she thought about it hard enough, but she was sticking with it.

Pearl's phone dinged, notifying her of a text. She took two steps over boxes and stretched her body toward her computer table to grab it.

Trenton: Downstairs.

On my way. Her face broke into what she knew was a silly grin. The worry about the flan and the business fell away. After their one night together, Pearl had expected an awkwardness to ensue. That he would've stopped calling, or that she would've found a reason not to take his calls. But their relationship held steady. They were still good friends. Good friends who happened to have slept with each other.

Admittedly, Pearl was content without a label. Now with a professional line in the sand between her and her sisters, she didn't want more pressure. The fact that he was her best friend's brother was a pressure point in itself.

Barefoot, she flew down to the first floor and unlocked the front door. Trenton stepped into the foyer, dressed in his work clothes today: dress shirt and slacks. His smile was bright and infectious, and Pearl reacted as she always did in his presence—like a giddy little girl in front of her crush.

He lifted a to-go coffee cup in one hand and a little brown bag in another. "I bring sustenance."

"Aw, thank you." She rolled onto her tiptoes and kissed him. He smelled like a fresh shower and toothpaste, and she savored the moment and the ease. She took the coffee and bag from him. "This is a surprise."

"Was down for a meeting in the area, and I thought I'd pass by."

"On a weekend?"

"I work when my boss works. But I'm still on for coming to Pio's party this afternoon."

"Good, because you know what we have to do."

They hadn't yet come out to Kayla. Her call schedule was hectic, and this was the kind of news one didn't reveal over the phone.

Okay, so maybe Pearl was being a scaredy-cat, too. What would she have said?

Hey, so your brother and I hooked up. Whoops!

Or: *Know that crush I've had on your brother since we were kids? Well, yay, we're sleeping together.*

Or: *Remember the time you said it would be gross for me and your brother to get together? Guess what!*

His face darkened. "I know. How about we talk to her about us after Pio's party."

"All right." She exhaled, though it didn't do anything for her nervousness. Because what was *us*? They'd expressed the nebulous idea about being there for one another, of "doing us." But they hadn't dated "for real" before they slept together. Technically, they were still at the beginning stages of a relationship.

"What's wrong? Did I say something?" Trenton said.

"Oh. No, you didn't." She heaved a breath. "I'm running on fumes. It's all adding up, this pressure to do good not only for Daphne, but for me."

"You've got this. You have me. You have your sisters."

"Uh . . . no." She looked askance at Mari's door. She lowered her voice. "It's precarious. I'm competition."

"I would not categorize this as a competition. I'm a hundred percent sure they don't want you to fail. If you don't want to ask Mari for help, then ask Jane."

"Jane has her own issues at the moment . . ." She didn't want to talk about it now, not because she hadn't thought of it, because she had, but because she wasn't sure how to broach the fact that she wished she had someone to help guide her. "I think it's just going to take some time." She turned her face up to him and channeled optimism. "But I love the coffee and the treat. Thank you."

His lips lifted into a smile. "Call you later?"

"I can't wait." Her insides brightened at the thought. She loved that there would be a later, that despite all the effort of these computerized systems to find her a match, hers had come through friendship.

He kissed her on the cheek before heading out the door. With a final wave from the driver's seat, he pulled away from the curb, leaving Pearl to stare at the empty space and relish in the fact that despite all her struggles these last couple of months, she had him.

A black Audi slid into the spot, snapping Pearl out of her thoughts. Reid Quaid stepped out in dark glasses, a plain white tee, and jeans. He grabbed a bag of groceries from the back seat and tucked it under his arm.

Pearl's interest was piqued. He was back for the weekend. Normally, Pearl would have been up in her sister's business; she would've begged for details. Did Mari think Reid was datable? If so, would he be the one?

Pearl's tummy hollowed out. How much had she missed? Would her sisters still share with her if something big happened in their family? And if ever Mari were to get married, would Pearl be part of the planning?

Would Pearl be in the wedding?

Of course she would.

Wouldn't she?

twenty-two

Mood: "If You Leave"
by Orchestral Manoeuvres in the Dark

Pearl's and Trenton's voices in the building's foyer brought Mari to her front door and she peeked through the peephole. She had been curious as to what her sister was up to the last couple of days, now in the transition of setting up Pearls of Joy, Inc. She'd passed by Pearl's former office yesterday and had paused at the stark space, now empty of her sister's touches, of her blinged-out pillows, her vases burgeoning with fresh flowers, and her trademark piece: an impressionistic and bold canvas painting she'd picked up from a street vendor at the Washington DC Art Festival.

Aside from what Mari had deduced—okay, she'd been stalking Pearl's personal accounts online, too—nothing seemed amiss. Pearl gave no indication that something had significantly changed in her life. Pearl gave no clue that her relationship with Mari had cooled significantly, that days had passed since they'd texted one another aside from their sister group text. Pearl's tone in her social media posts was still as relaxed and positive as ever, without revealing an inkling of the stress running through the shop.

So Mari drank in Pearl's interaction with Trenton, thirsty for a glimpse of her sister's true emotions despite their muffled and indiscernible conversation through her closed apartment door. She witnessed Trenton's kiss, a sweet one, so loving it forced Mari to look away, to walk to the window and watch Pearl's new man getting into his car.

A month ago, Mari would have known when Pearl and Trenton had decided to make their fake relationship real. They would have talked about it—the teasing would have been relentless.

An Audi drove into the empty spot Trenton's car had occupied, snapping Mari out of her nostalgia.

Reid was home.

Mari stared at her phone and willed it to ring, even while in the middle of mixing up the batter of a chocolate sheet cake for Pio's birthday this afternoon. Forty minutes had passed since she'd backed away from her window, letting the sheers fall in between her and the view of Reid's back. Mari had promised herself one hour. An hour of restraint before throwing herself at Reid. Make one dish, post one picture on the Rings & Roses Instagram account, and *then* call him.

And, geez, have some chill.

Chill, she didn't have. Instead, the gamut of emotions invaded her: anticipation and excitement that they'd pick up where they'd left off, but also a melancholy that their relationship had an expiration date. Despite her growing feelings for him, he called Atlanta home, and Mari wasn't about to get in a relationship with a guy who would take her away from her life, not even one as kind as Reid. Logistically, the distance would be a problem. Emotionally—well, that was another issue.

For now, she pushed these concerns aside and focused on the positives. He'd given her a rose.

Mari hummed, surprising herself. God, she was turning into a sap. Grinning, she poured the batter into a sheet cake pan, tapped it against the counter to eliminate those dang air bubbles. Her mind wandered to the guest list: three sisters, Pio, Trenton and Kayla Young. A group of eight of Pio's friends and their parents.

You can invite Reid.

She shook her head at her conscience. Kid parties were personal, and while her sisters knew about Reid, it didn't mean their relationship was bring-home-for-family-parties worthy.

She stuck the pan into her preheated oven, setting the timer for fifty minutes. Oven door, and subject, closed.

One hour turned into an hour and a half, and Mari still didn't have a picture to post on Instagram. She was standing on her couch, holding the phone level to take a picture of one of Just Cakes's cupcakes that they'd purchased for Pio's party. Her planned caption: *Carolina from Just Cakes not only makes your wedding confections, but your birthday ones, too!*

Except, despite dozens of shots snapped with her phone, not one was of any quality remotely close to Pearl's previous photos.

"Damn it," she said aloud, when she realized the shot she just took captured a lean shadow created by her body blocking the light. She grunted, eenie-meenie-miney-moed a filter, clicked to post it, and called it a day.

Mari took her previous statement back: social media was hard. Pearl had made it look so easy.

She sure missed that pain in the butt sister of hers.

Finally, Mari untied her apron and jumped into her flats, and before she could talk herself out of it, went out of her back door to knock on Reid's.

She halted in her tracks. Her body softened.

Reid was already in her backyard, fastening the rope to the top of Pio's piñata. "Oh, hey. Looks like a party today, so I thought I'd help. That's a pretty high branch." He pointed up at their trusty oak tree.

Mari dropped her head but couldn't keep herself from grinning. "This wouldn't be the first time I've slung a piñata up there. I think I could've handled it."

"I never doubted that. But since I'm here, why not make myself useful, right?"

She walked up to him and watched his fingers tie the rope into an intricate knot. "That's an impressive knot there, Mr. Quaid."

"I can do more with my hands. Besides cook and tie knots." He grinned, sly. "I also play the guitar. And I'm a badass bowling king. Now where's your ladder?"

"Over there." She gestured to the fence and laughed, holding the piñata. "Who knew you were so talented?"

"I could tell you, if we spent more time together." She held the ladder still as he climbed it to the fourth rung and then slung the rope up. One try was all it took. He descended holding the rope. "Where should I tie the loose end?"

"Around the trunk of the tree is just fine."

After he tied it with expert precision, he went to the patio table, to Jane's basket of activities. He picked up the package of balloons and tore it open.

"Thank you," she said, watching him stretch the balloon out straight. "For helping out, and for the rose."

He smiled and stuck the open end of the balloon in his mouth.

"Reid?"

The balloon inflated as he blew, cheeks puffing out. He twisted the end into a knot, then batted the balloon to Mari so it hit her on the forehead. "Yeah, Marisol?"

"What do you want from me?" At the sound of her words, Mari laughed. "That sounds terrible how I just said it, but the rose, the patio conversations, you helping me today. I don't want there to be any confusion between us."

"I'm not confused." He smiled. "And I think I've been pretty straightforward. I like spending time with you. It's easy to be around you—I don't have to guess what you're thinking and feeling because you simply tell me. Coming here, to your patio, is relief. Look at me, I'm blowing up balloons for a birthday party. When was the last time I did something so . . . family? I can't even remember. My feet feel like they're on solid ground when I'm around you. So even if you don't want to or aren't ready for anything more, that is truly fine with me."

Her cheeks warmed, but this time with appreciation.

"But my expectation?" he continued. "Only one thing—honesty. I mentioned a near stroll down the aisle. I don't want to be fooled, ever again. If I wear out my welcome, will you tell me?"

"Of course." She swallowed back giddiness. "Well, I . . . like spending time with you, too."

"Good." He grabbed another balloon from the bag and made like he was going to blow into it, then paused. "Can you just tell me one thing?"

"Okay." She fiddled with a balloon.

"If my sister wasn't your client, and if we'd met by happenstance, would it be this complicated? Would you have simply shown me where the Whistling Pig was? Would you have said yes to dinner?"

Mari grinned and reflected on his question, on her love life the last ten years, or the lack of it. What exactly was she available for? A commitment when she had no room for one? A relationship that would've put any man second to her business? Anything beyond—the idea of marriage and children of her own—was a dream that maybe, just maybe, wasn't in her cards. "I liken being a wedding planner to being a teacher, how they're mothers to dozens of children—I live the happily ever after almost every week through my clients or my sisters' clients. Whenever my clients fight, I feel their anxiety. Their joys are mine. I'd like to think I'd take their same risks. But—"

"You don't believe in happily ever after."

"No, that's not it. Of course I believe in it. I just don't think that mine has to match theirs. I have my own history and expectations. I'm not an easy woman, Reid. This is all so cute and exciting because you're only here on the weekends. I'm your next-door neighbor, and you see me in my profession as the beacon of couplehood, but that's not all me.

"Your sister is important to me, too, and that's a big factor in this." She tripped on her thoughts, seeing a window where she could've given him a clue of what she felt about Brad. "I want for her to feel open and comfortable, always."

"Likewise."

She didn't know how else to proceed, where the line was between fact and bias. Where her own experience had clouded her professional judgment. Where client confidentiality stopped, and where friendship began.

No, she couldn't tell Reid anything yet. Not until she'd spoken to Hazel first. "I'm just saying. I wouldn't want to lose her trust. Especially after the pregnancy news that I was supposed to have kept secret."

"I think she's already forgotten about it. And knowing my sister, she wouldn't mind . . . us." He brushed a leaf off her shoulder and let his hand linger. His thumb grazed the line of her jaw. She leaned into it, savoring the touch. A buzz of electricity traveled between them. The draw, and his smile, and his amazing ability to make her feel like right now was all that mattered—it was undeniable. But he retrieved his hand as if remembering his place and blew into the balloon until it was taut, then knotted it.

"Here's a garbage bag." She pulled a clear bag out of a box and opened it wide. "We're having the kids do a balloon game where they sit on and pop as many balloons as they can in a minute. The one who pops the most balloons wins."

"Sounds like fun." He stuffed the first balloon into the bag. Fiddled with another balloon. "Marisol, you think too highly of me. Everyone has a history that has shaped them."

"Yes, but I think I still have to work through mine. I set rules for myself, and in the last couple of weeks, I've realized the rules were all wrong. I've let these rules hold me back."

"So don't let them. Jump in."

"Not that easy."

"Yes, it is." He blew up another balloon. "Know this, though: categorizing yourself as a tough woman to deal with isn't a deterrent." He tied a knot in the balloon and stuffed it into the bag. "But I'll respect your boundary. No more pressure from me, except, damn, de la Rosa, I'm beating you at this balloon game. You'd better catch up."

"Is this how it's gonna go?" She stuck the end of the balloon into her mouth, beaming from his dare, from him. "You're on, Quaid."

"I'm not doing a dang thing until you tell me the truth. You like him. Like more than a little. Like enough to date." Jane was visibly giddy, chatty while Mari iced the cake. With an hour left before Pio's party, she said with a hoarse voice, "Be honest. I saw you guys. You were right outside my kitchen window."

"You were spying," Mari said.

"No. I was cooking." She rolled her eyes. "Fine, yes, okay, so I was spying."

"I was there with Jane, and I concur. Though, you guys were loud enough." Pearl said at the doorway, arms overflowing with Nerf water guns. "Ate Jane, where do you want this?"

"Outside, please. And tell Pio not to play with them."

"You've got it. And hold that thought, I want to do the sprinkles." Pearl passed them and exited through Mari's French doors to their backyard.

"Speaking of, let me go find the candles." Jane marched toward Mari's front door. "I can't keep my list straight. It's this decongestant, I'm walking around in a fog."

Pearl returned and grabbed the sprinkles from the cupboard. "Ate Mari, Reid seems like a really nice guy."

"I know. He's patient and persistent all at once. And you? Things with Trenton are good, yes?"

"How did you—"

"This is a small building." She slid the cake to her left, and Pearl uncapped the sprinkles and dumped half the bottle into her palm. "I've always liked him. A little part of me wants to give him the third degree though, just to make sure he knows how to treat you."

"Same here, to Reid, that is."

Mari's heart squeezed. She braved the moment by addressing the big elephant in the room. "So how . . . are things, with work, with Bling?"

Pearl had covered most of the top of the cake with sprinkles. "Good." A pause. "Great, actually." She took out her phone. "Oops, a call, I'll take this outside, but I'll be down in time for the party. Tell Ate Jane that if she needs anything else, to text me, okay?"

Except Pearl's phone hadn't buzzed, hadn't rung. Mari felt her sister tearing herself away, running in the opposite direction.

"Yeah, okay." Mari sighed as she watched Pearl walk out the door.

Their conversation was far from normal, but it was better than nothing.

The first of the guests arrived at Jane's apartment ten minutes before the designated party time of 4:00 p.m. As one of two assistants for this important party, Mari was assigned to the food area. Her job was to refill the buffet dishes with Pio's requested party fare: *lumpia*, or Filipino egg rolls; Cheetos; Doritos; marshmallows; and grapes. For the parents, Jane had prepared more *lumpia*; vegetable *pancit*, a Filipino noodle dish; a spinach-and-artichoke dip; an eight-layer dip; and barbecued chicken wings. Pearl had made an impressive *leche flan* that was the star of the tablescape aside from Mari's sheet cake. Jane hadn't held back in the matching blue and gold decor—these families were coming to a party put together by three wedding planners after all. It had to be Pinterest worthy.

Soon, Jane's apartment was packed, the noise rave-level from eight eight-year-olds, mostly boys, who commandeered the space like it was their bachelor pad. Somewhere out in the crowd was Pearl, who was in charge of making sure everyone had something

to drink—a choice of a water bottle, juice box, or can of soda—
and that the kids hadn't wandered elsewhere in the building.
Kayla and Trenton were stationed outside to mingle with parents
and encourage the kids to stay outdoors.

About an hour into the party, Jane took out a whistle and
blew it to get everyone's attention. "Time to sing 'Happy Birthday' and cut the cake!"

The crowd cheered; they migrated and surrounded the
kitchen island. Mari got to work and put the number eight candle on the cake, and lit it. Pearl dimmed the lights.

Then the doorbell rang.

"I'll get it," Mari said. She was closest to the door.

"Ate Mari." Jane called out as if in warning.

Mari turned the knob and threw the door open, arms wide
for a welcome. "Hello, you're right on—"

A man was on the other side of the threshold. "Hi, Mari."

"Marco." Mari took a step back. The next second, she
seethed. "What are you doing here?"

"I was invited to Pio's party."

It was only then Mari noticed the wrapped present in his
hand. Here on the threshold, he didn't look like an off-Broadway
star to Mari. He was the deadbeat dad, a man who had lots to
make up for.

She steadied her breath, spun around, and caught Pearl's
eyes, which reflected back her anger.

But Mari said nothing else; she simply stepped aside. The
crowd had been watching their interaction. Mari realized: Jane
did this on purpose. She knew Mari and Pearl would not make a
scene in front of guests.

Next to Pio, Jane said, "I'm so glad you could come. We're
just about to blow out the candle."

twenty-three

Mood: "Stand by Me" by Ben E. King

As Pearl had feared, they'd become a cliché overnight, the kind of family that suffered through awkward family gatherings.

Pearl avoided Mari because she didn't want to discuss work.

Jane avoided her sisters because she'd invited Marco.

Mari avoided Jane because Jane pissed her off by inviting Marco.

Marco avoided Pearl and Mari knowing he wasn't welcome.

Pearl avoided all compliments about her *leche flan*, because the one she brought to the party was made for her at the last minute by Barrio Fiesta. Her homemade flan hadn't set; it was runny and disgusting and would have caused food poisoning. Anyway, it *was* made from scratch. Just by somebody else.

Kayla passed Pearl at the buffet. The front of her shirt was wet, and she grabbed a kitchen towel and dried herself off. "Those kids are cutthroat with their Nerf wars. They all ganged up on me back there. They even made alliances."

The crowd had migrated to the backyard twenty minutes

ago and finished up the final activity of the day, the piñata, and the kitchen was empty of people. Sweat pooled at Pearl's neckline. There was one last thing she was avoiding, and that was being alone with Kayla. She'd agreed to wait until after the party to tell Kayla about her and Trenton, but every minute without the mention of their relationship felt like an act of betrayal.

"Look at all this food. I'd better eat now before you run out of *lumpia*." Kayla ditched her towel and grabbed a paper plate.

"De la Rosas running out of food? Surely you jest!" Pearl helped scoop a little bit of everything onto her friend's plate, and Kayla dug in. Pearl found random things to do to avoid her friend's eyes, like wiping the counter down and picking up big crumbs on the floor.

In between chews, Kayla gave Pearl the side-eye. "What the hell is going on with you all?" Pearl swallowed what felt like a ball of rubber bands as Kayla continued, "I mean, everything's out the in open now, right? You have your own client. You and Mari made up. Is it because Jane's ex is in town? What's up? I'm missing something, I can feel it."

The group in the backyard exploded in laughter, breaking the moment.

Think, Pearl.

"It's the *leche flan*," Pearl said, grabbing onto that small bit of truth. "I . . . I didn't make it. Mine didn't set, and so I bought this one and I'm letting everyone think it's mine. And it's been hard, getting my business off the ground. I know it's only been a couple of days, but it's been weird doing all of this on my own. It's not what I had expected." The swell of emotions rose inside of her. "I sound so weak, I know. I wanted this, but now that I'm here, it's just not what I expected. I feel so alone at times."

Kayla's body relaxed; her expression softened. "Honey, I'm here. I always am."

"I know you are. And I know I'll get used to things, and this will all get easier. I just wish my sisters and I could get back to normal."

"I hate to tell you, but normal for you all always included a layer of bickering." She scooped *pancit* into her mouth and swallowed. "But I understand. Not to worry, you all will get it together, soon. Look at this party you all threw—this was teamwork, too. Give it time. But your secret is safe with me. Both secrets." She stood and refilled her plate with more *pancit*. "But why not tell them how you feel? If you don't talk about it, it can snowball. They're your sisters, P. You're not on opposite sides."

"You sound just like"—*like Trenton*—"my conscience."

"Like your conscience, I am right. Listen to it."

God yes, Pearl was listening, but listening in theory was entirely different from reality. Kayla nudged her with a shoulder. "In the end, honesty is the best policy. Doctor's orders."

Pearl swore an entire day had passed though the party was only two hours long. Soon, guests took their leave, and in their wake was a mess that rivaled a frat party's day after. She started on the dishes while Mari picked up outside, filling the garbage with tiny balloon and piñata pieces.

Jane rested her elbows on the countertop. Her face had a sheen of sweat. "You don't need to stay and clean up."

"Of course I will, silly. Your place is destroyed. Besides I have backup, right, Kayla?"

"Who, me?" Kayla said while she lounged on the couch. "I'm sorry but I can't. I'm expected elsewhere in a bit, so I have to run."

"I'll help you, Pearl," Trenton added while pulling out the kitchen garbage from the receptacle. "No worries."

"Besides, you look like you need a nap, Ate Jane," Pearl noted. "Go sit."

A wry smile came across Jane's face. "No time for that. I'm going to take Pio for a walk. With Marco. Just us."

"Oh my God." Pearl clutched her sister's arm. "Are you telling Pio that Marco's his dad?"

"Not yet. I want them to hang out a little and then decide. Marco's in between shows. He said he's willing to come down and spend time with us."

"Are you sure this is what you want?"

"No. I don't know what I'm doing. This isn't numbers. I can't get a handle on this, so I'm flying by the seat of my pants. Just . . . if Ate Mari asks for me, make up something."

"Oh no, Ate. You can't ask me to lie." Pearl pleaded. "You know it's weird right now between us. I can't do anything remotely sneaky." But when her sister's face switched to desperation, Pearl folded. "Okay, fine. I will do my best to avoid a conversation about you. But after this I'm totally absolved of taking you to the speed-dating event, okay?"

"Thank you." She kissed Pearl on the cheek, laughing. "They're already outside waiting for me. I'll be back in an hour."

As soon as Jane walked out the door, Mari entered from the backyard. "I just got an SOS text from my top. Do you mind me taking off? I need to freshen up and meet her at the shop."

"No, it's fine." Pearl doubled over with relief. Mari was a human lie detector. With having to speak to Kayla today, she didn't want one more person to worry about.

Pearl's phone buzzed in her pocket. Christina Gonzales, from the Gonzalez fortieth wedding anniversary celebration: OMG I may need you. My parents are fighting. Again.

This was getting out of hand.

"What is it?" Mari asked.

"Gonzales. Not an emergency at this point, but I may have to mediate today."

"When it rains." Mari nodded. "You've got this, though."

Pearl waited for another word of advice or a nag about one of Mari's lists, but it didn't come. Pearl grinned at her, surprised at the support, that she was trying for peace. She repeated her sister's favorite motto. "No rest for the ambitious."

Pearl stacked the plates by the sink while Trenton rinsed and filed them into the dishwasher. Kayla brushed past her brother, barely acknowledging him and hugged Pearl. "Sorry I have to rush off. It's to the boss's for an early dinner."

"What? I thought you were kidding." Pearl flashed Trenton a look; panic jolted through her. She'd prepared to have all evening to sit Kayla down. "You can't go now."

"Excuses, excuses. You all just don't want to do the dishes." Kayla waved a hand at her brother. "You need to make up for the seven years you've been away. Besides, when the chief attending says jump, I say, how high." Her eyes lit up. "I love Calvin, but if you saw Dr. Nguyen, you'd say how high, too."

"No, she wouldn't," Trenton objected from behind her.

"Who are you to say?" Pearl teased. Except, now with more between them, it came out as something else altogether. It came out as a dare. Pearl sucked in a breath despite herself.

"Exactly. Pearl is, after all, her own businesswoman." Kayla walked to the counter where her bag was sitting, and slung it around her forearm. She winked. "Enjoy the dishes."

"Are you coming back?" Pearl chased after her best friend,

guilt settling on her shoulders. "She should come back here, right, Trenton?"

He nodded. "Pio asked me to watch him open presents. I can't say no to that kid."

A smile spread across Kayla's face. "Aw. That sounds fun. Okay, I'm in." She leaned in and kissed Pearl on her cheek. A trace of Kayla's vanilla lotion wafted across her senses. She'd used the same one for as long as Mari remembered, the predictability a comfort in this life that had suddenly become so complicated. "Love you. See you in a bit."

"Love you, too." Pearl breathed out her anxiety. Later—she would deal with Kayla later.

Pearl tapped the door so it closed lightly and turned to Trenton. His V-shaped back was to her, and among the sounds of water and the clanking of dishes was the song "Stand by Me"—he was humming.

Pearl latched onto his soothing voice like a child to the Pied Piper, and on the way to the kitchen, picked up littered plates and napkins. At the sink, she and Trenton worked efficiently, though her mind was ping-ponging between random thoughts. Time felt of the essence with too many things left unsaid to her sisters, to Kayla.

"You're quiet." Trenton rolled in the lower rack of the dishwasher. At his cue, Pearl handed him a jug of the liquid detergent, which he squeezed into the cup on the door.

"I'm worried."

"She'll be back here soon enough, and we'll tell her about us."

"And what will we tell her?" Pearl leaned a hip against the counter and watched Trenton stand to his full height. There was surely something about a man in an apron. Trenton was wearing one of Jane's, a fifties-style flowered apron, with a pocket in front and a ruffle at the hem. Right now, Pearl was tempted not to take this conversation any further and instead lure him upstairs. She shook her head free of the thought. Kayla was right: honesty was best. "What are we, Trenton?"

He took a step closer, and his hand rested casually on her hip. A thrill shot through her as his finger grazed the small space of exposed skin between the hem of her shirt and the waistband of her long skirt. "Is that a serious question?"

She swallowed. That was the thing—she didn't know what she was asking. Romance had never been this easy, never this natural. It had never meant this much. "We're good friends, that I know for sure."

"Do you think I would have slept with you, with *you*, if I was just going to mess around?"

"I don't know. It's been a long time since we've seen each other."

"People don't change."

"They could."

"I didn't." He dipped his head down lower, eyes captivating Pearl, and all she could focus on were his lips and the expectation of those lips on hers. "And I know you haven't either. Our friendship means too much for us to treat it so casually."

"Then we're together."

"Absolutely." He blinked. "Do you feel the same way? Because this is serious for me." Trenton's words were matter-of-fact, said without hesitation, so forthcoming that they knocked her sideways.

The time they'd been together, fake or otherwise, had been a dream. She was happy, content, thrilled, but she hadn't bothered to ask herself if she was ready for it. "We're serious?"

"Serious meaning I'm not playing games, Pearl. I wouldn't do that with you."

"Oh."

"Is that a good 'oh'? Or a bad 'oh'?" The smile on his face was hopeful, and Pearl locked onto it. This was what she wanted, right?

"It's a good 'oh.' I'm just a little overwhelmed."

He frowned. "Overwhelmed isn't exactly a positive response." He rested a hand on each of her shoulders. "I wanted to wait to say this until we told my sister tonight. But, I love you."

Love.

The room spun with emotions that ran the cavernous space of the past and present. In her silence, Trenton added, "I want to scream us from the rooftops. I need to know if you're in this. With me."

The request was made so casually, but the context was enormous. It was bigger than this room, bigger than both of them.

She wasn't sure what romantic love even meant, what it required. She could barely keep those she loved happy. The pressure to get another relationship right when all of her current ones were in limbo . . .

But Pearl understood that she had the potential to lose Trenton forever if she said no.

She spoke from her heart, forcing honesty into her words. "I love you, too, Trenton. There has never been anyone else." Suddenly, she couldn't breathe, and it wasn't because she was out of words, but because she was scared. Someone once said to be careful what you wished for, because you may get it someday. With Trenton, and now her new business, she felt this lesson down to her bones. "But." She pushed on as his expression fell. "I don't know about serious. About serious right this second."

"I'm confused. You said you felt the same way."

"I do feel the same way. But I don't know what serious is, what tomorrow will bring . . ."

"What is going on here?" A woman's voice rose from the front of the room. Trenton straightened at the shrill voice, eyes widening.

Pearl turned to meet Kayla's stunned expression.

twenty-four

Mood: "Fire Burning" by Sean Kingston

In her bedroom, Mari dressed, then sat at her makeup vanity. She looped her hair into a bun and applied her makeup. As she leaned into the mirror and touched up her eyeliner, a crayon drawing taped on the corner of her mirror tugged at her attention. Drawn by Pio when he was six, it was of the three sisters, labeled by name. A different shade of brown was used for every figure. Even without the labels anyone could tell who was who. From when they were children, they'd been starkly different, in looks and personality.

But what the hell was going on with them? What kind of example was Mari setting? Why couldn't she get over this? Why couldn't she be happy for Pearl? Sure, she let her go like her mother had suggested, but it felt like it was too late. What she should have done was to trust Pearl from the start. Yes, today had been a great day, but it was a celebration. Pearl wasn't even fully out of the business yet. What would it be like once she was gone for good?

She stood, shaking off her mood. Her mind shifted to Hazel,

and what she could want on a Sunday. Her text had been brief: Can we meet today? No pressure.

As Mari approached her apartment door, the sound of arguing voices echoed from across the hall. Kayla, maybe? Then Trenton's voice. Then Pearl's.

Mari frowned, opening her door slowly. The three were in Jane's living room. Kayla stood in Jane's doorway, her back to Mari and blocking her view of her sister and Trenton.

"What was that I saw and heard? What do you mean you love each other?"

"Kayla—" Pearl said.

"How could you keep this a secret from me? I'm supposed to be your best friend. And I'm your sister. How long were you going to keep it between you all? No, forget it, don't answer that, because it won't take away the fact that you both lied to me. I would have been happy for you. I'm out of here . . . no, Trenton." She backed up as her brother approached her. "Just give me space. You're my family, you're not supposed to lie."

Meanwhile, Mari's feet were glued at her doorway. Kayla shot out past her and into the foyer. Mari caught her eyes—they were stricken with anger, with grief. Backing up to the building's front door, Kayla blindly reached for the knob and stepped out. "I'm sorry for yelling. I have to go."

A second later, Trenton stepped out and hesitated when he saw Mari. He opened his mouth, then shut it, and instead followed his sister out the door.

When Mari finally entered Jane's apartment, Pearl was at the kitchen counter, dumbfounded, with tears in her eyes. "I messed up," she said.

Mari took Pearl in her arms. "It's okay. We've all done our share of that, Pearl. I'm here."

There was no rest for the ambitious, all right.

As soon as Pearl calmed, Mari's cell phone rang, and Pearl's buzzed. It was back to business. Without another word about the debacle between her and Kayla, they both headed out to their respective clients—Pearl to the Gonzalez home, and Mari to Rings & Roses to meet Hazel.

Old Town buzzed with shoppers. The weather had soared to a balmy eighty degrees. This weekend was rumored to be the height of bloom for the cherry blossoms, and the ones in Old Town flourished. Petals drifted in the warm air with every mild gust of wind. A sheen of pollen from oak trees covered the tops of cars.

Hazel was sitting in her parked car half a block away from the shop when Mari arrived. Mari knocked on the passenger-side window and leaned down. Her client was blowing her nose.

Not a good sign. "Hey. Are you okay?"

She got out of the car wearing dark glasses. She shook her head. But instead of Mari inquiring about it, she led the way swiftly to the privacy of the shop. She held the door open for Hazel and stepped into the sunlit foyer. Walking to the back office, Mari asked, "Care for something to drink? Juice? Tea? I have decaf."

"Tea, please." Hazel's voice trailed as Mari filled and turned on the Keurig. "I'm sorry to take you away from your nephew's party."

"How'd you know?"

"Reid told me."

"Ah. It's fine. We were done, just cleaning up. So, you saved me from it." Mari grinned, popped a tea pod into the Keurig, and pressed Brew. "How was your weekend?"

"It was okay." Her voice grew louder, and Mari turned. Hazel was at the break room door, glasses now removed. Her eyes were rimmed in smudged black eyeliner.

Nope, not a good sign at all.

"And how's the baby?"

This got Mari a smile. Hazel's hand automatically rested on her belly. "Good. I had an appointment yesterday and everything seems to be going well."

"Have you decided if you want to know the sex?"

"No, not yet." Hazel gazed at her through her lashes. "I want to know, but Brad wants the big reveal at the end."

Mari pressed her lips together into a smile to keep a comment from bursting through. Of course her fiancé would chose to take the opposite stance. He couldn't just give her what she wished for without a fight.

The tea finished brewing, and Mari loaded their cups and a small jar of cubed sugar and spoons onto a silver tray and turned. "Let's hang in the lobby, shall we? The shop's closed for the day. I don't expect us to be bothered."

They each took a seat in the upholstered chairs, the silver tray set upon the glass tabletop.

Hazel linked her fingers in her lap. "I texted you because I wanted to discuss a couple of things without Brad, if that's okay."

"Of course. That's what I'm here for." Mari's gaze scoured her client's face. The bells in her inner conscience chimed. Was this the first time a client had wanted to discuss their wishes separately from their partner? No. But in conjunction with what she'd witnessed—Brad's temper, the way Hazel cowered in his presence, how swiftly she changed her mind when Brad showed displeasure—Mari stilled with dread.

"First. I want to tell you that I'm totally okay with you and Reid."

The insinuation took a second to sink in. Mari cleared her throat. "Oh, but I wouldn't—"

Hazel put a hand on Mari's knee. "He told me today how much he likes you, and I love the idea of you and him. I consider you a friend, and the thought of two of my favorite people coming together . . . I think it's perfect. I get it—you don't want it to come between us. You're a professional through and through. But I need to get it out there that I approve."

"I . . . I'm stunned."

"I know. Me, too. My brother has never been this giddy about anyone." She grinned, but just as quickly, her eyes dimmed. "The second thing—the dress."

"The dress?"

She bit her lip. "Is it too late to choose another?"

Mari's hands began to shake on her lap, so she clamped them together. Squeezed. "You want another dress? Why?"

Hazel waved away Mari's words like she hadn't pulled the rug from underneath her, but her eyes were glossy and regretful. "It's so . . . tight and so . . . suggestive, you know?"

"I see." Mari bit her cheek to silence her conscience that wanted to respond with "No!" She gathered logic like the tendrils of her hair during a windstorm, and reminded herself that this was Hazel's life. Not hers. Not even her sisters', where she could've meddled.

Think.

From her purse, Hazel retrieved a folded page torn from a bridal magazine. "I was thinking a traditional gown, princess style."

"We're a little less than two months away from the wedding."

"This is what I want." Hazel shook the page at her; agitation laced her voice.

Mari accepted the page. The dress on the model was beautiful, but it bore no similarity to the first dress Hazel had picked.

This was not okay. She set the page on her lap. "This concerns me. As your wedding planner. As your friend."

Hazel inched backward in her chair in what Mari knew was a defensive posture. Knowing she could chose to leave at any moment, Mari took a deep breath and said, "This is something I don't disclose to many, but I was in . . . I mean, in a position in which I was being . . . managed." *Just say it, Marisol.* "Emotionally abused."

"What are you talking about?" She stiffened.

"I want you to know I'm here for you, Hazel."

"How dare you even assume? I came here for help, not accusations. For the record, Brad and I are perfect."

Mari kept her voice neutral. "Okay . . ." Seeing that Hazel was a breath away from fleeing, Mari stood and grabbed a Post-it note from the front desk. She scribbled a 1-800 number on it, pulled easily from memory. She peeled the page off and held it out for Hazel to take.

Hazel became a whirlwind, refusing the Post-it, rising from the chair, and backing away. She pushed her sunglasses back onto her face and slung her purse onto her shoulder. "This is preposterous. You are overstepping your bounds. I'm going to go. Forget about all this, the dress, our contract is cancelled, and stay the hell away from my brother."

"Hazel!" Mari called out, following her out the door. Down the street, Hazel's car engine growled to life; the running lights flipped on. The car pulled out of the spot, speeding away with the screech of tires.

Seeing her go sent Mari's physical world spinning. The memory of her own family's intervention materialized. Her father, mother, and Jane in the living room at five in the morning. They'd waited up for her. She was warm from drink, hair a mess from a night of the drama she'd become addicted to, of having this man who wanted and hated her at the same time. Saul had become her whole world. He'd surprise her with fear or with goodness; the adrenaline and the rush of emotions had been a high.

Mari knew now that the high was fear, but back then, she'd thought that was living. She'd been convinced that no other love would've thrilled her as much. She'd believed Saul's assertion that it was them against the world.

She'd moved out of 2404 Duchess Street that night, first crashing at Saul's before finally finding that third-floor apartment in Falls Church. All her life, she'd been the frugal type. She'd saved all her paychecks. Despite her partying ways, she'd been a bear of a student, earning a full ride to GW. She was twenty-one, an adult, and obviously around a family that hadn't wanted to accept the one person she loved.

No, Saul hadn't asked her to choose, but he didn't have to. She did it all on her own.

Of course, there had been manipulation and fear, couched in between hot passionate lovemaking and the promise of forever. She paid for it with that horrible night with Pearl.

She was still paying for it. Now her mistake had cost her a top client, the commission of which they were depending on to keep the shop afloat through the summer. First Pearl, the Bling wedding, and now Hazel—these two months had been an open fire hydrant of loss.

Mari entered the shop once again, grabbed her purse, and

focused on what she could control, knew that she'd done all she could.

Digging her phone out of her purse as she locked up Rings & Roses, key chain dangling from her thumb, she discovered that she'd received two voicemails and over a dozen texts during her twenty-minute meeting with Hazel. The texts were all from Jane. Each an SOS.

The huge fight between Pearl and Kayla.

Hazel breaking their contract.

Terrible things came in threes.

twenty-five

Mood: "Sunrise, Sunset"
by Jerry Bock and lyricist Sheldon Harnick

Pearl dropped her purse and jacket at the door and kicked off her Toms. She kissed her cousin Christina Gonzalez on the cheek. "Hey."

"Thank God you're here." Christina gestured to the right, to the sunken living room, where the rest of the family milled, a couple of heads peeking into the kitchen on the far side. "They both want a divorce." She rolled her eyes. "This time they said it's for real."

"Ah . . . and for what reason?"

"You know my mother had her heart set on their first dance."

"Yes."

"Papa backed out. He said that"—she curled her fingers as if quoting—"'It's our fortieth anniversary. I've earned my choice.'"

"Oh dear." Pearl stepped down into the living room, parting the crowd like Moses parted the Red Sea. The quiet murmuring added to the loud argument in the kitchen, and with it the aftermath of her own day fell away. There would be time to go after Kayla, time to fix things with Trenton. David and Imelda Gonzales had a fortieth wedding anniversary next Sunday with two hundred guests attending, and it would be ideal for them to still be married. Right now, Pearl had to fix this.

The Gonzales family were not blood relatives, but their clans were entwined in the way people of the same culture gravitated toward one another, with ferocity and loyalty. Pearl called Christina her cousin; she considered Christina's parents her aunt and uncle. Hence, Rings & Roses had agreed to provide day-of coordination for this party at half the service cost, arranged pretransfer of ownership. Otherwise, Pearl would've charged them double—they had been so high-maintenance.

She walked into the brightly lit kitchen, in the midst of what looked like lunch cleanup. One was accusing of the other of smashing their dreams.

"Finally. You can talk some sense into this man." Imelda smacked the air with her hand.

David's arms were crossed and rested on his tummy that poked out from his short-sleeve dress shirt. "I'm the one with sense. Who wants to watch us dance anyway? It's overrated."

"This is my wedding!"

"It's mine, too. You get everything you want. See this house? And the furniture, and your precious Mercedes MLK with white leather seats that stick to my legs in the summertime? All I want is no dancing."

"I don't care about the Mercedes. Take the Mercedes. The dance is more important to me."

"You choose the dance over the Mercedes?" He laughed, then caught himself. "No. Absolutely not."

"That's enough." Pearl shot a hand out to each side of the

room. "I've about had it with the both of you. First of all, this is not a wedding. This is a vow renewal."

The crowd in the other room gasped. *Nice. Thanks for helping out, people.* "Which means you are already married, and there's no way you're allowed a divorce, else there won't be a party."

The two seemed to put away their claws, and she gestured for each of them to take a seat. They both sank into breakfast table chairs across the room from each other. Imelda refused to look at her husband.

Pearl brought an empty chair, set it next to Imelda, and gestured for David to take it. After a huff, he moved to her side.

Pearl swore under her breath. It didn't matter how old couples were, when it came to planning something so close to their heart, they held on tight to their wishes.

She perched on the breakfast table. "What happened today?"

Imelda jumped in. "After months of not caring, suddenly, he thinks he gets to have a say. The party is in a week!"

He growled. "How can I care if I'm not informed of the plans?"

Pearl eyed the man. "Is that true? I think half the family knew the plans."

He looked sheepish. "Well . . . but . . . I was hoping she'd listen to me. I said all along that I hate to dance."

Imelda raised a finger. "That's not true. Today with the karaoke—"

"That's different. It wasn't in front of everyone *everyone*," he gruffed. "And another thing. I hate the song 'At Last.'"

"I see. Tita, would you consider changing that song?" Pearl asked.

"No."

Her gaze darted between the two. The frustration came off

them in waves. They were at a standstill, much more than they'd been the last few weeks. Pearl had since employed all the tactics: logic, being understanding; she'd done her share of pleading. She only had one last card to pull, a card she'd never thrown faceup into a ring before, a card her mother had thrown once and won, at a wedding she was so sick of planning because the families were contentious. Her mother had been willing to lose the entire account. Pearl had watched from the sidelines as it all unfolded in their mother's office like the quarterback's Hail Mary throw in the final seconds of a Super Bowl game, in painful slow motion. Luckily, her mother had won.

Pearl lowered her hands, shoulders sagging. "Fine, then. I'm done."

"What?" the two asked, first glancing at each other, and then at her.

She made a commotion of fixing her hair back up into a bun, as if she herself was in the fight. "I'm not here to make you want to walk down the aisle again. If this was your wedding, I might've stuck this out, considered that maybe you were making the wrong decision, but you are two grown individuals—I mean, you're retired! You both want the same things. You both want this party. You want to celebrate, and yet you continue to argue. I can coordinate, I can plan for contingencies, but I can't make you see what is so obvious to all of us. That you love each other, that you're committed. Shouldn't that be enough to set all these little things aside?" She planted a kiss on each of their cheeks, her words catching up with her. Her eyes watered at her mistake, at her horrible judgment. How could she have even doubted that she wanted Trenton? How had she let fear drive her actions?

She had to call him. But first . . . "I love you both. You know that. I also respect you. But maybe I'm not the woman for this job."

Her aunt's face skewed in pain. "Iha."

Pearl's heart leapt at the small victory but she kept up her charade. "It's clear you aren't happy, and I'm at my wit's end. I'm not sure what more I can do." She moved toward the doorway. "I'm going to forward your contract to Ate Mari."

She stepped into the living room and was met by a shocked crowd. Christina emerged from it with widened eyes. "What the f—"

Pearl stopped her with a hand on her elbow and directed her to the front door, away from the discerning ears of the others. "Don't worry."

"But—"

"They should come to their senses soon." She unzipped her purse and took her keys and phone out. A message flashed on the screen.

Mari: Need you at Alexandria General SOS.

Pearl's voice choked. "Or, hopefully, anyway. Look, I've got to go, but I'll keep my phone on me. Text me to update. Okay?"

"Okay." Christina's voice was tenuous, trailing behind her as Pearl scrambled to put on her shoes. "Sorry, for grabbing you out of Pio's party to deal with a couple of wannabe teenagers."

She hugged her cousin. "Hey. It's what family's for. No judgment. Love you."

But as soon as Pearl stepped out from under the home's covered porch, her mind was already on Mari's texts.

Mari never sent SOSs.

~

Damn this Volvo without Bluetooth capability—Pearl couldn't check her phone as it beeped. She couldn't call Trenton to beg for him to hang on, to not give up on her. Couldn't text Kayla and ask for forgiveness. Her eyes solely on the road, she swerved through the busy streets to Alexandria General Hospital. Her thought: Pio, and his need to get on high structures. Did he fall off the monkey bars? Did he break an arm? He had nine lives, that kid, but he had the attention span of a pup.

She streaked through the hospital valet driveway. A pretty penny to pay, but she couldn't think, much less park. She threw the attendant the keys.

Finally, she checked her texts, all from Mari.

Jane's in the ER. Pio is with one of his friends.

Where are you? We're moving up to the ward.

nvm. I'll meet you in the lobby.

Drive safely.

Sure enough, when the hospital's automatic doors opened, Mari was on the other side. Her face was taut—worry was never one of Mari's emotions. She was serious or stressed or triumphant. Never worried.

"Ate Mari." Pearl's voice shook.

"Don't cry." She enveloped Pearl in a hug. "She's okay for now. C'mon. It's a ways to her room."

Was she crying? Pearl swiped her cheeks, then hopped to her sister's side, and yet the heaviness in her heart remained. "What happened?"

"Jane didn't feel good at the playground. She was dizzy and unsteady, short of breath. She passed out. Marco called an ambulance and used her thumb to get into her phone before she was taken here, to text me." Mari's voice shook. "After they stabilized her in the ER, they transferred her up to the internal medicine unit."

Pearl clasped her sister's hand, gripped it tightly.

"It was an asthma attack."

Pearl shook her head. "I don't get it. She doesn't have asthma."

Mari's eyebrows turned downward. She pressed the button for the elevator. "They have to do tests, but her oxygen was low when she came in." She swallowed. "Her oxygen was low. How did I not notice it? She's been coughing for weeks. The doctor said her bronchitis on top of her allergies might have triggered it."

"God," Pearl whispered. The door opened and they stepped in. She clicked on to her texts, and sent a group text to Kayla and Trenton: Jane at Alexandria General Hospital. I know you're both mad at me, but I thought you should know.

"We were too damn worried about stupid things," Mari said.

"I know." Pearl repeated. "I know."

The internal medicine floor was full of the bustle of medical personnel and the chatter of televisions from patient rooms. Pearl followed Mari to the right-most room on the west wing, her Toms squeaking against the white linoleum floor.

The room was tiny, just big enough for the hospital bed and a chair on its left side. Jane's skin was pale, in concert with the faded blue hospital gown. A skinny plastic tube below her nose ran to a spout on the wall—her oxygen.

Pearl brushed past Mari to get to her sister, tears coming once again. Overwhelmed by the need to calm her nerves, to feel that her sister was real, she threw her arms around her.

Jane's voice was hoarse. "I'm okay, Pearl."

"No, you're not, obviously."

A hovering shadow to her right moved. Marco was at the foot of the bed, silent. She hugged him, too. "Thank you for making sure she was safe."

"I wish I could have done more," he whispered, voice croaking, and he patted her on the back. He straightened, though his expression was wary and unsure. "I should . . . I should go now that you both are here. I'm due at the train station soon."

"I'll call you. I promise." Jane reached up and beckoned him. "I don't know what I would have done without you."

He leaned down and kissed Jane on the cheek. "Give the kid a high-five for me, okay?"

"Of course."

Pearl sat on the pink cushiony chair to make herself as small as possible during their exchange. She noticed Mari back up toward the window and look away. Marco had taken on a different role to her now. He'd saved her sister.

Once Marco left, Pearl wrapped her hand around Jane's. "Ate Mari caught me up. Have the doctors said more?"

"Did someone say doctor?" A man in a gray oxford shirt and black slacks came in. A smile spanned his entire face, a contrast to every sad face in the room. "How's our patient doing?"

Pearl squinted, pursed her lips. Examined his full dark hair, his posture and muscled build. "Wait. You look really familiar to me."

"Number Fourteen," Jane said.

"Number Fourteen?" Pearl repeated and slowly, the memory came back to her. Of him among a crowd. Of introducing herself as she sat down at a small circular table. Of a silver cuff bracelet around his left wrist. *The speed-dating event.* "Ohhh. Fourteen."

"That would be me. Dr. Gabe Mori. I had hoped this wouldn't be the way we'd see each other again, Jane, but here we are. Then again, I'm glad to be here to help as the pulmonologist on call. Can I answer any of your questions?"

"Me first," Mari said. "Why asthma and why now?"

"Numerous things could have triggered it. Environment,

predisposition." Dr. Mori's eyes were sympathetic. "It was the perfect storm, I think. First her allergies, then bronchitis, the sudden turn of the weather, and the high tree-allergen counts. I can't really say why now."

Pearl shook her head, remembering the pharmaceutical commercials that frequently ran during her Hulu shows. "There are medicines to treat it, right?"

He nodded. "It will take a bit of finding out what will work best, but yes, completely treatable. The asthma attack was serious, though. She had a breathing treatment at the emergency room, and she'll be on oxygen at least overnight."

Pearl glanced at her sister. "Have I ever said that you are so high-maintenance?"

They all laughed, grateful for the joke. Even Dr. Mori.

Jane squeezed her hand. "Not gonna lie, I was a little scared." Her gaze jumped to the other people in the room, her eyes filling with tears. "All I could think of was Pio, and what if?"

Mari jumped in. "You never have to worry about what if."

Pearl interceded, grabbing Jane's knee. She understood her worry—she'd felt so alone the last month. The family hadn't been this splintered in a decade. But no more; Pearl wouldn't let it go on like this. She squeezed her sister's hand. "Never."

"Wait. I have another question." Mari addressed Dr. Mori, now peering through narrowed slits. "You were Number Fourteen in what?"

twenty-six

Mood: "We Are Family" by Sister Sledge

It had taken doctors two nights to wean Jane off the oxygen and to give the final diagnosis of adult-onset asthma. And finally, after tests, a chest X-ray, twice-daily breathing treatments, follow-up examinations with Dr. Gabe Mori, and a comprehensive meeting with the patient educator, she was cleared to come home.

It would be up to Jane to take charge of her health. But it would be up to the sisters to pull together to take care of Jane.

Mari's phone buzzed on the hospital table as she packed up Jane's things. Jane was in the bathroom, changing back into fresh clothes. Pearl was in arm's reach of the phone and she peeked at the screen. "It's Reid. I'll answer and tell him you're unavailable."

Mari raised a hand to protest. Her meeting with Hazel the other day felt like a million years ago, and while she didn't have regrets about speaking up, there were sure to be repercussions. Mari hadn't wanted to think of them until they got Jane back home.

But Pearl had already pressed the green button and placed it on speaker. "Hello?"

"Hazel told me." Reid's voice was somber as it echoed into the room. "I don't know what to believe. She's denying any conflict with Brad and insists she is absolutely safe. And I don't know if it's my place to do anything about it at all."

"Reid—" Pearl interrupted. "This isn't—"

"I'm sorry, Marisol. My sister doesn't want me to even speak to you." He sighed. "I'm not in the habit of doing something just because my sister asked me to, but I feel like I need to support her."

"I don't regret what I shared." Mari's voice broke as she spoke up. "And I understand. I wouldn't want you to feel like you're even choosing. You have to take care of your family first."

Silence permeated the room. Reid cleared his throat. "Okay."

Mari choked her reply. "Okay."

Pearl pressed the red button to hang up, then enveloped Mari in a tight embrace. "I'm sorry."

"Eh." Mari feigned indifference.

Pearl stepped back. "You don't have to do that. You don't have to act like you don't care."

"It was stupid of me to think that there could've been something else. Nothing can come from being a hypocrite."

"Yeah, well, I didn't mean to call you that." Glancing up at Mari, she corrected herself, grinning. "Okay I meant it at the time. But I was also rooting for you and him. I know it takes a lot to cut through to your black heart."

"Ha." Mari perched on the bed and took a deep breath. "But worse is that I think I've lost our top." She explained what had happened with Hazel, and Pearl listened intently.

"You did the absolute right thing."

"I know I did. I only wish it didn't have all these consequences." Mari thought of the money, the lack of clients, the long winter months. How she'd have to buy Pearl out and then lose her talent on top of the cost. "I really made a mess of things."

"No, you didn't, I did."

"Stop." Mari halted her by placing a hand on her wrist. "I have something to tell you."

"Yes?"

"I never should have tried to hold you back. You were right. It was my own insecurity that got in the way. I wanted every-thing to run perfectly to show you all—" Mari stumbled, re-grouped her thoughts and tried again. "I didn't want to fail anyone. I don't want to be *that* Mari from a long time ago. I con-vinced myself that if I could control the transition to our owner-ship perfectly, I would make up for everything you had gone through."

"That was never your fault. It was solely Saul's and no one else's." Pearl shook her head. "Look, I wanted my space." She paused. "I felt like I was suffocating. All my life, I felt like I was watched. Like I couldn't make a mistake. I convinced myself that it was my way or no way at all. The control thing? It's not just you. It's a de la Rosa trait."

Beats of silence passed, and in the pause, Mari couldn't take it anymore. The last two days of worry was the final piece of per-spective she needed. Life was too short. She declared, "I don't want you to go."

At the same time Pearl said, "I don't want to leave."

"What?" they said to each other. "Jinx." They both laughed. "Jinx again."

Both exploded in a fit of giggles, and as they settled, Mari said, "I'm sorry, Pearl. I know your talent. I know what you're worth."

"Thank you." She patted the tears on her face with the back

of her hand. "I needed that. But how do we do this, Ate Mari? How do we make it so that we can work together? You and I know about the honeymoon period—"

"It doesn't last." Mari finished the sentence. "I don't know what we need to do. So let's ask for help. Let's get some advice. Restructure, set some real objective ground rules. Something. Okay? But I can't be in charge of social media, ever."

Pearl laughed. "Okay."

Mari leaned into her sister and held her tight. A crisis might have brought them here, but in this case, she'd take it. She'd take it to learn the biggest lesson of her life.

The past might've shadowed the future, but it didn't mean she couldn't shine a light on it. It didn't mean that she couldn't gain her footing. And it didn't mean that others couldn't help steer her in the right direction.

"Thank the freaking heavens!" a voice said behind them. Jane was at the bathroom's doorway now, in a T-shirt and sweats, face wide with relief. "This made my life. Can we please stay together forever?"

Mari looked at Pearl and answered with words that would be forever and binding. "I will."

Pearl nodded without hesitation. "I will."

———

To Mari's chagrin, Jane did not follow doctor's orders. The day after her discharge, she had insisted on taking Pio to an after-school playdate, which deposited her right back into bed.

Mari now hovered over her while Gabe, apparently now the de la Rosa doctor on call, listened to her heart and lungs.

"My asthma attack was days ago," Jane said. "I don't get why I'm not better. I'm using my inhalers."

"Yes, but it was an asthma attack with a side of bronchitis." He slung the stethoscope around his neck. "Which means you have to listen to your body and take it easy. Promise me you'll stay in bed, just for the rest of today. Start again tomorrow, and slowly. A walk around the block, not an event surrounded by elementary schoolers."

She pouted. "Fine."

Pearl snorted from the doorway. "And don't even think you can sneak around. One of us will be watching. You can come with me to yoga . . . when you're well." She grinned. "I did all kinds of research last night. Yoga is beneficial to people with asthma."

"You guys are ganging up on me," Jane said.

"And that's my cue." Gabe stood. "I'll check on you tomorrow, okay?"

"I'll walk you out," Pearl said, but before she exited the bedroom, she shot Mari a look of collusion.

And Mari agreed—the man was definitely interested in their sister. Cupid had struck again.

As soon as the two were out of the room, Mari's eyes widened at Jane. "House calls, huh?"

"They're unofficial," Jane said. "But sweet. Don't you think?"

A smile crept onto Mari's face. "I do. And then there's Marco, who hasn't stopped calling. I think you have yourself a love triangle."

Jane's face twisted into confusion. "Yeah, it's all levels of complicated. What a week."

Pearl burst into the bedroom. "What did I miss?" She leapt to the foot of the bed.

Mari straightened the comforter Pearl had wrinkled. "Jane was talking about her love triangle."

"I don't want to talk about that anymore. I want to talk about you, Ate Mari," Jane said. "Tell me about Reid. Did you call him back?"

Mari shook her head. "It's taking everything out of me not to, but he's got to figure things out with Hazel. I'm still a little sad, though. He gave me a glimpse of possibility."

Pearl's eyes widened. "Of love?"

"Yes? I don't know. What we had was respectful. Good. Different." She sniffed. "But I should be grateful it all ended when it did, right? Better now, early in the relationship. Before I got in too deep."

"I'm sorry, but I object." Jane pushed Mari's flyaway hairs back. "Seriously. I don't think you should give up. If the relationship means what it looks like it does to me. This expression on your face—we don't see it often."

"She's right," Pearl added. "You almost look . . . friendly."

Mari cackled, grateful to laugh freely, to be seen and called out for exactly who she was. No one could do that but her sisters. "Anyway, I don't want to talk about it anymore. How about you, P? Have you spoken to Kayla?"

"She won't return my calls." Pearl's lip twitched downward. "And Trenton—the guy said he loved me, and I totally froze. So yeah, it's been radio silence from him, too."

"Oh no." Jane frowned.

"I thought I wasn't sure if I was ready for love. It's taken my whole life to get here and I'm just getting to know myself. Now, after thinking it all through, I wonder if there will ever be a perfect time."

Jane answered quietly, though firmly. "No, there isn't. When I got pregnant with Pio, when I gave birth, when I realized I had to raise him as a single mom, and at every junction, I questioned myself. I doubted my ability, and I was scared to death. I'm still scared sometimes knowing I have to guide this child to be who he's meant to be. But guess what? When there's love, you make it work. And when there's family, the unknown isn't as frightening. Speaking of." She blinked at the two of them and cleared her throat. "I have something to tell you both. It's serious. I don't know if Mommy and Daddy are going to support me, but I hope you both will. I've decided to give Marco a chance to get to know his son. A true chance." She raised a hand. "I don't want to hear your arguments against it. This is just an FYI. I was hospitalized. I could have . . . died. All I thought of while I was lying there out of breath was that I *couldn't* die. I didn't want the only parent Pio knew to leave him. Pio wants a father, and his father wants his son."

Mari bit at her cheek and nodded. "I don't judge you, Jane. So much that I'm not going to add a caveat to that statement with a threat against the man, but if he hurts Pio's feelings, so help me God."

"Same," Pearl answered.

Jane smiled. "I don't expect any less."

"Mama. You're awake!"

They turned to the voice at the doorway. Pio, still with his shoes on, bounded in, the heat radiating from him. He held a brown bag with Barrio Fiesta's logo.

"Hey, bud!" Jane opened her arms. "I missed you. What have you got for me?"

Pio handed Jane the bag.

"*Puto.*" She pulled out a tiny steamed cake and bit her bottom lip. "Oh my heavens."

"I told you to wait at the door!" Amelia stomped in, out of breath. Strands of hair from her high bun framed her face.

"Goodness. Your child can sprint, Jane." She presented a handful of napkins.

"God, if I knew I'd get all of your undivided attention, I would have gotten sick sooner." Jane accepted a napkin and passed the bag around.

"Better watch out, you might get what you wish for," Pearl said. "I have a feeling you will be getting a ton of attention from the two points of that triangle."

"Yeah, we're going to have to take sides," Mari said.

Pearl rubbed her cheek mischievously. "We can even start a hashtag. Team Fourteen—"

"Or Team Beefcake." Amelia waggled her eyebrows. Mari and her sisters laughed, and as if the act of laughing alone released the tension all of them had been holding the last month, their cackles rose to a full crescendo before they ebbed to the rolling wave of giggles.

Pio shook his head. "I don't get it."

"It's us being us, *iho*," his mother said, ruffling the top of his head.

It was them being them. As it should have always been.

part six

The Rose is without an explanation; She blooms, because She blooms.

—Angelus Silesius

twenty-seven

Mood: "Let's Stay Together" by Al Green

Pearl coughed at the increasing smoke in her flat. She ran to her windows and opened them fully, bringing in the warm air and the current thunderstorm. Grabbing a dish towel from her kitchen counter, with concentrated effort, she flapped the air under the smoke detector, praying that it wouldn't go off. She didn't have time for this, not with what she had planned for this evening.

Then, above her, the ceiling fan turned on.

"Thank you. I swear I looked away from the stove for a sec—" Pearl turned toward the front door to thank whichever sister had arrived in the nick of time. Instead . . . "Kayla! You're early!" She ignored the stench of the apartment and dropped her arms, her body relaxing at the sight of Kayla's not-surprisingly smug face. Who cared about the smoke? Her best friend was here. "Hey."

"I got some face time with Jane downstairs and dropped off an early Mother's Day present," she said, reading Pearl's mind. "I thought I would make this a twofer." She crossed her arms but didn't budge from her spot, and her face was soldered into a frown. "So, I'm here."

"Thank you for coming. I—" Pearl gestured upward at the lingering smoke. She pointed at the cast-iron skillet of impossibly burnt bacon for fried potatoes—Kayla's favorite comfort food—and threw her hands up. "I give up. Want a drink?"

"Why am I here, Pearl?"

"Because I wanted to talk. And have a good meal; obviously, that's not going to happen. I can order pizza." She was met with little expression. "Sushi? Chinese? Mexican food!" Her floors were getting wet, so she shut the windows. It was the Friday before Cinco de Mayo, and it had thus far been a stormy month. She was lucky that they didn't have an event for tomorrow—it would have been a monumentally wet occasion.

Kayla shook her head, but the mere fact that she was still standing in her apartment gave Pearl some hope. It had taken almost three weeks, a series of novel-length texts, a dozen of her favorite macarons, and a five-minute voicemail message for Kayla to finally agree to dinner.

"Greek? From Nikos!" Pearl declared, bringing out the big guns. Greek was Kayla's fave, though not Pearl's. But she would eat all the tzatziki to get the woman to stay.

With a nearly imperceptible nod, Kayla agreed.

The first part of her plan was complete.

They sat across from each other at the kitchen table, each with a drink in their hand. The air still reeked of burnt bacon, and the minutes had ticked by at a molasses pace. Kayla spun her glass of gin and tonic on the table, making condensation rings on the wood, and Pearl, watching her, ran through her apology in her head.

She'd planned for days on what to say. She planned to apologize and promise her undying loyalty. She'd reveal the God's honest truth of why she'd kept her relationship with Trenton a secret and admit her reasons were still no excuse. She shouldn't have lied to Kayla.

Except the words were stuck in her throat, because even if she apologized, she didn't know how to make up for it.

She also wasn't sure if Kayla was going to like what the rest of the night entailed.

"So." Pearl broke the stalemate and promptly patted herself on the back for having the fortitude to do so. "Refill?"

Kayla's drink was still three-quarters full; she raised the glass as if to emphasize.

"Right." She sighed. *Think, Pearl.* "Thanks for checking on Jane."

The vibe cracked. An honest smile appeared. "I was glad to see her back to her normal self. Her apartment was buzzing in there, with the music on and Pio running around." Then, as if realizing she was still angry, her expression clamped down like a vice. "Pearl, can we get started, please?"

"Okay." She spied the time on her wrist. Ten more minutes.

"Why do you keep checking your watch?"

"Food delivery. I'm starving. Aren't you?"

Kayla eyed her suspiciously. "Whatever you have to say, say it now. Let's get on with this so that I can go home. I've got work waiting for me."

A car rumbled outside her window, bringing Pearl to her feet. "Okay, uh, hold that thought."

Kayla huffed though she didn't bother to get up.

Pearl jogged down the stairs and opened the front door to Trenton. His smile was twisted into worry though she couldn't blame him. The last time they'd seen each other, he'd professed his love and she'd basically rejected him. Since then, they hadn't spoken. She hadn't tried to contact him and vice versa, as if they'd both known that without Kayla's blessing, there couldn't be a relationship.

Behind Trenton was a waterfall of rain. The tops of his shoulders were wet. A drop of water ran down his cheek. His Uber sped off, tires sloshing through the street.

"Hi, Pearl," he said.

She stood aside and he walked in, though he hovered by the doorway. She breathed in the sight of him. "Hi . . . um, food should be here soon. I had a culinary emergency a bit ago."

With perfect timing, Nikos's delivery truck rolled up, and a guy popped out with two steaming grilled-meat smelling bags, safe under an umbrella.

Trenton grabbed both bags. They climbed the stairs in silence, coming to her apartment door. Pearl entered first, bracing herself as she opened it.

"What are you doing here?" Trenton asked of the woman sitting at Pearl's dining room table.

"I was here first. What are *you* doing here?" Kayla fired back, eyes then cutting to Pearl. "What is this?"

Pearl all but pulled Trenton inside. Hurrying, she lifted her priceless antique armchair from its normal spot in the corner of her living room, shut the door, and blocked it with the chair.

"I'll tell you what it is." Pearl sat on the chair, crossed her legs underneath her, and slung her arms across her chest. "I'm not moving until I apologize so much that you all can't take it anymore."

A triad of sad people, that's what they were. Pearl at the door, Kayla at the kitchen table, and Trenton seated on the couch.

Pearl unfurled her arms and leaned down, elbows on knees.

"Kayla, I'm going to speak for myself, and myself only. I. Am. Sorry." She took a deep breath. "I should have told you right away. I should have said something the moment things between Trenton and me shifted. I was scared. It felt like I was losing things left and right, and Trenton was there, and the whole kid-crush thing blossomed into something bigger than I ever expected." She swallowed her excuses. "I messed up. But I love you. And I love you, Trenton. Like, down to the bone, since the beginning of life. I'll do anything so it can be the three of us again. But the most important thing to me is that the two of you are back to being close." She looked at Trenton. "I want all of us to try to work this out. I see my future with both of you at my side. Not one or the other. But your family comes first. I know the strength of that now more than ever. So if I have to step away from the both of you, I will.

"Nothing can replace family, blood or otherwise. I don't want to be the cause of breaking up yours. But at the same time, I can't walk away without showing you something, Trenton." Pearl stood, face tingling with the start of tears, and went to her printer. "You both knew my sisters gave me a Love Unlimited gift certificate. It included two matched dates and the speed-dating event. With everything that's gone on, I completely forgot about the second matched date. Davina, the owner, emailed me several times, and even when I refused that last matched date, she felt compelled to send me who the match was, in case I changed my mind. It came last week." She handed Trenton the piece of paper.

Trenton bit his bottom lip, eyes on the paper. He fell silent.

"Well, who is it?" Kayla asked.

"It's me," Trenton said. "I signed up for this service too when I moved back. I thought it'd be a good way to get back into the groove." He folded the paper in half and stood.

"Where are you going?" Kayla stood, too.

Panic rose within Pearl—he was going to leave. The man

meant to walk out and she hadn't said everything in her heart. "No, you can't go yet. Because I need to tell you that I love you. As in, more than friendship. I was stupid and scared. It felt too good to be true, so I didn't believe what I felt."

Trenton advanced toward the exit, and Pearl backed up to the door, arms splayed out to block it. "It's all excuses, I know. But I'm not letting you out until I say this: I'm willing to wait until you forgive me. Even if it's not today, or for days, or for weeks. For years." Her eyes shot to Kayla. "Both of you."

Kayla had a hand on her chest—her tell. She was torn, but her next words were unexpected. "Oh, hell, Trenton. Are you just going to let her stand there?"

"No, I'm not," he growled, taking the last two steps to reach her. His hands cradled her face; she melted into his touch. He kissed her on the lips, chaste, pure, and perfect. "How can I, when you're the woman who's twisted my heart into a pretzel like one of your yoga moves? Even if I tried to forget you, I couldn't. I would have waited for you, too. I love you, Pearl."

Kayla's arms encircled the both of them.

"I'm sorry La-La," Trenton said. "I fucked up."

"You both are still on notice," Kayla said, face wet with tears. "But I'll get over it. I can't stay mad. These last three weeks have been the worst. I love you both too much." She sniffed. "But please, please, *please*, when you guys have drama with each other, keep me out of it."

"Okay." Pearl shook from relief and laugh-cried into her friends' arms.

In the background, the doorbell rang, but Pearl ignored it.

Everyone important to her was here, already inside 2404 Duchess Street.

twenty-eight

Mood: "I'll Be There for You" by The Rembrandts

Friday nights were crunch nights, usually spent finalizing last-minute details and calming her anxious clients. Mari had often spent it dragging brides and grooms from the proverbial ledge that would've otherwise kept them from walking down the aisle. She'd barely sleep; she'd run on fumes combing through every line item on her checklist. Wine was not earned until the event's end.

But tonight, tonight Mari was having her wine early. It was only 7:00 p.m. and her feet were propped on her ottoman. Jane was settling in for a movie night with Pio. Pearl was having Kayla and Trenton over at her apartment. Music played in the background, her secret boy band music playlist. She had a cookbook on her lap with Post-it flags sticking out from some of its pages, marking recipes for their planned barbecue for Memorial Day. The sound of the rain brought about a peace that she hadn't felt in a long, long time.

No, Mari didn't have an event tomorrow—she'd reminded herself of it throughout the evening, even rechecked the calendar to make sure. Besides it being a bye week, her work schedule had changed dramatically. The last three weeks had seen a major restructuring within Rings & Roses. Mari had stepped down as CEO, finally admitting her leadership style might not be the best among the three of them—and this compromise solidified Pearl's acceptance of her role at Rings & Roses as a full-time wedding planner and her newly minted title of chief of marketing. Jane stepped up as CEO with her logical thought process, even keel, and objectivity. Mari still could keep up her list and process obsessions as the chief of operations, in charge of building, maintenance, and procedures, which Pearl had agreed she would adhere to as part of the business's standard operating procedures.

In the last three weeks, Pearl had shouldered more of the business than Mari could've imagined. With Pearl's top, a new and affordable pricing strategy for family and friends, and new branding on the horizon, they were at the ground floor of a solid foundation. There would still be kinks to work through; their personalities were sure to clash at some point. But with Jane and her ever-steady hand, and Mari and Pearl's commitment to giving each other the benefit of the doubt, hope had trickled back into Rings & Roses and the de la Rosa family.

These days, Mari had found pockets of time for new hobbies like sitting. And resting.

And without the Glynn wedding to plan . . .

A hurt burned in her stomach and radiated up her chest. It could have been the Riesling or the coffee before it. It had been three weeks since she'd heard from Hazel, and the pain from losing her and Reid lingered.

"No regrets," she said aloud to her living room. It was what it was. This week, a wedding planner from Time of Your Life—

Mari's replacement—contacted her, requesting details about Hazel's current wedding plans. Mari passed along what she'd coordinated to ensure the wedding's success. While their standard contracts were ironclad and protected them from runaway clients—the Glynn couple had paid the necessary fees to cut ties—the act still caused her heart to ache.

Did she miss Reid? Absolutely. Yesterday, a For Sale sign had gone up in front of 2402, the metaphorical stake in her heart.

Halfway through her glass of wine, Mari spotted the lights of a car rolling up. It idled in front of her window before a figure made its way to the front door; the doorbell rang.

She set aside the cookbook on her lap, taking her time, when the bell rang again.

When the bell rang a third time, she yelled, "Goodness, I'll be right there!" She stood, passed her hallway mirror, and spied the unicorn pajamas, fussy topknot, and makeup-free face she sported. She smiled at herself.

Was this what it was to forgive oneself? For one to be able to open one's door despite their imperfections, their unkempt hair, and clutter in their home?

Whatever it meant, she might already be there. Two months ago, she wouldn't have been caught dead outside of her apartment in unicorn pajamas.

Mari went to the foyer and peeked through the building's peephole. "Who is it?"

The street and front porch light revealed little but rain and shadows. "Mari? It's Hazel," the figure said.

Hazel? Mari threw the door open.

Hazel wore a yellow slicker, and the rain cascaded off her jacket. Sopping wet tendrils of her blond hair whipped from under her hood.

"Hey. What's going on? Are you okay?" Mari's tone surprised even herself; there wasn't a hint of stiffness in it.

"I didn't know where else to go. Can I come in?"

Mari stepped aside. "Of course."

Mari led the way into her apartment. Hazel peeled off her coat and hung it on the coatrack and stuck her umbrella in the stand inside the front door. Mari gestured toward the couch. "Would you like to sit?"

Hazel did not sit. Instead, she paced, trailing a citrus scent. She spoke in a jumble. Mari had just begun to process that Hazel was here, in her apartment—a place she'd never stepped foot in when she was a client—and she couldn't keep up.

"Slow down," Mari said.

"I don't know what to do. I don't know what to do."

"You don't have to do anything."

"But I do, see." She wrung her hands. "I ended it. I couldn't go through with it, Mari. I couldn't marry him."

Mari pieced together Hazel's incomplete sentences and thoughts, her heart hammering in her chest. "You called off the wedding."

She nodded, crying now. "I walked out. He wanted . . . I picked up my dress. I decided not to change it after all, and he said he wouldn't walk down the aisle with me in it. He said he wouldn't have the mother of his child look like a . . ." She took a breath. "He was enraged, and I was so . . . so scared for us. I was already dressed—we were supposed to go to a play tonight. But I walked out. I literally . . . walked out."

"Wow." Inside, Mari wanted to give Hazel a high five, but she tempered her reaction. Right now, adrenaline was high. Sadness and mourning were sure to follow.

Hazel half laughed. "I know, right?"

"What can I do?"

"I dunno. Reid's in town, but he isn't home . . ."

"You can stay here until Reid gets back."

"Thank you. God, I'm shaking." She looked at her hands.

Hazel's emotions, her shaking, the crying, the noise—it started to unsettle Mari. Her own breathing had become erratic, her heart rate sprinted, and sweat bloomed on her back. It was the start of anxiety—she identified it, the first step—but there was more beyond it. Fear.

It didn't make any sense. Mari wasn't in trouble, there were no signs of danger directed at her, but the trigger had been pulled, and she foresaw herself twisting into panic if she didn't get help. Now. She was out of her league.

Mari picked up her phone and texted Reid. Hazel needs you. My house.

She looked at Hazel. "Wait here? I'm going to grab one of my sisters. I'm just going to step into the hall really quick. Okay?"

Hazel nodded fervently. "Okay."

But when she opened her apartment door, Brad was on the other side. He was halfway up the stairs when he spun around, eyes blazing. "I want my fiancé."

⌒

To Mari, time transformed from linear to multidimensional. Her past slipped into the present as seamlessly as cards appearing from a magician's coat sleeve. With her feet seemingly super-glued to the floor, her environment became fuzzy, and she was no longer in the town house's foyer but in her apartment in Falls Church, and the man descending from the stairs was Saul.

But the man's booming voice woke her from her trance. "Hazel, I know you're here."

Hazel.

Brad.

Still speechless, Mari backed into her doorway as Hazel whimpered behind her. With Brad taking the steps down in twos, she slammed her door shut, chest thudding.

Except the door didn't shut. Brad had gotten to it first and pushed against it from the other side, yelling obscenities. He eased his shoe into the doorway—Mari watched it appear like a ghost in a horror movie. And after a microsecond where the door seemed to give, Mari was slammed on her ass when Brad rammed the door open with his body.

Tears sprang to Mari's eyes at the stabbing pain in her tailbone, but that pain fell by the wayside when she watched Brad lumber to his fiancé and strong-arm her.

"No!" Mari's voice erupted like lava from a volcano. Instinctual, primal, in solidarity. Her body followed suit, scrambled to standing. She lunged at Brad—shoved him aside. He loosened his grip on Hazel, giving Mari enough time to get in between them. In between Brad and Hazel and their baby.

Pearl had just sat down with Kayla and Trenton for their meal.

Kayla scrunched her eyebrows downward. "Is your sister having a party downstairs?"

"Not that I know of." They all fell silent as Pearl focused her hearing, picking up a man's and a woman's voice. No, two women's voices, elevated and shrill. "It sounds more like a fight than a party."

"It doesn't sound good," Kayla said.

"I'll be right back." Without waiting for a response from Trenton or Kayla, she flew down the flight of stairs. A chaotic chorus of voices assaulted her senses, followed by the pounding of footsteps behind her and someone knocking on the front door. But Pearl took a deep breath to hold her nerves at bay, blocked out the noise, and followed the pool of light from Mari's doorway.

Upon crossing the threshold, déjà vu knocked Pearl back ten years, to Mari's smoke-filled college apartment. Her heart boomed in her ears as a scene unfolded in front of her, of a man hovering over Mari and Hazel. Mari shielding Hazel. The fear in her sister's eyes became a catalyst, spurring Pearl to action. She would not cower this time. This time, she would be the one to make this better. She reached for the first thing she saw from the umbrella stand next to the front door: Pio's Wiffle bat.

Shit. It would have to do. She held it up high and gave a warning. "Get off my sister!"

The man didn't turn, so focused on wrenching Hazel from Mari.

Pearl reeled back and swung the stupid Wiffle bat with all her might.

twenty-nine

Mood: "All of Me" by John Legend

This year was the first Mari let Pio—or anyone, for that matter—take charge of the de la Rosa family summer solstice tradition: making handmade soft pretzels. The kid had handled the measuring, the kneading, the rolling, and soon, the baking. Admittedly, when Pio had thrown flour on the ground like a magician, Mari almost took control of the process, but she held tight to her resolution to loosen the apron strings. She was so proud of this little boy. When the time came for him to leave home, Pio was going to be able to cook for himself.

Pio dropped the twisted pretzel dough into the boiling water mixed with baking soda. When the plump dough floated to the top, he announced, "It's ready!"

"Here you go." Mari handed him the tongs, then grabbed the parchment-lined cookie sheet, with five already-dunked pretzels on it, from the kitchen island. Pio wrangled the sixth pretzel and plopped it onto the sheet.

"Okay, ready to stick it in the oven?" She turned off the burner. Using oven mitts, she pulled out the top rack.

He nodded and, with Mari's help, settled the pan into the rack. After he shut the oven door and set the timer, he skipped to his aunt and mother outside in the backyard where they were container gardening, and threw himself into their midst.

Mari's kitchen was a mess. The island was covered in flour. From the KitchenAid mixer hung leftover pieces of dough, and dishes from their early dinner filled the sink.

Still, as she wiped down the island and spied the most important people in her life, Mari was overcome with gratitude. She almost didn't have this. She'd expected to have had only one sister in the business. After Brad's assault a little over a month ago, she'd anticipated that drama would linger.

It hadn't.

The shock had been enough for Hazel to file a restraining order and relocate to Florida with her mother. It had been enough for Pearl to decide to give all she had to Trenton. And it had been enough for Mari to then truly forgive herself.

Mari put a check mark next to *pretzel-making* on her calendar's daily checklist, open in front of her on her vanity. She stared at the next item, her belly a ball of nerves:

Date with Reid.

Jane stood behind Mari and curled her hair, eyes narrowed. "Please tell me you didn't write a checklist for tonight."

"No, because I have no idea what should happen, or what I want to happen. I don't even know what we're going to talk about." Mari bit her lip—good thing she'd waited to apply her lipstick. "Should I start with 'Hey, so were you impressed with how my sister whacked your almost brother-in-law on the back?'"

Jane giggled. "Yeah. That *is* slightly awkward." She lowered her voice. "'Hey, uh, do you have a friend who needs a wedding planner? We do full-service, complete with private security utilizing only the very best military-grade Fisher-Price gear.'"

She laughed. "Dear God."

"Right? But like any one of your lists: you're going to take this date one step at a time."

"One step at a time."

After that chaotic night, Reid came by at first to update Mari on Hazel, and then to discuss the town house when he'd found a buyer. Their texts blossomed from one liners to sentences, to full on conversations about their daily schedule. They video-chatted twice when he was in Atlanta.

Mari knew he'd wanted more; the hope was in his eyes, in his voice. He was patient, and when she had been ready to take the next step, she'd sent *him* a rose this time. His date invitation came quickly afterward.

"I see a car!" Pearl yelled from the kitchen.

Mari's legs jiggled with nervousness. She stood from the chair and accepted the lipstick from Jane. Applied it with precision despite her shaking fingers. She fixed her shirt against the mirror and tucked strands of her hair behind her ears.

"What if he tries to hold my hand?" she asked, then felt utterly foolish. She smiled weakly. "Is this stupid, going out with him?"

"Absolutely not." Jane gently ushered her out of her bedroom.

Mari expected Reid to be in the living room, but only Pearl and Pio were in her apartment. "Where is he?"

Pearl spoke up. "In the foyer."

"You didn't let him in?"

"Um. *No.* This is your first date." Pearl crossed her arms.

Mari rushed to the front door and opened it to Reid, who had a sheepish smile on his face. "Hi," he said.

"Sorry about that. Ready to go?"

Pearl yelled from behind, "Get her home on time, Mr. Quaid."

"Really?" Mari whined, then shut the door behind her.

"We're staying up until you get home!" Pearl's voice echoed from the other side.

"Pearl!"

"It's okay," Reid said. "I'm up for whatever you de la Rosas dish out." He held out his elbow. "Speaking of dish, are you ready to eat your heart out at your first DC Metro Food Tour, Ms. de la Rosa?"

One step at a time. Mari linked her arm with his.

"I'm ready."

thirty

Mood: "Single Ladies" by Beyoncé

Hey, slugger." Kayla entered Rings & Roses with a to-go cup of coffee in each hand. "Break time for you."

Pearl rolled her eyes at her friend's nickname for her and met her in the foyer. "If you weren't handing me a red eye right now, I would totally be disrespectful."

"As long as there isn't a bat around, I'm not worried about it."

The shop's newest interns snickered, each loaded with boxes of decorations and favors. Though only seven in the morning, it was full speed ahead for the Bling wedding this afternoon. The entire shop was dedicated to today's event, closed to retail customers. Her sisters had their marching orders on what needed to be accomplished before they descended on the Thatched Roof Winery. Her parents, who'd decided to visit through September this year, also had jumped into the chaos, volunteering to help in any way.

"Hey, mind your own business," Pearl cackled to the staff, jovially. It had been more than a year since she'd walloped Brad, but she was never going to live it down.

Admittedly, she didn't mind the teasing. That night had been a defining moment for her. The growth she'd experienced since then had been a whirlwind, from her official promotion to full-time wedding planner and chief of marketing, to today, the Bling wedding, which had been dubbed the "biggest wedding of this year" among DC's elite. Most important, that night, she'd learned to be part of a team with her sisters, with her best friend, and with her boyfriend. Together, they could take on anything.

"You know? I can totally tell when you're thinking about my brother." Kayla led the way outside. She had night shifts at the hospital, which meant she was free during the day. She'd known that Pearl was nervous about this wedding; it had been the only thing she'd gabbed about the last two months. Since their fight, they'd made more time for best friend dates, even for coffee.

"Sorry. I can't help it."

"Do you have time for a quick breakfast? I know you'll be hungry by ten a.m."

She glanced at her watch and surveyed the commotion in the shop. "I guess I could go for something quick."

"There's a food truck near the square. Wanna try it? It's a transplant truck from San Francisco called Lucianna. Ruby's sister-in-law's cousin-in-law owns it."

"Sister-in-law's cousin-in-law?"

She waved a hand. "I know. I don't get it either. The skinny is that her husband is an Army officer who works at the Pentagon, and she drove that truck clear across the country. She's serving breakfast paninis."

Pearl raised her eyebrows, stomach growling at the thought. "Breakfast paninis? Take me to it."

They walked the four blocks toward the square, though it only took two blocks to see the behemoth of a parked truck.

There was a line, a good sign. As they neared, Pearl noticed a trail of red.

"Where did all these . . . rose petals on the ground come from?" Pearl asked, distracted by them.

"Hmm, let's follow them."

Pearl glanced at her best friend, suspicious at the faraway tone to her voice. "Kayla?"

"Go with it." She linked an arm around Pearl's elbow.

"Okay." Pearl dragged a half step behind her, following the trail of rose petals to the front walkway of the Carlyle House of Old Town, where Trenton was standing. Behind him were her sisters and Pio and her parents. Reid. Marco. Gabe. Calvin. Ruby and Levi. And Mr. and Mrs. Young, who she hadn't seen in months.

"What's going on?" she whispered, hesitant to take a step.

Kayla nudged her friend. "Go on. It's time."

In the past, Pearl had been dubious at the idea that people hadn't a clue that they were going to be proposed to.

Yet here she was. Pearl hadn't known, not even when Trenton handed her a piece of paper with her picture on it.

"Trenton?" Her voice shook, eyes darting to the crowd around them. "What's going on? What's this?"

"It's my email from Love Unlimited," he said. "I had the printed email with me that night when we all made up. You were my match, too."

"That was over a year ago."

"It feels like yesterday." He dropped to one knee and retrieved a black velvet box from his pocket.

Pearl's lungs ceased to function.

"One night over a year ago, I walked you home. It was the first time we'd been alone together in years, and you asked me if there was anything wrong with wanting to be seen. That night, I told you that I saw you, and I was telling the truth. But what I didn't say was that I felt it in my core that you saw me, too."

He opened the box, revealing a vintage princess-cut diamond banked by square baguettes.

"I knew that night, Pearl. And now I humbly ask: In love and in friendship, will you be my one and only?" His eyes glistened, lips turned up into a smile.

"Yes. Yes. Yes." Pearl gasped, doubling over in joy and in tears. She dropped to both knees, lips meeting his for a long kiss. "Past, present, and future."

After the fanfare of the Bling wedding was no longer underfoot, Pearl's sisters brought her champagne. They sat on dainty white chairs under a castle-like white tent, looking out into darkness dotted by stars and a high full moon. Scratch that—her sisters were looking out at the view. Pearl couldn't stop staring at her ring. It was Trenton's grandmother's, an heirloom. Priceless.

Jane raised her glass. "Congratulations, Pearl. For an immaculately executed wedding, and for the next chapter: us planning yours."

Their glasses met in the middle, Pearl's face warm from adrenaline and pride. She sipped her champagne and reveled in what the next year would bring. New clients, a wedding of her own. Maybe a home of her own.

"I have something for you guys." Mari pulled two small boxes from a bag next to her and passed them out.

"I didn't know we were doing gifts," Jane said.

"Not a gift. More like an office necessity, part of our standard operating procedures."

Jane rolled her eyes. "Are you serious? Is this really the time to talk about procedures? I swear, Ate."

Pearl groaned, though part of her was unsurprised.

"Just open it," Mari said, deadpan.

Pearl opened the box and gasped. Inside was a skeleton key—*the* cherished key. She looked up; Jane had taken hers out, too.

"It took a while to find a craftsman to cast the key that Mommy gave me when they left," Mari said.

Pearl teared up, understanding this significance. Of Mari truly letting go. Of sharing the baton. She reached across to Mari's hand and gripped it.

Her ate squeezed back. "Rings and Roses belongs to each one of us. Without you all, there wouldn't be any of this . . . this happily ever after for our clients. It's only right for each of you to have a key, too. It's only right, because our family is my key."

Jane put her hand over both of theirs. "And so is mine."

"Mine, too," Pearl said, as sure of them as of the ring on her finger.

They were women who bloomed with different strengths, who had varying shades of personalities and unique souls, who had thorns of imperfections. But they would always be sisters.

Sisters who had finally found the keys to their happily ever afters.

acknowledgments

The de la Rosa girls were born from my love for my soul sisters: women who I've met and bonded with over the years, women who I've grown to rely on and hope I've been there for. Thank you for raising me, for opening your homes and lives to me, for coming into mine without judgment. I thought of you lovingly as I wrote Marisol, Janelyn, Pearl, Amelia, Regina, Kayla, Hazel, Ruby, and Daphne. You know who you are. In case I haven't said it in words: I love you.

Deepest thanks to my publisher, Jennifer Bergstrom, and editor, Kate Dresser, for the opportunity to tell this story. Kate, you know exactly how to push, how much to give, how much to ask. Thank you for taking this step with me. Rachel Brooks, cheerleader and agent: you are absolutely *the best*. The entire Gallery team, especially Molly Gregory, Christine Masters, the art department, and the marketing and publicity teams, thank you for bringing Key to the world! I appreciate each and every one of you! Publicist Kristin Dwyer of LEO PR: you are a gem! I'm lucky to have met you on this journey.

My girls: Stephanie Winkelhake, April Hunt, Annie Rains, Rachel Lacey, and Sidney Halston. Writer's coach Nina Crespo. Ladies of the #Thermostat crew. My early-morning writer's group #5amwritersclub. #TeamBrooks. Tall Poppy Writers. How lucky I have been to connect with all of you—you have my heart.

Amie Otto of Amie Otto Photography and Lauren Hidalgo: thank you for answering my SOS! To Sara Bauleke of Bella Notte for being a critical resource in the writing of this book. All mistakes are purely mine.

To the readers and bloggers who have recommended my books, who have reached out and given me encouragement: you fuel my fire!

To my fabulous four: yes, you may read this book before you're of legal age. ☺ Thank you for inspiring me with your sibling love and conflict. Also for not minding eating pizza and cereal for dinner. Finally, to Greg, always steadfast, a reed against the waves: twenty years together went by in a minute despite our own anxiety-filled wedding. Thank you for holding the key to my happily ever after.